## WENDIGO MOUNTAIN

Suddenly a pebble fell near Touch the Sky's feet.

Another pebble, and now fear coated his tongue in a coppery dust, for he had recalled something—a "game" Sis-ki-dee had once played when Touch the Sky had sighted the railroad spur through the San Arcs. The renegade had remained in hiding, tossing pebbles and making rattlesnake noises to unnerve the Cheyenne, letting him know that he was a mere bug inching along the face of the mountain—a bug he could flick off at any moment.

Just as he could flick him off now again.

A hard wind whipped up and simultaneously pushed the clouds away from the moon while also parting the tendrils of ghostly mist. Just enough for Touch the Sky to see that he was completely ringed in by a grinning Sis-ki-dee and his well-armed warriors!

## DEATH CAMP

Touch the Sky dismounted, threw the horse's bridle, and watched the animal stretch its long neck out to drink from the little streamlet. Everything was a blur, as if his tired eyes saw things underwater. For a moment, just a blessed moment as the horse drank, the tired Cheyenne let his head fall forward and closed his eyes.

When he opened his eyes again, a shock wave of fear slammed into him. He saw that Ladislaw had wandered well away from cover to relieve himself, and none of the others had yet noticed him.

Touch the Sky shouted a warning even as Little Horse looked up and also spotted the danger. Touch the Sky steeled his muscles for the jump, then saw Wolf Who Hunts Smiling stepping from behind a deadfall, an arrow notched in his bow.

Touch the Sky leapt at the same moment Little Horse did. They crashed down onto Ladislaw and toppled him. But they were an eyeblink too late to completely avoid the deadly arrow—as Touch the Sky landed on the doctor, he felt a pain like white-hot fire rip into his back.

# CHEYENNE

## DOUBLE EDITION
## WENDIGO MOUNTAIN/
## DEATH CAMP

### JUDD COLE

LEISURE BOOKS     NEW YORK CITY

A LEISURE BOOK®

January 1999

Published by

Dorchester Publishing Co., Inc.
276 Fifth Avenue
New York, NY 10001

ISBN 0-8439-4479-X

# WENDIGO
# MOUNTAIN

# Prologue

In the year the white man's winter-count called 1840, a Northern Cheyenne warrior was born to face a great but bloody destiny.

His original Cheyenne name was lost forever after a bluecoat ambush near the North Platte killed his father and mother and 30 other Cheyennes riding under a truce flag. The squalling infant was the lone survivor, and his life was spared by the officer in charge. He was taken back to the Wyoming river-bend settlement of Bighorn Falls near Fort Bates. There, he was adopted by John Hanchon and his barren young wife, Sarah.

Owners of the town's thriving mercantile store, the Hanchons named the boy Matthew and loved him as their own son in spite of occasional hostile looks and remarks from other settlers. But

5

their affection couldn't save Matthew when he turned 16 and made the mistake of falling in love with Kristen, daughter of the wealthy and hide-bound rancher Hiram Steele.

Steele had Matthew severely beaten when he caught the Cheyenne youth and Kristen in their secret meeting place. Steele also warned Matthew to stay away from Kristen if he wanted to live. Frightened for Matthew's safety, Kristen lied and told him she never wanted to see him again. Although he was full of hate for the white men who meant to harm him, Matthew loved his parents and Kristen too much to leave Bighorn Falls.

But an arrogant young lieutenant from Fort Bates was also in love with Kristen. He altered Matthew's life forever when he issued an ulti-matum: Matthew had to leave Bighorn Falls for good or his parents would lose their lucrative contract with Fort Bates—the backbone of their business.

Thus began the odyssey of the brave but lonely Cheyenne youth trapped between two worlds and welcome in neither. His heart sad but determined, Matthew set out for the upcountry of the Powder River—Cheyenne territory.

He was immediately captured by braves from Chief Yellow Bear's Northern Cheyenne camp. His clothing, manners, and speech marked him as an enemy. Declared a spy for the blue-bloused soldiers, he was tortured and sentenced to die. But just as a young brave named Wolf Who Hunts

Smiling was about to gut him, old Arrow Keeper intervened.

The tribe shaman and protector of the sacred Medicine Arrows, Arrow Keeper had recently experienced an epic vision. His vision foretold that the long-lost son of a great Cheyenne chief would return to his people—and that he would lead them in one last, great victory against their enemies. This youth would be known by the distinctive mark of the warrior, the same birthmark Arrow Keeper spotted buried past the youth's hairline—a mulberry-colored arrowhead.

Keeping all this information to himself to protect the youth from jealous tribal enemies, Arrow Keeper used his influence to spare the prisoner's life. This infuriated two braves, especially the cunning Wolf Who Hunts Smiling and his fierce older cousin, Black Elk.

Black Elk, the tribe's war leader despite his youth, was jealous of the glances cast at the tall young stranger by Honey Eater, daughter of Chief Yellow Bear. And the proudly ambitious Wolf Who Hunts Smiling had turned his heart to stone against all whites without exception. He believed this stranger was only a make-believe Cheyenne who wore white man's shoes, spoke the paleface tongue, and showed his emotions on his face like the woman-hearted white men.

Arrow Keeper buried the youth's white name forever and called him Touch the Sky. But the youth soon found that acceptance did not come as easily as his new name. At first, as he trained to be a warrior, Touch the Sky was humiliated at every turn. And his enemies within the tribe tried relentlessly to prove Touch the Sky was a spy for the whiteskins.

By dint of determination, guts, and the cunning he learned from whites, Touch the Sky not only became the greatest warrior of the *Shaiyena* nation, but also made great progress in the shamanic arts, thanks to Arrow Keeper's training. His fighting skill and courage won him more and more followers, including the ever loyal brave, Little Horse.

But with each victory, his enemies managed to turn appearances against him, to suggest that he still carried the white man's stink, which brought the tribe bad luck and scared off the buffalo. And although the entire tribe knew that Touch the Sky and Honey Eater were desperately in love, Honey Eater was forced into a marriage with Black Elk—who chafed in jealous wrath, plotting revenge against Touch the Sky and the woman.

But most dangerous of all—a graver threat than Pawnees, land-grabbing renegades, whiskey runners, buffalo hiders, Crow Crazy Dogs, mad turncoats, the U. S. Cavalry, and the other enemies he defeated—was the treacherous and ambitious Wolf Who Hunts Smiling. Having formed secret alliances with Comanche and Blackfoot renegades, Wolf Who Hunts Smiling planned to raise the lance of leadership over the entire Cheyenne nation and lead a war of extermination against the whiteskin settlers. Only one obstacle prevented his final bid for absolute power: the tall brave named Touch the Sky.

# Chapter One

Early in the Moon When the Green Grass Is Up, Touch the Sky rode out with other braves to hunt for antelope in the valley of the Little Bighorn. The hunters returned in five sleeps, their travois piled high with fresh meat. But even as the hunting party crested the last rise before reaching camp, Touch the Sky's shaman sense pricked at him like a cactus spike, warning of new trouble.

Their Sister the Sun had gone to her resting place, and Uncle Moon owned the sky. Touch the Sky spotted Gray Thunder's summer camp the moment they topped the long rise. The village was located in the lush grass where the Powder River joined the Little Powder west of the Black Hills.

Even from there, he could hear the crier racing

up and down through the camp, announcing their arrival. Touch the Sky's muscles felt heavy and tired from the journey and the arduous hunt. It would be good to bathe and sleep. Yet as he glanced below at the welcome and familiar sight, something again seemed amiss. But what?

The tipis were erected in their ancient clan circles, all with their openings pointed toward the rising sun, the source of all life. The hide covers had become parchment-thin as they'd aged, and the tipis looked like glowing orange cones because they had fires burning within.

As he rode down following River of Winds, Touch the Sky's eyes automatically sought out the biggest and finest tipi in camp, one with bead-inlaid entrance flaps and several meat racks out back. Spotting the elongated shadows of Black Elk and Honey Eater, he glanced quickly away again, his heart racing.

Thinking of Honey Eater trapped in that tipi with the fierce and jealous Black Elk made Touch the Sky forget whatever had bothered him upon spotting the camp. He fell into a gloomy reverie as the hunters left the meat in the care of Tangle Hair. A Bowstring soldier respected for his honesty, he would distribute it in equal piles to the clan leaders.

"Little brother!" Touch the Sky called out, spotting a youth of 16 winters named Two Twists. "Where is Little Horse?"

"You will see him soon enough," Two Twists replied evasively, hurrying away.

This odd behavior made a deep furrow appear between Touch the Sky's eyes. Two Twists admired him greatly. Why would the young brave suddenly avoid him like this? Clearly, there was something he was afraid to tell him.

Touch the Sky rubbed his pony down with sweet grass and turned her loose in the common corral, then crossed to his own tipi. Since he belonged to no clan in Gray Thunder's tribe, his tipi stood by itself on a lone hummock near the river. He paused beside the light of a huge fire and stooped to borrow a piece of glowing punk. The lurid orange reflection limned his sharply defined features. He was lean, straight, and tall, with a strong hawk nose and piercing black eyes. His hair fell in long, loose locks, cut short over his brow to keep his vision clear. He wore beaded leggings, a doeskin breechclout, and elkskin moccasins. He also had a wide leather band around his left wrist for protection from the sharp slap of his bowstring.

Touch the Sky threw back the hide flap over his tipi entrance, using the glowing punk to ignite the shredded bark kindling in his firepit. The bigger sticks soon flamed to life and shot orange spear tips up, pushing the shadows back. Then he glanced down and saw atop the heap of his sleeping robes a pictograph message made with claybank war paint on a flap of doeskin. Puzzled, Touch the Sky at first paid only scant attention to the series of crude illustrations: a lone mountain peak shrouded in clouds, an eagle tail feather, what appeared to be an underground tunnel. He was more concerned with figuring out who had left it there—a friend or a foe.

The message must have something to do, he decided, with Two Twists's odd behavior. And perhaps with that nagging premonition Touch the Sky had felt when nearing camp.

If anyone in camp knew about this, he thought as he left his tipi and started across the camp clearing, Arrow Keeper would be the one. Although Touch the Sky had barely 20 winters behind him, he knew that a man was not wise simply because he was old. There were plenty of old fools among the red men. But Arrow Keeper was undoubtedly a wise Indian. Age had not dulled the vital spark in his eyes or his dagger-sharp insight into the human heart. As a shaman, he had medicine that was respected from the banks of the Powder River to the Land Beyond the Sun. He had been the tall youth's first friend in the red man's world, and it had been he who had initiated Touch the Sky in the survival secrets of the warrior and in the esoteric arts of the shaman. Many times his help had pulled Touch the Sky back from the jaws of death.

Touch the Sky glanced ahead, then pulled up short in confusion. The hummock upon which Arrow Keeper's tipi had always stood was empty! Instead of the familiar tipi with its cooking tripod out front, Little Horse waited for him.

"How was the hunt, brother?" his sturdy little friend greeted him, handing Touch the Sky a loaded clay pipe.

Despite his agitation, Touch the Sky knew the custom. Clearly, Little Horse had something important to tell him, something much too important to broach immediately. So they sat upon the ground and smoked for a time, speaking of inconsequential matters. Finally Little Horse laid the pipe down between them, the signal that he was ready to speak.

"Brother," he said solemnly, "I have a thing for you."

Every important transition in Indian life was marked by the giving of a gift. Little Horse handed Touch the Sky something small, hard, and highly polished. Touch the Sky leaned into a shaft of silver moonlight to examine it.

"Why, it is Arrow Keeper's magic bloodstone! He told me once that it made his tracks invisible to his enemies. Then, has he. . . . Is he—"

"Brother, every warrior in this tribe would have cropped his hair short in mourning if Arrow Keeper had crossed over to the Land of Ghosts. Be easy. We may yet speak his name aloud without fear his ghost will answer. He is alive."

"Then, buck, where is he? Where is his tipi?"

"He left. As for his tipi, he said in good time it will become his death wickiup."

"Brother," Touch the Sky protested, frustration creeping into his tone, "this is no time to speak like a peyote soldier. You say I may still pronounce Arrow Keeper's name, but then you speak of his death wickiup. Where is our tribe's shaman and Keeper of the Arrows?"

"I am looking at him, buck."

Touch the Sky shook his head impatiently. "The whole world knows I am only Arrow Keeper's assistant. I would need twenty more winters behind me to even dream of attaining his medicine."

"I have no ears for this. And neither does Arrow Keeper. He told me to tell you this thing. His magic bloodstone—do you understand that it was his prized possession? It is yours now because you are the tribe's shaman. And buck, I have the Sacred Arrows. I am holding them for you."

This last pronouncement left Touch the Sky speechless with confused wonder. This was all too much, all too sudden. Little Horse spoke again, his voice urgent.

"Pick up these words, Cheyenne, and carry them in your sash always. Arrow Keeper bade me speak them to you. You know that he was ailing, that red speckles had lately appeared in his cough?"

Touch the Sky nodded.

"Just before you rode out for the hunt, Arrow Keeper decided he had to leave to build his death wickiup and make his preparations for the Last Path while he still had strength to do so. He intended to wait until your return to hold private council with you. But then, he told me, he experienced a powerful medicine vision, one that foretold new suffering for you—and for Honey Eater."

"Honey Eater?" Touch the Sky cut in sharply. "What manner of suffering for her?"

"I know not, buck. Only his words. 'There will be trouble ahead for Touch the Sky, trouble behind for Honey Eater.' That painting you clutch in your hand is a key to Arrow Keeper's vision and this new trouble. He said to tell you that, after this vision was placed over his eyes, he realized you must now act on your own or you will never survive the schemes and dangers your enemies have in store for you."

Arrow Keeper gone! Touch the Sky still could not register that brutal fact. Always, when all had seemed lost and Touch the Sky's last breath was in his nostrils, the old shaman had been there with just enough medicine to help the beleaguered young brave defeat his enemies.

"But brother," he said, "how can I safely guard the Medicine Arrows? You know my situation in camp."

Little Horse nodded. "Arrow Keeper spoke of this. He said you have too many enemies to keep the Arrows in your tipi as he did. But you will be the Keeper of the Arrows. No one else has your gift of visions, your strong medicine. No one else can fight harder to protect them. He has selected a temporary hiding place near camp where you must keep them.

"Tonight, even before you visit the sweat lodge and then sleep, you must take the Arrows to their new place. They will be safe enough there until you decide on a permanent spot known only to you."

"I will, certainly. But what have the others said about having White Man Runs Him as their shaman?" Touch the Sky asked, his tone becoming scornful as he used the name Wolf Who Hunts Smiling had given him.

"For now only Chief Gray Thunder knows. Though Gray Thunder plays no favorites, he has grown to admire you. This will be discussed at the next Council of Forty."

"Expect a lively council, buck! Now let us go get the Arrows from your tipi while you tell me their new hiding place."

Dark clouds blew in from the west, and the breeze grew cooler as a threat of rain filled the night air. Thunder rumbled and bone-white tines of lightning danced on the horizon. From behind a thick deadfall, Wolf Who Hunts Smiling and Medicine Flute silently spied on Touch the Sky.

Periodic lightning flashes illuminated the young warrior clearly. He knelt in the middle of a small willow copse located beyond the first bend in the Powder north of camp. A flat rock shaped like a box lid had been lifted away from a neatly dug hole beneath it. Now the two spies watched Touch the Sky lift out a piece of bright yellow oilcloth.

He spread open the weatherproof cloth, then carefully laid a coyote-fur pouch inside it and wrapped it tightly. Wolf Who Hunts Smiling knew full well that inside that pouch lay no less than the very fate of the tribe: four stone-tipped arrows, their shafts dyed bright blue and yellow and fletched with scarlet feathers—the sacred Medicine Arrows.

"Did I not tell you we need only watch him close?" Wolf Who Hunts Smiling gloated in a whisper. "Now the future belongs to us, shaman!"

Wolf Who Hunts Smiling had been aptly named. He was a compact, powerful buck slightly younger than Touch the Sky. His furtive sneer was matched by swift-as-minnow eyes that darted everywhere at once, always watching for the ever expected attack.

In contrast, Medicine Flute watched Touch the Sky from indolent, heavy-lidded eyes. He was the only brave in camp who had challenged Touch the Sky's claim to the title of shaman. Slender, lazy, and untested as a warrior, Medicine Flute was named after the human-bone flute upon which he constantly piped his eerie, toneless notes.

While still young, the intelligent and perceptive youth had realized that visionaries were highly respected by red men, that they did not have to hunt and fight and work as other braves did. So he pretended to have visions and eventually convinced most of his clan that he possessed medicine. With Wolf Who Hunts Smiling goading him on, he had once awed the entire tribe by performing a miracle: setting a star on fire and sending it blazing across the heavens.

But in fact, Wolf Who Hunts Smiling had talked to a reservation Indian educated in a whiteskin school. This so-called miracle was really a comet, and the whiteskin shamans had predicted its passage. Nonetheless, Medicine Flute claimed credit for the spectacular celestial demonstration, which had struck many in the tribe dumb with awe. Wolf Who Hunts Smiling had ambitions to set Medicine Flute up as tribal shaman, thus wresting control of the tribe from Touch the Sky and his allies.

"But, brother," Medicine Flute objected now in a whisper, "surely you do not intend to harm the Arrows?"

"Harm them, buck? Of course not. But we will use them to send a white man's dog to his funeral scaffold."

Despite their nefarious schemes and lack of faith in most of the Cheyenne spirit lore, neither brave was so blasphemous as to actually harm the four sacred Medicine Arrows. Every Cheyenne was taught from birth that the fate of the Arrows was the fate of the tribe. It was the Keeper of the Arrows' solemn duty to protect them with his life, to keep them forever sweet and clean. Once, a Pawnee band had stolen the Sacred Arrows. Until the tribe had managed to retrieve them, every sort of ill luck and tragedy befell the Cheyennes.

"But if we are not going to harm them," Medicine Flute said, "what is left? Surely you are not so soft-brained as to steal them?"

"Steal them is exactly what I intend to do."

Medicine Flute's heavy-lidded eyes shot open wide. "Brother, have you been struck by lightning? The Council of Forty will feed our livers to the camp dogs if they catch us with the Arrows!"

"We will not have them, buck. Rest easy on that score."

"Who will?"

Another flash of lightning revealed the lone brave in the clearing as he pulled the flat rock back into place. It fit naturally under a thick bush of nettles, safe from animals and curious humans. That same lightning flash revealed Wolf Who Hunts Smiling's lupine grin and hateful, scheming eyes.

He gazed off toward a dark and indistinct mass on the horizon—the rugged Sans Arc Mountains. One peak rose high into the night sky. Fine threads of lightning wrapped the craggy summit like a nest of writhing snakes. Again Wolf Who Hunts Smiling thought about the Blackfoot Indian word-bringer who had recently searched him out with a message.

"You will soon meet the brave who will hold the Arrows," Wolf Who Hunts Smiling promised. "The same brave who is finally going to help us send White Man Runs Him to sleep with the worms."

# Chapter Two

"Of course I know what they are," said the Blackfoot renegade named Sis-ki-dee, gazing down at the Medicine Arrows. "You Cheyennes have many foolish beliefs. If I started to piss on them right now, both of you superstitious warriors would try to kill me."

Sis-ki-dee threw back his head and roared with laughter when he saw how nervous his comments made the two Cheyenne visitors. He had no patience for supernatural foolishness. Men kept their weapons to hand and feared no god but the gun. But this wily Wolf Who Hunts Smiling, Sis-ki-dee reminded himself, was a useful ally. Best to humor him and his canny-looking companion, Medicine Flute.

He spoke in the odd mixture of Sioux and

Cheyenne used as a lingua franca among Plains
Indians. "No need to pale, bucks! Foolish or not,
your magic Arrows are safe with me. We must all
cooperate to flush out our quarry and close the
net on him—this tall brave they call the Ghost
Warrior and the Bear Caller."

"Ghost Warrior!" Wolf Who Hunts Smiling spat
into the fire to show his contempt. "He is merely
clever at deft tricks mistaken for magic. No one
in my camp, except his constant shadow Little
Horse, claims to have seen this great battle up
north where Touch the Sky turned Bluecoat
bullets to sand. I call him Woman Face and
White Man Runs Him."

"He is called many things—behind his back,"
Sis-ki-dee remarked quietly in his own language
to his lieutenant, Takes His Share, who sat beside
him.

Sis-ki-dee commanded a band of 30 battle-
hardened warriors. The number had been closer
to 50 until his first encounter with the tall
Cheyenne. That had been in these same Sans
Arc Mountains, when Sis-ki-dee had attempted
to exact tribute from the whiteskin miners who
were building a railroad spur. Unfortunately for
Sis-ki-dee, Touch the Sky had served as the miners' pathfinder—and left the mountains strewn
with dead Blackfoot warriors.

The four braves were holding council near
the craggy summit of Wendigo Mountain. The
highest peak in the Sans Arc range, it was also
considered a tabu spot by most Plains Indians—

the very reason Sis-ki-dee had chosen it for his defensive bastion. Wendigo Mountain was steep and virtually unscalable. It had been scoured by wind and rain for millennia until it was worn down to sheer cliffs except for one narrow, talus-strewn approach. The Cheyennes had ridden up that approach to get here. The camp was further protected by sentry outposts, natural obstacles, and man-made pitfall traps.

The Blackfoot looked at Wolf Who Hunts Smiling, his eyes aglitter with the sickness in his soul. Also called the Contrary Warrior and the Red Peril, Sis-ki-dee had once roamed the rugged country around the Bear Paw Mountains in the northern Montana Territory. But his ruthless, murdering attacks on immigrant trains and bullwhackers had earned a high bounty on his scalp and sent him fleeing south to the Sioux-Cheyenne ranges.

"This plan of yours. I agree it might work."

"It *will* work, Contrary Warrior. The old shaman, Arrow Keeper, has finally dragged his rotting carcass off to die. Now the Council of Forty must decide who will be my tribe's new shaman and Keeper of the Arrows. It will come down to only two choices, the only two braves in the tribe said to possess medicine: White Man Runs Him and Medicine Flute here."

Sis-ki-dee grinned. Big brass rings dangled from slits in his ears, and heavy copper brassards protected his upper arms from enemy lances and arrows. His face was badly marred by smallpox scars. In defiance of the long-haired tribe that had banished him forever, he and all of his contrary braves wore their hair cropped ragged and short.

"You," he said to Medicine Flute. "Do you believe in medicine too?"

"Dangle all the red man's medicine from an empty coup stick," the young brave replied, "and you still have an empty coup stick."

Sis-ki-dee approved this with another grin and a crazy-brave glint to his eyes.

"Unfortunately," Wolf Who Hunts Smiling resumed, "White Man Runs Him will almost surely be selected. Sentiment for old Arrow Keeper runs high among the elders, and this Touch the Sky was the doting old fool's favorite. Yet if I am to take command of the people, I must have my own shaman in power. That means White Man Runs Him must be killed. My ransom plan will accomplish this thing. Then, Contrary Warrior, we two will command a red empire between us."

Sis-ki-dee risked a swift exchange of ironic glances with Takes His Share. We two indeed that glance said. Sis-ki-dee shared power with no one. And the cunning sheen to Wolf Who Hunts Smiling's eyes said that he, too, was not one for dividing up an empire. This was the way the insane Sis-ki-dee liked things to be: treacherous and dangerous, with worthy enemies locking horns in a bloody fight to the death.

But more than anything else, he wanted this tall Cheyenne sent over forever. He had once, in front of the Contrary Warrior's entire band, defeated Sis-ki-dee in a Blackfoot Death Hug: a knife fight with the two opponents' free arms bound together at the wrists. Not only did Touch the Sky win the fight, he humiliated Sis-ki-dee by knocking him out but not killing him—saying, in effect, that he was on a level with soft-brains and women, not worthy of killing.

And that had been a serious mistake. For it was always better to kill a man outright than to humiliate him, to leave him alive to seek revenge.

"We both want this Ghost Warrior killed," Sis-ki-dee said. "He deprived me of a generous peace price from the whiteskin miners. And you say he was the cause of your being stripped of your coup feathers. But medicine or not, he is a warrior who fights like ten men."

"You speak straight-arrow," Wolf Who Hunts Smiling said. "I have raised my battle axe against him for life. May that white man's dog die of the yellow vomit. But I am the first to say it, he stands behind no warrior when the battle cry sounds. My plan is good, yes. But be prepared for a bloody fight, Contrary Warrior. He will not forfeit his life—nor those Arrows—cheaply."

Sis-ki-dee glanced around at his mountain bastion. Huge boulders provided excellent natural breastworks. A fresh deer carcass hung high in a tree, protected from predators. There were also plenty of stores of dried venison and jerked buffalo. Well-armed braves lounged in small groups before their curved wickiups, drinking

40-rod whiskey and gambling with stones. He glanced further up, toward the very pinnacle of the mountain. Should all else fail, there was a secret escape route known only to him.

A smile creased his scarred face. "Not cheaply, perhaps. But count upon it, buck. He will forfeit his life."

"But not the Arrows," Wolf Who Hunts Smiling reminded his secret ally. "They must be returned after his death."

Sis-ki-dee chanced another sly glance at Takes His Share.

"Of course," he reassured his two visitors. "No harm will come to your Sacred Arrows."

Touch the Sky was working his pony in the common corral when he and Little Horse heard the camp crier announce the arrival of a word-bringer.

News was always an important occasion. The two young braves turned their ponies loose and stepped under the buffalo-hair ropes forming the corral. They joined two of their friends, Tangle Hair and Shoots the Bear. Both belonged to the Bowstring Soldier troop, one of several Cheyenne military societies responsible for enforcing the ancient Hunt Law during the annual buffalo hunts. Together, the four braves headed toward the hide-covered council lodge at the center of camp.

Touch the Sky felt Little Horse watching him closely. No doubt he could see clearly that his friend looked distracted, lost in some private worry.

"You have shed much brain sweat lately, brother. Have you been studying Arrow Keeper's painting?" Little Horse said.

Hearing the old shaman's name quickened Touch the Sky's sense of sadness—and hopelessness. Arrow Keeper was gone, probably forever.

"I have, Cheyenne, and done little else. But I might do better to cut sign in the clouds. I cannot even guess what manner of trouble is headed my way."

He didn't add what really cankered at him: Nor what manner of trouble is headed Honey Eater's way. But as if timed to coincide with this thought, he spotted Honey Eater walking with her aunt, Sharp Nosed Woman.

Her jealous mate Black Elk was nowhere in sight. Taking a chance, the two of them exchanged a long glance, their eyes thirsty to drink each other in. Once more Honey Eater's startling beauty caused a sharp pang in his heart.

Her skin was the shade of flawless topaz, her cheekbones delicately and perfectly sculpted. She wore a pretty blue calico dress, made with cloth from the annual treaty goods Touch the Sky had earned for the tribe when he served as pathfinder for the white miners' spur track. The soft material molded itself to her breasts, to the long, sweeping curve of her hips. She had adorned it with elk's teeth, painted shells, and dyed feathers. Honey Eater had also braided her long hair with fresh white columbine petals.

Quickly, almost in an eyeblink, Honey Eater crossed her wrists over her heart. This was Cheyenne sign talk for love.

"Buck," Little Horse warned him quietly. "This is no time to dream. Black Elk has eyes everywhere."

Touch the Sky spotted Lone Bear, leader of Black Elk's Bull Whip Soldier troop, walking with several of Black Elk's troop brothers. They were watching him closely. Quickly he cast his eyes away from Honey Eater.

"Brothers," Tangle Hair said, staring ahead, "which tribe sent this strange messenger? I can tell any tribe by its style of hair. But never have I seen Indians wear their hair like this."

Touch the Sky and Little Horse spotted the word-bringer at the same time, sitting his buckskin pony in front of the council lodge. His face was set in defiant scorn. Immediately recognizing his raggedly cropped hair, they exchanged a wordless glance. They alone of Gray Thunder's tribe had faced these fierce renegade Blackfoot marauders. Now they knew that, true to his promise, the Contrary Warrior had returned to terrorize their homeland.

Sis-ki-dee's words drifted back to Touch the Sky now from the hinterland of memory, his final words after Touch the Sky had defeated him. *You have won the day, Noble Red Man. But Sis-ki-dee swears this. His trail will cross yours soon enough. And then I will skin your face off and lay it over mine with you still alive to see it!*

Now Touch the Sky at least knew the source of this new trouble Arrow Keeper had foretold. He also spotted Black Elk among the warriors ringing the word-bringer. The Blackfoot rode under a white truce flag. But Black Elk was the tribe's battle leader, a fierce warrior who never trusted a potential enemy inside camp.

Black Elk's younger cousin Wolf Who Hunts Smiling stood nearby, his rifle aimed at the messenger. Both braves darted hateful glances at Touch the Sky as he edged closer. Black Elk's scowl was made even fiercer by the wrinkled, leathery flap of his dead ear, which had been severed by a Bluecoat saber. Black Elk had killed the soldier, then calmly sewn the ear back on himself with buckskin thread.

The word-bringer waited until Chief Gray Thunder emerged from his tipi. His refusal to pay homage to a chief or dismount and smoke to the four directions made it clear that these were not friendly tidings. But by strict Plains Indian custom, no word-bringer— not even an ill-behaved enemy—was ever insulted or harmed.

"Cheyenne people!" he announced. "I have been sent by my war chief, Sis-ki-dee, the Contrary Warrior. Attend well to my words, for they are his words and therefore important."

Touch the Sky watched Black Elk's contemptuous scowl deepen. Who was this arrogant Sis-ki-dee? Only Chief Gray Thunder's curt glance convinced him to remain silent. But Touch the Sky noticed that Wolf Who Hunts Smiling had registered no surprise at hearing the renegade's name. He felt the danger-net tightening, for Touch the Sky knew these two treacherous schemers were secret allies.

"Whatever words you have for my people," Gray Thunder replied, "I have ears to hear. There they stand, attending you. Speak them."

"Cheyenne people, know this. You are now a tribe with a new God. For my leader, the Red Peril of the North, the Contrary Warrior named Sis-ki-dee, has your sacred Medicine Arrows!"

These unexpected words landed on the people with the force of buckshot. Numb shock, then a collective gasp of disbelief, ran through the crowd.

"Look to your Keeper of the Arrows," the messenger added, "and ask him if this is not so."

Everyone in Gray Thunder's camp knew Arrow Keeper had left, that Touch the Sky, as his assistant, would be in charge of the Arrows. Now every face turned to stare at him.

Touch the Sky felt warm blood rush into his face. In that moment his eyes flew straight to those of Wolf Who Hunts Smilings'—and the cruel betrayal in the latter's mocking eyes was as clear as a blood spoor in new snow.

Could he? thought Touch the Sky. Could this ambitious monster have done the unthinkable? Not only sullied the Sacred Arrows, but actually have played the turncoat and given them to an enemy?

"Prove this thing is so," Touch the Sky demanded of the word-bringer.

"Prove it is *not* so," the messenger taunted. "Produce the Arrows."

"Do you take us for a camp of soft-brains? I should remove them from hiding now in front of enemies?"

"Never mind then, buck. You may confirm the truth of it when you will. For now, look on this."

Another collective gasp passed through the crowded clearing when the Blackfoot word-bringer stabbed one hand into the pouched front of his clout and produced a piece of soft coyote fur. It was dyed in the intricate geometric patterns of Gray Thunder's band, distinguishing it from the nine other Cheyenne bands that also possessed a set of Medicine Arrows. Everyone instantly recognized it as the cloth used to wrap the Arrows.

"You traitorous dog!" Black Elk roared, closing on Touch the Sky. "You have ruined your tribe! Now I swear by the four directions I'll send your soul west for good!"

But Chief Gray Thunder, a vigorous and stout warrior though well past his fortieth winter, caught Black Elk's arm before the bone-handled knife could leave its sheath.

"Hold, buck! Do not wade in further until we have looked for snakes."

"Father, there stands the snake. Do you realize what this turncoat has done?"

"I realize what he *appears* to have done. I swear it now by the sun and the earth I live on, and this place hears me: If Touch the Sky has indeed let our Arrows into enemy hands, he has no place to hide from Cheyenne justice.

"But place my words in your sash, Black Elk and any others whose thoughts now run to blood. My first duty is to save those Arrows if Maiyun the Good Supernatural will grant it. Now hold, all of you, until we have some sign to guide our way."

The chief looked at the word-bringer again.

"Your leader did not send you merely to taunt us. We are red men, not slyly bargaining Mexicans who come at a price by indirection. Speak like a man and state your leader's terms for the return of the Arrows."

"The mighty Cheyenne demands plain talk? Very well. Here are words you may pick up and examine. Your tribe claims the fate of your Arrows is the fate of the tribe. Within four sleeps your sacred Medicine Arrows will be bloodied, then burned to ashes, unless a ransom is left where Sis-ki-dee tells you to leave it."

His words stunned the tribe into utter silence. Only Gray Thunder spoke, his voice steady but clearly apprehensive.

"What ransom, buck?"

## Wendigo Mountain

The messenger's face divided in a wide grin as he whirled his pony to point at Touch the Sky.

"Within four sleeps. And only one price will get them back. The severed head of that tall buck!"

# Chapter Three

Takes His Share was still half asleep when a sharp kick to his thigh instantly cleared the cobwebs from his eyes. In a heartbeat he sat up in his sleeping robes, a big-bore Lancaster rifle at the ready.

"Wiser to shoot at the Wendigo than at Sis-ki-dee," his leader greeted him, adding his crazy-brave laughter. "Bring a bloody portion of that deer meat over there and follow me."

The sun had barely begun to rim the eastern horizon, but Sis-ki-dee, whose men swore he never slept, was wide awake and keen for sport. His .44 caliber North and Savage rifle, sheathed in buckskin, protruded from under his left arm.

Takes His Share had learned never to question his insane master. He obediently crossed to a cedar brake just beneath their camp and untied a rope made of braided human hair, lowering the deer carcass and using his twine-handled knife to slice off a hind quarter.

"Time is a bird, stout buck," Sis-ki-dee said as the two braves ascended on foot toward the granite peak of Wendigo Mountain. "And now that bird is on the wing. Four sleeps, and the tall Ghost Warrior's head will roast in our campfire until his brains bubble. Four sleeps, if I play the fox well, and *these*—" (he raised the oilskin-wrapped bundle in his hands) "—will be nothing but a thing of smoke, a memory smell. We will have our ransom *and* the pleasure of destroying these pretty-painted sticks."

Sis-ki-dee's pocked face was ugly in the new day's light, the crazy sheen already clear in his shrewd eyes. As they picked their way through the loose talus, he glanced back down the mountain. His camp was in a cup-shaped hollow just below. Further down, the eerie wisps of mist that always shrouded this accursed mountain moved and shifted like something sinister and alive.

"Takes His Share, you fought this Ghost Warrior alongside me once before. Tell me, buck. Can he penetrate our camp?"

"If it were any Indian but that one, I would laugh at the very thought. A titmouse could not slip in unobserved. But truly, Contrary Warrior, they say his life is charmed, and I believe it. I believe that one could penetrate to the heart of a Bluecoat fort and steal their Star Chief's wife from her bed without waking either of them."

Sis-ki-dee approved these wise words with a nod. Takes His Share's ability to size up a situation, and his penchant for straight talk, were the reasons the Blackfoot leader kept him close to the heart of his schemes.

"Your thoughts graze in the same direction as mine. This is a warrior to be feared and respected as well as loathed. So I will not keep the Arrows in camp. They must be hidden in a manner and place equal to his cunning. I know just the spot."

Soon, their breathing ragged from exertion, the two renegades reached the furthermost peak of the rugged mountain. From here the Wyoming Territory stretched out to infinity around them, the mountains folding into foothills, then flattening to the broad brown plains. The Yellowstone and Bighorn Rivers formed winding silver threads twisting north toward the land of the Mandan, Hidatsa, and Assiniboin tribes.

"Now, buck," Sis-ki-dee said, pointing to a slight opening in the rocks. "See that place? A mountain lion lives in there, a she-bitch with hungry cubs. She needs red meat to give them rich milk. Tear that meat you have into tender gobbets. Then make a trail from the opening across to that rock spine over there. Once you have done it, look sharp and move quickly away downwind. This bitch is in a fighting fettle to protect her cubs. If she pokes out while you are near the opening, I will send her back inside with a shot."

Takes His Share did as he was ordered. Sis-ki-dee took up a position out of sight behind a massive boulder. Takes His Share scrambled nimbly from rock to rock, leaving bloody pieces of meat. Tawny fur soon filled the opening, then a magnificent mountain lion peeked cautiously out, twitching her nose, sampling the air.

Ravenously, she devoured the meat and moved out after more. When she disappeared behind the rock spine, Sis-ki-dee hurried into the den.

It was actually a huge underground cavern, most of whose entrance had been obliterated by a rockslide. Sis-ki-dee had explored it well when he had selected this tabu mountain for his stronghold. Now he held his rifle close to his chest and squeezed through the narrow entrance.

He ignored the squirming cubs in their bed of leaves and debris near the entrance. The cavern opened up into a vast chamber illuminated from surface shafts above. From the rear of this chamber a series of tunnels led to the backside of Wendigo Mountain. They emerged onto cliffs, but with ropes a man could descend. Sis-ki-dee had stashed many things at the end of the tunnels.

Hurrying so as not to meet the she-bitch mountain lion, Sis-ki-dee stepped into the cool air of one of the tunnels. Then he lay his rifle aside and, seeking out rough hand and footholds, climbed high until he reached the wet, cold limestone at the top of the tunnel. When he could climb no further, he secreted the slicker-wrapped Medicine Arrows inside a narrow fissure.

*There,* he thought as he climbed down. *Those Arrows are now lost to the world.* He didn't really expect the tall Cheyenne to simply offer his head for the Arrows. He would be coming after them. And Sis-ki-dee planned to be ready. For if he killed this Cheyenne with his own hands, there would be no need to return the Arrows.

Sis-ki-dee had lost face in front of his men when the Cheyenne had defeated him. Now the Cheyenne would literally lose his, for Blackfoot warriors often skinned their enemies' faces off instead of taking scalps. They did it while the victim was still alive, and then laid the bloody facial skin over their own, the tormentor's mocking eyes staring at the victim through his own eyeholes.

Grinning his crazy-by-thunder grin, Sis-ki-dee slipped back outside just in time to avoid the returning mountain lion.

"Fathers! Brothers! Have ears for my words, for you know I speak only the straight talk."

The council lodge fell silent when Black Elk stood and spoke these words. He was their war leader and sat behind few men in council. This important emergency meeting of the Council of Forty had been called the morning after Sis-ki-dee's word-bringer announced the ransoming of their Sacred Arrows.

Touch the Sky recalled the joy that had swept

through the ranks of his tribal enemies at the word-bringer's chilling pronouncement. That same sneer of celebration lighted Black Elk's stern face as he spoke.

"You know me well," Black Elk said. "My lips have touched the common pipe we just smoked. I have strewn enemy bones from here to the Marias River, I have counted coup on Apaches, Utes, Pawnees, Crows, and blue-bloused soldiers. When did Black Elk ever hide in his tipi when his brothers were on the warpath?"

Touch the Sky felt the fierce warrior's obsidian eyes search him out as he added:

"Cheyenne bucks! Do you finally see now the results of our foolish indiscretion? Do you finally understand what my cousin, Wolf Who Hunts Smiling, has been warning us all along? Do you finally realize that the well-being of our tribe cannot be entrusted to a white man's dog? Now we are up against it! These are the blackest days our tribe has faced, and there sits the cause of this new woe!"

Touch the Sky felt the hostile glances directed at him. He sorely missed the presence of old Arrow Keeper, always his best and most influential ally in council. But things were not the same as they had been during his early days in the tribe. He also had supporters now in that sea of red faces. Some of them were important supporters.

"This Sis-ki-dee," Black Elk continued. "We know not what manner of man he is, nor even where to find him. We cannot even renew the Arrows as preparation for fighting him. He has the Arrows, thanks to this one."

Now Wolf Who Hunts Smiling rose.

"Fathers and brothers, have ears! I have no desire to speak in a wolf bark against old Arrow Keeper. But everyone knows he grew soft-brained in his frosted years and doted on this Touch the Sky. Otherwise the sacred Arrows would never have been entrusted to him. They should have been left with Medicine Flute, whose big medicine was witnessed by all in the tribe when he set a star on fire. What has this one ever done except lay claims to 'visions' no one but he has seen?"

This was greeted with many approving murmurs. Chief Gray Thunder, presiding over this council of the clan Headmen, folded his arms until it had quieted down.

Now Little Horse rose. Everyone paid attention, even his enemies, for here was a brave honored in council for his fighting courage when he had only 15 winters behind him.

"I have no ears for this! Everyone knows that Black Elk, Wolf Who Hunts Smiling, and many in their Bull Whip Soldier troop have turned their hearts to stone toward Touch the Sky.

"Black Elk, consumed with jealousy, claims that Touch the Sky wishes to put on the old moccasin by bulling his squaw. Wolf Who Hunts Smiling claims Touch the Sky is a spy for the *Mah-ish-ta-schee-da*."

Little Horse had used the Cheyenne word meaning Yellow Eyes, the name his tribe had given to white men because the first palefaces they ever saw were mountain men suffering from severe jaundice.

"Both of his accusers are warriors to be reckoned with. Indeed, Black Elk trained me and Touch the Sky in the combat arts. But neither brave has truth firmly by the tail. Arrow Keeper is no fool. His medicine is respected throughout the Red Nation. If *he* selected Touch the Sky to be Keeper of the Arrows, then count upon it, the best brave was picked."

Arrow Keeper had many friends in the tribe. This speech, too, was greeted with approving murmurs.

Again Chief Gray Thunder folded his arms until the lodge grew quiet. He looked frustrated. His tribe faced a crisis unprecedented since Pawnees had stolen those same Arrows. Yet this bitter, acrimonious meeting was doing nothing to get the Arrows back.

And get them back Gray Thunder knew they must. The Medicine Arrows were the great flywheel that regulated Cheyenne moral life. An angry brave considering the murder of another Cheyenne, for example, knew that such a crime would also bloody the Arrows, and thus the entire tribe. It was the thought of the Arrows that held most troublemakers in check. Without them, lawlessness might soon descend on the tribe.

"Brothers! I speak as your Chief. The duty of

a chief is not to take one side against the other within his tribe. Rather he must determine the collective will of his people.

"This is what I propose now—that we give over this useless trading of accusations until this emergency is behind us. In good time we will have a special council to select our new shaman and Arrow Keeper. Certainly this is important. But for now, bucks, only think! Four sleeps, and then our fate may be horribly sealed. First things first. For now, our every word, thought, and deed must be aimed at saving those Arrows."

These wise words drew approval from all assembled. Now Touch the Sky rose. He had carefully selected his words. His eyes searched out Wolf Who Hunts Smiling.

"Fathers and brothers, have ears for my words. Count upon it, there is treachery for our tribe, but I am not the source. However, our chief has spoken, and I agree. There will be time later to deal with traitors. For now, only one question looms. What do we do about our Arrows? Rather, what do *I* do? The tribe cannot mount a large war-party for fear of endangering the Arrows. And truly, traitors or not, I must admit that somehow my carelessness led to the loss of our Medicine Arrows. I might simply do the manly thing and offer my head now. But brothers, I know this mad renegade called Sis-ki-dee. I have fought him, and so has Little Horse. He is no brave to trifle with. I tell you now, and this place hears me: He will not return those Arrows no matter how we try to appease him."

"Notice how convincingly this one argues that his own death would be pointless," Wolf Who Hunts Smiling put in scornfully. "No coward, he!"

"And *you* have walked between Touch the Sky and the campfire," Tangle Hair said angrily, alluding to the Cheyenne way of announcing one's intention to kill another. "Now you seize the first opportunity to see him killed."

Again the lodge erupted in noisy debate. Touch the Sky silenced it.

"As our chief said," he resumed, "this occasion is too urgent for pointless fighting. So hear me well, then take my words away with you and examine them later. I have four sleeps to locate those Arrows. If they are not safely returned to our tribe before the time expires, my enemies can hold their victory dance. For even though I know Sis-ki-dee for a liar, even though I know he will not return those Arrows after my death, yet my head *will* be severed in payment."

# Chapter Four

"Black Elk! I would speak with you, cousin."

Wolf Who Hunts Smiling's voice sounded loud and clear outside the raised elkskin entrance flap of the tipi. It was late morning, shortly after the council meeting broke up.

Black Elk glanced up from the whetstone he was using to sharpen his knife. He watched Honey Eater, who was gathering her beadwork into a basket woven of willow stems.

"Your war leader hears you," Black Elk called out to his cousin. Then, to Honey Eater: "Where are you going?" he demanded.

"Where I always go at this time of day with my beadwork. To my aunt Sharp Nosed Woman's tipi."

Her disrespectful and resentful tone sent dark blood into his face.

"I know full well why you go there so often. That way, the spindly colt Two Twists can bring you honeyed messages from your randy buck, White Man Runs Him."

"You call him a spindly colt, yet that did not stop you from ordering your Bull Whip brothers to savagely beat him for befriending me. But as you say," Honey Eater continued coldly, "why should I deny it, for clearly Black Elk knows everything."

Quicker than an eyeblink, the hot rage was on him. Black Elk rose and pinned her by both arms. His nostrils flared wide with his suddenly heavy breathing.

"Only one thing makes me forbear from killing you now," he told her in a low, dangerous voice. "I know that Touch the Sky, your stag-in-rut, is now doomed. I am going to let you live to see his death confirmed. But once he is sent across the Great Divide, defiant daughter of a great chief, you will learn exactly what your 'pride' is worth. For I will kill you with my own hand."

"You *would* kill a woman," she shot back defiantly. "Just know this, bold warrior who threatens those he has sworn to protect. What you do to me is of no consequence. I know not if you are involved in this foul business of stealing our Arrows. I know you are no coward, nor do I think you are a traitor. But I know your evil cousin who is out there right now waiting for you. I know he had a wolf's paw in this business—I see it all over his shrewd face. If Touch the Sky is killed for ransom, then I swear by the four directions I will kill your cousin! And one way or another, I will kill anyone else who was involved."

This was so brazen and astounding that Black Elk forgot to feel anger. He uttered a harsh bark of laughter.

"Woman, have you eaten peyote? True, my cousin is as glad as any man must be to know that this tall dog is finally marked out for death. But he had nothing to do with giving our Arrows to our enemy. Your pretend Cheyenne is the treacherous culprit with that sin on his head."

"Cousin!" Wolf Who Hunts Smiling called impatiently. "Are your moccasins picketed to the ground? I am waiting."

Black Elk stepped outside, his dark eyes snapping sparks.

"Does the calf bellow to the bull? I trained you, buck."

Wolf Who Hunts Smiling bit back a sharp reply. In truth, he no longer feared his older cousin, whom he considered too stupid and loyal to do anything except command a battle—which, admittedly, he did second to no brave. But leading an entire nation of Indians, shaping them to a man's purpose—that required a shrewd brain indeed. For now, though, he needed Black Elk and his fellow Bull Whips with him, not against him.

"You trained me, indeed, and a good job, too. My ghost will never cry for lack of good training. But tell me, cousin, do your meat racks need inspecting?"

This was the signal that he wanted to discuss something in private. They moved out behind Black Elk's tipi.

"Cousin," he gloated when they had moved out of Honey Eater's hearing, "Touch the Sky can make the he-bear talk in council. But it is all over now except for the dying!"

"Familiar words. But he has outfoxed death before. This Sis-ki-dee, who is he? We know nothing of his mettle. Why should this Blackfoot renegade succeed where legions have failed?"

Wolf Who Hunts Smiling was careful to tread lightly now. Only Medicine Flute knew of his secret connivance with Sis-ki-dee. Black Elk was covered with hard enough bark but respected most of the Spirit Ways. He would never cooperate in a plot to steal the tribe's Sacred Arrows, no matter how much his jealous wrath desired the death of Touch the Sky. And in fact even Wolf Who Hunts Smiling did not want to see those Arrows harmed. He had begun to have second thoughts about trusting Sis-ki-dee.

"As you say," Wolf Who Hunts Smiling agreed. "But cousin, this mystery brave was wily enough to obtain the Arrows. He may well see this thing through."

Honey Eater emerged from the tipi. Watching her cross the clearing, heading to her aunt's tipi, Black Elk felt the heat of his earlier anger returning. His wily younger cousin watched his face closely and saw which way the jealous buck's thoughts drifted.

"Black Elk," he said, "have you noticed how Woman Face's unbelievable carelessness with our Arrows has turned many against him? Many who had merely been indifferent before?"

"Of course. Who could not notice this? I have eyes."

"As you say. And clearly, if this thing goes badly, it would also tell against those who are loyal to him. Little Horse, Tangle Hair, Two Twists, Shoots the Bear—certain others," he added meaningfully, not having to say Honey Eater's name.

"It would, Cheyenne." Black Elk's tone was more curious, less impatient now, for he realized his cousin was homing in on a target.

Wolf Who Hunts Smiling weighed each word carefully. He was taking a chance here. But this was one of his chief skills: Knowing the soft places where he could grab hold of a man.

"If, for example, a number of reliable braves were to come forth and speak a thing. Say, the fact that a certain married Cheyenne woman lifted her dress for him in secret, that they witnessed this thing. Perhaps more than once. Well, then. . . ." Wolf Who Hunts Smiling shrugged one shoulder. "Why, the Star Chamber might well absolve a squaw's husband should he understandably become violent and, in a fit of just rage, somehow punish her. Perhaps even slay her."

A long silence followed as Black Elk mulled over his cousin's hints. In the Cheyenne tongue, the word 'murder' was the same as the word 'putrid,' for the murder of a fellow Cheyenne caused the internal corruption of the individual and the tribe. Thus the murder stigma was strong. Even if a murderer was not banned—for the Cheyennes were loathe to banish their own—he could never again smoke from the common pipe or eat from a common utensil. He could never participate in the Renewal of the Arrows or the Spring Dance or the annual buffalo hunt.

Wolf Who Hunts Smiling was reminding him, however, that if Honey Eater were charged with adultery, especially with such a heinous criminal as Touch the Sky, then the Cheyenne Star Chamber would almost certainly absolve him of the act of wife-slaughter. The braves taking part in this secret court of last resort were known only to Chief Gray Thunder, nor could their judgments be questioned.

Black Elk once more recalled Honey Eater's arrogant tone, and her increasing defiance of him. How much humiliation had her love for Touch the Sky caused Black Elk? How many jokes had been spawned by his failure to get her with whelp? He could have crawled off like a whipped dog when Touch the Sky had saved Honey Eater from her Comanche and Kiowa captors after Black Elk had failed. It would be satisfying indeed to finally feel her delicate neck snap in his grip.

He met his cousin's eye. That look sealed a silent agreement.

"Straight talk, buck. As you say, it would go hard for all who were loyal to one who jeopardized the Arrows. Even for a woman."

*There will be trouble ahead for Touch the Sky, trouble behind for Honey Eater.*

Arrow Keeper's words set up a ghostly refrain in Touch the Sky's thoughts, goading him to action. But *what* action? His only clue was the crude pictograph warning. Puzzle over it as he might, it was like trying to make out the bottom of a muddy river.

*You must now act on your own or you will never survive the schemes and dangers your enemies have in store for you.*

Never had he felt so alone in a hostile world. Even during his earliest days with the tribe, even before he had learned that Indians mount their horses from the right side, Arrow Keeper had been there with his loyalty and his magic. Touch the Sky's own shaman sense told him that Arrow Keeper was still alive. But it was useless to look for him when he chose not to be found.

As he studied the pictograph while readying his battle rig to ride out, he held his face impassive in spite of the shame he felt. Yes, the wily Wolf Who Hunts Smiling was involved in this thing. But even so, Touch the Sky knew he had somehow been careless. Now the Medicine Arrows were in enemy hands.

As the result of some hard and bloody fights to prove his bravery and loyalty, Touch the Sky had earned a growing number of supporters within the tribe. Now only a few would visit him with a loaded pipe or even look him in the eye and nod. True death for an Indian, Arrow Keeper had taught him early, is to be alone forever. Until he returned those Arrows, he was alone. And if he did not do it soon enough, he would be dead.

Death, Touch the Sky told himself as he secured an axe to his pony's rope-rigging, he could accept. He feared it, of course, as any sane man does. But he could face it. However, Arrow Keeper was not one to raise an alarm lightly—and how could Touch the Sky protect Honey Eater once he was sent under?

"Brother!"

Startled, he glanced up. It was Little Horse who called to him. He was accompanied by Tangle Hair and his Bowstring Troop brother Shoots the Bear. Also with them was Two Twists, the young warrior named after his habit of wearing his hair in double braids. All four warriors led ponies rigged for battle.

"When do we ride out?" Little Horse called out boldly. "I am keen for sport, nor do I plan to die in my tipi."

Touch the Sky opened his mouth to protest. But then he knew it would be useless. Each one of these braves would gladly die for him. They had made up their minds to ride out. And truly, he welcomed them. He would not embarrass them with thanks.

"When do we ride out?" Touch the Sky lifted the doeskin flap. "As soon as Arrow Keeper's mysterious art yields a first clue."

His friends hobbled their mounts and gathered round him. Touch the Sky opened the simple claybank painting up in the grass in front of his tipi. Each brave crowded close and studied the crude illustrations: a mountain peak, an eagle's tail feather, a dark, curving line.

"Truly," Little Horse said, glancing at the sawtooth horizon all around them, "there are mountains enough in or near our hunting grounds. Nothing about this painting helps us tell which one."

Two Twists squinted and bent closer to the doeskin. "Why did Arrow Keeper smudge this with charcoal?"

"Where, little brother?"

"Here." Two Twists pointed at a spot about halfway up the painted mountain. Touch the Sky looked closer. He had assumed that that smudged girdle was simply dirt that had got on the painting before it dried. But now he saw that Two Twists was right: It was charcoal. Some of it came off on his finger now as he rubbed it.

Little Horse frowned and glanced northwest, toward the Sans Arc range. His eyes narrowed thoughtfully.

"Maiyun grant that I am wrong," he muttered.

Touch the Sky met his eyes. "Wrong about what, brother?"

"This ring about the mountain. It is halfway up. There is a peak in the Sans Arc range, one you cannot see from here. You were close to it when you sighted the track for the iron horse through the Sans Arc pass. You may have noticed it—mostly steep cliffs and loose talus, and it is constantly shrouded in a ring of mist about halfway up."

Touch the Sky nodded. "As you say. I remember it. I remember I was glad the track ran past it, for it was as treacherous as any I have seen."

"Not merely the slope," Little Horse said grimly. "Have you heard the people talk of Wendigo Mountain?"

A cool feather tickled the tall brave's spine. "I have, though I know little about it."

"I should have thought of it before," Little Horse said, musing out loud. "It is exactly the spot that one as cunning as Sis-ki-dee would pick."

"Bad medicine protects that place," Tangle Hair put in, glancing off toward the northwest. "The Cheyenne, the Lakota, the Arapaho, even the mountain-loving Ute—all avoid this place. It is said that any brave who touches its slope will never leave Wendigo Mountain alive."

"What caused such bad medicine?" Touch the Sky said. "The mountains are a gift from the Day Maker, Maiyun. Only a great evil could taint gifts from the Powerful One."

"Only the greatest," Little Horse agreed. He glanced uncomfortably at the rest. Touch the Sky had not grown up with them, hearing the old stories. Reluctantly, Little Horse untied the chamois pouch hanging from his sash. It contained rich brown tobacco traded from whiteskins. He had been saving it for a special occasion. Now, reluctant to talk about such unholy things without paying tribute to the spirits, he scattered it on the ground. Watching him, Touch the Sky felt another chill.

"It happened after the Pawnees stole our Medicine Arrows," Little Horse explained. "Before we were even children on our fathers' knees. A group of Cheyenne hunters were trapped out on the plains by a huge Crow war party. Crow Crazy Dogs—you know them well, buck."

Touch the Sky nodded grimly. Crow Crazy Dogs were highly feared suicide warriors. Once engaged in an attack, they were sworn to either defeat their enemies or die. Touch the Sky and Little Horse had fought them in a fierce skirmish while serving as voyageurs on land-grabber Wes Munro's keelboat.

"The Cheyennes fled into the Sans Arc range. They selected the peak now known as Wendigo Mountain because it was the most formidable. Because of the mists, they did not realize the opposite side was all cliffs."

"The relentless Crazy Dogs," Shoots the Bear took up the narrative, "locked onto the Cheyennes like hounds on a blood scent. They backed them on to the cliffs. The Cheyennes used all their musket balls and arrows."

"Then," Tangle Hair took over, "rather than give the Crazy Dogs the pleasure of torturing them, the Cheyennes all sang their death song. As one, all twelve hunters locked arms and stepped off the cliffs and were impaled on the basalt turrets far below. The bodies were never recovered."

All five Cheyennes made the cutoff sign, as one did when speaking of the dead.

"They died unnatural deaths after dark," Little Horse said. "Bad deaths. Now all twelve are souls in torment, doomed to haunt Wendigo Mountain. Indeed, some swear you can hear their groans in the moaning of the wind. It would be Sis-ki-dee's nature to pick this place, knowing he is safe from attack there."

Touch the Sky looked at the rest. "I am convinced now, brother, that you have truth firmly by the tail. And so I must attack this Wendigo Mountain, tabu or not. Now are the rest of you still keen for sport?"

Indeed, there was little bravado in their manner now. The same Cheyenne who would ride unflinching straight into a stampeding buffalo herd would flee from an easy fight if he were not correctly painted to please the Holy Ones. Nor would he be called a coward, so great was the belief in matters supernatural.

Abruptly, Little Horse thrust out his lance. After the slightest hesitation, the others, too, laid their lances across his.

"We ride after our Arrows," Little Horse vowed. "My life, my honor, are pledged to them. If I fall, it will be on Blackfoot bones. No matter how hard the battle, no matter if I must face the Wendigo himself, I will not flinch. Our enemies have no place to hide from me!"

One by one, the others added their pledge.

"I am riding with the best," Touch the Sky said simply. "Ipewa. Good."

He grabbed a handful of the calico's mane and swung up onto her back. His eyes dwelled one final time on the jagged granite peaks of the Sans Arc range.

"May the Holy Ones ride with us," he prayed softly, and with that the small war party rode out, singing a battle song.

# Chapter Five

The five Cheyennes made good time across their familiar ranges. They crossed the flat tableland near the rivers, then the rolling tall-grass plains. Their mounts were strong from the new grass, and rivers, streams, and runoff rills were plentiful.

Even with the imminent danger they faced, Touch the Sky's senses were alert to the beauty around him. The fertile green river valleys dotted with bright verbena and golden crocuses; the pure, quick-flowing water of the Powder and the Little Bighorn; the Yellowstone, teeming with trout and bluegill; the fathomless blue sky, opening like an infinite dome above them. The Cheyenne spotted distant herds of antelope, their white tails flashing in the sun, while pronghorn sheep grazed in the lush bunchgrass.

Time was critical, so the normal routine based on the rising and setting of the sun and moon was abandoned. They simply rode and camped, rode and camped, sleeping briefly; otherwise they paused only to rest and water the horses. They made simple cold camps, killing no fresh game and subsisting on dried venison and pemmican. Following this dogged schedule, the hardy band reached the foothills of the Sans Arc range within one full sleep.

Good time, Touch the Sky knew, but it also meant that only three sleeps remained until Sis-ki-dee's deadline. It was the deadline for his death, certainly, but Touch the Sky couldn't stop reminding himself even his head would not purchase those Medicine Arrows from a brave as hateful and insane as Sis-ki-dee. Touch the Sky would die *and* the Arrows would somehow be destroyed if that crazy renegade had his way.

And Honey Eater, his death would somehow entail her destruction as well. Truly, thought Touch the Sky, it would go hard for anyone who ever showed him friendship and loyalty, including every brave now riding with him.

"Brothers," Little Horse called back as he debouched from a narrow ravine, "ahead lies Wendigo Mountain."

Even before Touch the Sky caught a first glimpse, Little Horse's muted tone alerted him to the daunting nature of this mission. Together they had faced 200 buffalo hiders armed with

Hawken rifles, been mercilessly tortured aboard Wes Munro's keelboat, fought their way out of a whiskey-trader's fortress. But then they had faced only death; now they faced a *bad* death, the kind that left an Indian's soul crying in the wind for eternity.

Touch the Sky's pony flexed her strong hindquarters, leaping up onto the flat, and the young Cheyenne felt a ball of ice replace his stomach.

The Sans Arc range towered before them, rising above steep headlands and deep gorges scrubbed by white-water rivers. The railroad spur that Touch the Sky had sighted through for Caleb Riley and his crew lay far over on the northern slopes. But Wendigo Mountain itself could not be missed at this distance. Its tall peak disappeared into the low gray belly of clouds—and that eerie belt of mist circled it just beyond the halfway point.

"See?" Shoots the Bear pointed. "Only one slope goes up."

"The rest," said Tangle Hair, "is all worn away to cliffs."

"If our enemy waits up there," Two Twists added, "they are as safe as eagles in their nests."

"They are waiting." Touch the Sky believed this even though they had spotted not one sign so far of Sis-ki-dee's band. He saw this thing with the eye Arrow Keeper had taught him to use, the shaman eye, which read sign even the best scouts missed.

"But eagles die, too," he added. "Two Twists is right. Anyone watching that slope could pick us off as if we were turkeys on a log. It hints at a bloody business, brothers. Though time is scarce, we must make a fast scout all the way around the base of the mountain. Scour every piece of it. If there is any other way up, we must take it."

The rest agreed. They divided into two teams, Touch the Sky and Little Horse setting out to the west, Tangle Hair, Shoots the Bear, and Two Twists circling to the east.

The sun tracked further across the sky, and more valuable time slipped away as the two teams circled the mountain. But an alternate route appeared out of the question. With the exception of that one narrow slope up the southern face, only rugged cliffs were visible. And the base of many of these was rendered inaccessible by massive heaps of scree—fallen and broken rock, some of it on the verge of forming dangerous slides. Touch the Sky felt something else during this quick circuit of Wendigo Mountain: the unmistakable presence of great evil. Not just the evil represented by Sis-ki-dee and his murdering band, which was evil enough for this world. What he felt now, even more strongly, was an evil of place—a sense that bad medicine haunted this mountain, a poison waiting to infect any fool who headed up that steep slope.

"The Contrary Warrior knows his business well," Little Horse complained bitterly.

The preliminary scouting was finished, and all five braves had assembled again beneath the southern slope. By now the sun was low in the west, their shadows long and growing purple behind them.

"Did you see any sign of them up there?" Tangle Hair said. "We did not."

Touch the Sky shook his head.

"Perhaps," Shoots the Bear suggested, hope lifting his tone, "they have no sentries on the slope. Perhaps they feel too secure up there to bother."

Tangle Hair and Two Twists nodded at this, as did Little Horse, but Touch the Sky believed they were wrong. Shoots the Bear, however, was a respected Bow String trooper who had distinguished himself in the fight against the buffalo hiders. A Cheyenne leader did not impose his will on his men—he determined the collective desire of the group. Thus, whatever happened later, they had spoken as one and no individual was blamed.

"We will see about this slope," he agreed. "But first let us see if we can outfox the foxes."

Since this was not to be a battle fought on the open plains, the Cheyennes had brought no remounts—only two packhorses in the event they had dead or wounded to haul out. Working quickly, Touch the Sky borrowed a buckskin shirt and trousers from Tangle Hair and Two Twists. Working out of sight of the slope, he stuffed them well with grass and then tied them to the extra mount. A stuffed, feathered headdress was secured to the sham warrior with rawhide whangs.

"Nothing fearsome at this range," he admitted when the crude Indian was ready. "But perhaps he becomes more dangerous with distance." He slapped the pony's rump and sent her up the slope.

For some time the sturdy little high-country mustang picked its way carefully through the talus, as nimble as a mule. The braves watched anxiously from below, unsure how to interpret this.

"Perhaps our enemy is not up there at all?" Two Twist said.

"He is up there," Little Horse suggested, "but there are no sentries on the slope."

"Unless," Shoots the Bear reminded them, "they have recognized our trick. They may be holding back to lure a real Indian target that bleeds."

Touch the Sky opened his mouth to speak. Suddenly he spotted a bright flash of light above, a flash too powerful to have been the mere glimmer of quartz or mica. A flash he recognized as a mirror signal.

A heartbeat later a rifle shot split the silence. The feathered headdress flew from the mock warrior, dragging grass stuffing with it. The pony shied, crow-hopped sideways as it had been trained to do under fire, then turned and raced back down the slope.

Two Twists ran to catch the pony's hackamore. The rest stared at Touch the Sky. Now the sun was a dull orange ball balanced just above the western horizon.

# Wendigo Mountain

"What now?" Little Horse said. He nodded at the setting sun. "Your trick may have saved one of us, brother. But only three sleeps remain now, and we have done nothing except make them waste a bullet."

Touch the Sky's mouth formed a grim, determined slit.

"We have done nothing, you speak straight-arrow there. As much as I am loath to do it, buck, I see no other course. Our Cheyenne way forbids fighting after dark. But we have no choice. Any brave who wishes may return to camp now and know he is not a coward. For after Sister Sun goes to her rest, we move up that slope."

"Contrary Warrior," Takes His Share said to his battle chief, "I have noticed a thing. You have hidden the Cheyenne Medicine Arrows well. Even I do not know their exact spot. You handled them with great care, I noticed. Do you believe there is medicine attached to these Arrows?"

The sun had flamed out in a fiery blaze of red glory, and now Wendigo Mountain belonged to the night. Despite the warm days, nights were cool up in these altitudes, especially with the constantly shrieking wind. Legend claimed that the shriek was the death cries of those Cheyenne warriors who had plunged off the cliffs long ago.

Sis-ki-dee flashed his crazy-by-thunder grin in the gathering darkness.

"Believe? Would you ask a hawk if it believes a mouse should not be eaten? Stout buck, if I believed their other-world nonsense, I would have destroyed their 'Sacred Arrows' the moment they filled my hands. It is *their* puny faith that grants value to those pretty sticks, not mine. I play their game to keep that value high."

Ten of Sis-ki-dee's best fighters were positioned behind the rocks flanking the narrow slope. The belt of mist around Wendigo Mountain was in fact steam from underground hot springs. A huge fissure had opened above the springs, and steam constantly escaped. Conflicting wind currents formed the permanent belt. Now it lay just below the Blackfoot position. They had pulled back after realizing how the resourceful Cheyennes had tricked them with the dummy warrior.

The night was dark; a cloud-mottled sky and a weak quarter moon made little illumination. Sis-ki-dee had slid his North and Savage .44 from its sheath and now held it at the ready across the top of a boulder. Takes His Share's big-bore Lancaster rifle lay beside it.

"Go remind the others one more time," Sis-ki-dee said. "They may kill any but the tall Ghost Warrior. He is to be taken alive."

Sis-ki-dee knew Touch the Sky would eventually have to die, of course, and it would be a hard death. He had lost status with his men when this tall Cheyenne had defeated him in the Death Hug match at the railroad camp. Sis-ki-dee's authority was based on fear—his men's fear of his own invincibility. Now, every time he failed anew to kill the Cheyenne, he risked his position of unquestionable authority.

Takes His Share materialized beside him out of the grainy blackness.

"They have all been reminded," he assured his leader. "The tall one will be taken alive."

"Good. Their little ruse earlier with the decoy shows they mean to play children's games with us. But soon enough they will not feel so playful."

Sis-ki-dee's tribe did not waste human scalps as trophies. They had discovered that human-hair ropes remained stronger in rain than buffalo or horse hair. Thus scalps were taken to make ropes. As for war trophies, it was their custom to remove an enemy's entire facial skin.

Just thinking about it made Sis-ki-dee grin like a happy baby. How his men would howl and praise his name when he danced around the fire, that tall Cheyenne's wrinkled visage worn over his own face—his own triumph-gleaming eyes peering through the empty holes!

# Chapter Six

Touch the Sky's band made a temporary camp in the foothills, waiting for full darkness to settle over the mountains.

As they prepared for their dangerous ascent, they could still make out the dark, looming presence of Wendigo Mountain. Even here, back in the hills, they could hear the terrible shrieking of those winds up on the slope—winds that raised eerie human cries, cries of pain and desolation, but also cries of warning.

How many wise Indians, Touch the Sky wondered, had heard that warning and heeded it?

Not one brave in this band of five had ever shown the white feather. All had been tested in battle, even young Two Twists, who had only 17 winters behind him. Touch the Sky knew they were warriors, each of them straight grain clear through.

And yet none of them had ever faced such a test as this. They had all grown up believing that Wendigo Mountain was a place of terror, suffering, and death, a place to be avoided at all costs. "If you do not behave," Cheyenne mothers often threatened their children, "I'll send you to Wendigo Mountain." They were up against not only a formidable physical foe, but powerful bad medicine as well.

Little was said as they inspected their weapons. Sand was carefully wiped from crimped cartridges, their animal-tendon bowstrings were tightened and closely scrutinized for frayed spots. Little Horse ran all four revolving barrels of his scattergun around to check the action; Touch the Sky made sure he had a fresh primer cap behind the loading gate of his Sharps.

They had no idea what they might encounter, if or how long they might be pinned down. So they stuffed their parfleches and legging sashes with dried venison and bitterroot, as well as strips of cloth for binding wounds. The slope was hard and littered with plenty of sharp rocks and flints. They took the precaution of stuffing their moccasins with dead grass.

As was the custom, each brave said a brief, silent battle prayer as he touched his personal medicine, which was the totem of his clan. These totems were kept in small rawhide pouches on their clouts. Touch the Sky had no official clan.

But Arrow Keeper had presented him with a set of badger claws—the totem of Chief Running Antelope of the Northern Cheyenne, killed in the year the white man's winter-count called 1840, the year Touch the Sky had been born. Arrow Keeper called this chief Touch the Sky's father, and Touch the Sky had never known Arrow Keeper to speak bent words.

"Brother," Little Horse said curiously, who had seen his friend remove the badger claws and pray over them, "I would ask you a thing."

"I have ears to hear you, buck. Ask this thing."

"Brother, we have saved each other's lives more than once. We fought Bluecoats and whiskey-traders and land-grabbers and Pawnees, fought all of them side by side and then smeared our bodies with their blood. We stood shoulder to shoulder at the Buffalo Battle and sent many white hiders' souls across the Great Divide. So tell me only this.

"You know that I have seen the mark of the warrior buried in your hair. An arrow point so perfect it might have been fashioned by Maiyun the Day Maker. And I recall when the Bull Whips set upon you during the buffalo hunt, beating you after Wolf Who Hunts Smiling played the fox and accused you of violating Hunt Law. You told them your father was a great warrior, greater than any in Gray Thunder's tribe."

Touch the Sky nodded. "Certainly I too recall this. The Bull Whips mocked me for a liar."

"They did. But others did not. You fight like

five men—clearly you descend from a stout warrior's loins! But brother, when you sought your great vision at Medicine Lake, was it revealed to you the part you are meant to play in our tribe's destiny? How much was made known to you?"

Touch the Sky thought for a long time. As he did, he sharpened his obsidian knife and stared out toward the shadow of Wendigo Mountain.

"Much was revealed," he finally answered. "But it was like shadow pictures on snow. The shape of things was there, but not the substance."

If this answer confused him, Little Horse did not show it. He merely nodded, accepting these words.

"Truly, I have heard this about visions and medicine dreams. That they convey great truths, yet little that can be told with words."

"As you say. They are felt more than known."

The Cheyennes' final preparation was to wrap their heads in blankets or buffalo robes. This was to prepare their night vision for the moonless trek up that dangerous slope. An hour spent in total darkness would dilate their pupils so much that objects now hidden to sight would take on linearity and depth.

Little Horse's questions had set Touch the Sky thinking about his harrowing vision quest to Medicine Lake. The voice of Chief Yellow Bear, Honey Eater's dead father, had spoken to him from the Land of Ghosts. He had warned him that great suffering was in store for him before he would ever raise high the lance of leadership.

But that vision—which also hinted at a crimson clash of war for the *Shaiyena* nation—did not tell him whether or not Honey Eater would ever share his tipi. Nor, he thought now as he lay in a burrow of grass with his eyes tightly covered, had it warned of any suffering for Honey Eater.

And yet, according to Arrow Keeper, she too now had a grisly share in his danger. That gnawed at the young brave like sharp incisors, for truly Honey Eater had already suffered enough for his sake, especially unfair abuse from the jealous Black Elk.

All these reminiscences about Arrow Keeper brought the old shaman's wrinkled-as-a-peach-pit face firmly into his mind's eye. The wind rose again, a hollow groan that lifted to a shriek. Touch the Sky felt the fine hairs on his nape stiffening when, suddenly, the image of Arrow Keeper was all at once shrouded in wisps of smoke.

No, he realized. Not smoke. Thin tendrils of steam. For Arrow Keeper sat naked in a steaming sweat lodge. And mysteriously, the old man was vigorously shaking his head no, vigorously waving his young assistant back from something.

A strong hand gripped his arm, and Touch the Sky flinched violently.

"It is time now, brother," Little Horse told him. "Wendigo Mountain is waiting for us."

They muzzled their ponies with sashes and belts, wrapped their hoofs in rawhide to quiet them. Then Touch the Sky made the final inspection of his warriors.

"Shoots the Bear?"

"I have ears, brother."

"Remove your bone choker. If the clouds blow off, it may glint in the moonlight."

He glanced at Two Twists. "Smear more mud on your face, buck. It too will glint."

Now he addressed all of them.

"We ride up single file, using the scree as much as possible for cover. Keep wide intervals in case they have a rockslide planned. No one plays the big Indian. If enemy are sighted, try to avoid the fight. Maiyun has forbidden treading the war path by night. Do not goad His wrath by rashly trying to count coup or draw first blood.

"Our mission is to retrieve those Arrows. So the first step is to get up that mountain and near their camp. Hatred, revenge, glory—none of these matter now. The fate of the Arrows is the fate of the people. Keep a keen eye and a steady hand, and commend your soul to the Good Supernatural.

"May the High Holy Ones go with us."

"May it even be so," the rest intoned when Touch the Sky closed on that line of prayer. With that they hit the slope.

Their sure-footed ponies were well grazed and took the rock-strewn slope easily. Touch the Sky took first turn riding point. His tough little calico was rebellious at first as she fought her muzzle. Then she settled into the steady climb, powerful haunches bunching as the slope narrowed and steepened.

The wind howled and screamed and sometimes died down to an eerie whistle before again rising in a shriek that made Touch the Sky's pony sidestep nervously. There were constant, sudden movements in the corner of his vision. But each time he pointed his rifle, there was nothing out there but the black maw of the night.

He was nerved for action, every muscle like a coiled spring. Now and then a scud of clouds blew away from the moon. Then Touch the Sky would glance back down to see his companions moving up behind him.

He led them around a pinnacle, then down into a hollow. He felt it before he saw it: huge, billowing wisps of warm fog. Then he realized it wasn't fog, but steam escaping from the underground hot springs.

They had reached the necklace of 'mist' that encircled the mountain.

Visibility was abruptly reduced; Touch the Sky could only see a few feet ahead. He pulled back on the calico's hackamore, debating. This ring of billowing steam clouds would have to be traversed if they were to ascend.

But it felt wrong. That familiar numb prickle of warning moved up his spine. And he recalled the brief vision he'd just had of old Arrow Keeper. True, the old shaman had been in a sweat lodge, not here on the mountain. But had he not waved him back from clouds of steam?

Time was critical. But only a fool, he decided, ignored spirit signs.

Touch the Sky dismounted and hobbled his pony's legs. Then he called the rest of his band around him.

"I do not like the feel of it, brothers. Wait here. I will sneak through the steam on foot to see if a trap awaits us."

"You hog all the sport," Little Horse objected. "Let me go. I have the best ears in the tribe."

This was true enough, but on this point Touch the Sky did not yield to debate. After all, it was *his* carelessness that had somehow placed the Arrows in danger.

"I will go, and no further discussion of it will stand. Listen for the owl hoot. If I make it up, I'll signal back for the rest to advance. Someone lead my pony."

Holding his rifle close to his chest, Touch the Sky disappeared into the roiling cloud of steam.

Between the steam and the new-tar darkness of the night, Touch the Sky was forced to rely closely on his warrior training.

Arrow Keeper had constantly emphasized the dangers of too much thinking, which distracted a man when he ought to be attending to the signals from his senses. Now, with vision practically useless, Touch the Sky freed his mind of thoughts and paid attention to the language outside of him.

He kept his ears pricked for the slightest noise.

But he heard only the hollow shrieking of the wind—no hidden horses snuffling, no bit-rings clinking, no rifle bolts snicking home in the darkness above him. Nevertheless, more sweat broke out on his back with every step he took.

He sniffed the air carefully and constantly, alert for the familiar smell of horses, the stink of unwashed human bodies.

Nothing. Just the clean, damp smell of the mountain. Still his skin grew goosebumped as if he were lying naked in a snowbank.

Shadows seemed to move in and out of the distorted periphery of the trail. But the lazy feathers of steam made it impossible to tell what was real and what wasn't. Everything was dream-distorted, so he couldn't tell how close or far things were.

Suddenly a pebble fell near his feet.

Had he kicked it loose?

Another pebble, and now fear coated his tongue in a coppery dust. For he had recalled something, a "game" Sis-ki-dee had once played with him when Touch the Sky had sighted the railroad spur through the Sans Arcs. The renegade had remained in hiding, tossing pebbles and making rattlesnake sounds to unnerve the Cheyenne, letting him know that he was a mere bug inching along the face of the mountain—a bug he could flick off at any moment.

Just as he could flick him off again now.

Nature often seems to abet the schemes of men. Now, even before Touch the Sky could fight down the blind panic caused by his helplessness, a hard wind whipped up and simultaneously pushed the clouds away from the moon while also parting the tendrils of ghostly mist.

Just enough for Touch the Sky to see that he was completely ringed in by a grinning Sis-ki-dee and his well-armed warriors!

# Chapter Seven

"So! Once again the Contrary Warrior comes face to face with the noble champion of red pride! I promised you, the last time I saw you, that our trails would cross again soon enough. And see, I have kept my word!"

It was a tableau from a nightmare. Touch the Sky saw that familiar visage, mocking and ravaged by smallpox, as it seemed to float toward him out of the swirling, moonlit mists. But the Cheyenne held his face impassive, kept his tone defiant, as he answered.

"You did indeed make that promise. But you spoke those brave words even as you fled for your life."

"That was then, this is now. I also promised," Sis-ki-dee added, the mocking grin easing into a wide smile of triumph, "that I would skin your face off and lay it over mine with you still alive to see it. That time has come, Ghost Warrior. Or would you turn our bullets into sand even now, as the superstitious Cheyenne grandmothers claim you once did to Bluecoats in the Bear Paw Mountains?"

"I need not bother," Touch the Sky replied, "so long as my own bullets are real."

What followed was a move of pure desperation. Touch the Sky suddenly whirled and shot point-blank at the nearest brave. The round struck just above his navel and blew an exit hole the size of a fist in the man's back. The shot was still ringing in the damp air when the Cheyenne jumped through the space left open when the brave dropped dead.

It took less than two seconds. By the time the surprised Blackfoot renegades realized it, the tall Cheyenne had slipped from their net and back into the swirling vapors.

"Capture him!" Touch the Sky heard Sis-ki-dee bellow. His voice was tense from fear of losing this prize catch. "Good whiskey and white man's tobacco for the brave who tackles him!"

The tall youth bolted with reckless abandon into the protective but disorienting steam. His feet landed hard on sharp flints; twice he banged hard into big boulders and almost went down. His flight was reckless now as he heard the pursuing feet behind him.

Rifles cracked, bullets splatted hard or whanged

from rock to rock, zwipping close to his ears. His wild retreat took on all the features of a fever delirium: objects were obscured in vision, sounds distorted, directions nonexistent in this eerie and warm fog. He knew his men below could hear the guns discharging, perhaps even see the brief muzzle-flashes. But they were holding their fire, fearful of hitting Touch the Sky in the steam and confusion.

A bullet struck so close it sent rock dust into his eyes. Touch the Sky groped blindly, fell hard, felt himself tumbling downslope; it was like being kicked over and over in all the vital places. Then somehow he was back on his feet, bloodied and limping, groping ever downward as bullets continued to thicken the air around him.

"Brother! Do you hear me?"

Little Horse's desperate voice was somewhere just ahead.

"I hear you!" Touch the Sky managed to shout back.

"We are covered down and ready, Cheyenne! As soon as you break clear, tuck low and stay down, for the air will be humming above knee level!"

Even as Little Horse finished speaking, Touch the Sky hurtled forward from the necklace of ghostly steam. He had a momentary glimpse of his fellow warriors in their defensive positions among the scree. Then he was on the ground, and his four companions turned that steam dangerous when they opened fire.

The rifle shots found only boulders. But Little Horse made all four of his barrels roar, the scattergun peppering the pale vapor with deadly buckshot.

Loosing an agonized scream, one Blackfoot renegade dropped like a stone right beside Touch the Sky. Nothing was left of his face but a scarlet smear. Another caught buckshot in his belly and stumbled. Touch the Sky had his obsidian knife out in a heartbeat. He rolled fast toward the renegade and caught him even as he started to rise again. The Cheyenne sliced his throat open before his enemy could rise past the first knee.

The unexpected resistance broke the Blackfoot attack. But any further advance by the Cheyennes was clearly impossible. Battered, sore, but grateful to have breath in his nostrils still after that harrowing escape, Touch the Sky joined his band in a retreat down Wendigo Mountain.

"We killed at least two of them," Little Horse boasted, rallying the others. "True, Touch the Sky here forgot his name and touched the ground more than the sky—one time too many, from the look of his cuts and bruises. But his blade made a Blackfoot dog's throat bay at the moon! And here we stand, while our enemy are two less! They call us the Fighting Cheyenne, and they are right to do so."

"We stopped them," Touch the Sky agreed. "You turned your shotgun into a Bluecoat regiment. But I know this crazy killer Sis-ki-dee, and so do you, Little Horse. You fought him and his men. You know he is not one for a hoop-and-pole game, where each side makes its move in turn."

"Straight words. I learned he is called the Contrary Warrior because he prefers to strike on his own terms, in his own time."

Touch the Sky nodded. "Honor and the Warrior Way mean nothing to him. There is no soft place in him. He once bragged of braining an infant against a tree, making its mother die on the spot of shock and grief. No man who can speak of such a thing while smiling deserves to live."

The Cheyennes had returned to their meager camp in the foothills. Attack from the mountain was unlikely, since only one clear path, the narrow trace down the southern slope, led to their camp. The Cheyennes took turns on sentry duty, the rest managing only fitful sleep.

As a new dawn limned the eastern horizon, no one said it directly. But all were aware: Only two sleeps remained until the all-important deadline.

Touch the Sky knew this mission would be desperate under the best of conditions. With the present urgency, however, it took on the face of sheer madness. Each man had spoken in a grim battle council. They agreed on one important point: They would never get up that slope alive. And their deaths, no matter how glorious, would do nothing to return those Arrows.

"Yes, and Sis-ki-dee has found the right home," Little Horse agreed. "For he is the very Wendigo himself and has nothing to fear from this accursed place."

"He has Cheyennes to fear," Touch the Sky reminded them. "And count upon it, brothers, he fears us. He is too smart not to."

The new sun gave off little light, but embers still glowed in the firepit. Touch the Sky had been studying Arrow Keeper's pictograph. A sinking realization had come to him as he puzzled over the crude painting of the eagle. He studied it again, then gazed back over his shoulder toward the mountain. One eye was swollen shut from his tumble down the talus slope.

Little Horse watched his friend.

"What is it, brother? You suddenly look like a much older Indian."

"And feel like one, buck, for I think I now understand more of the meaning of Arrow Keeper's warning."

"If you understand it better, then why not smile, for it must also mean you have a plan for us?"

The rest watched him expectantly.

"A pale sort of plan," Touch the Sky reluctantly conceded.

"Nothing is as pale as nothing, buck! And nothing is all we have. Speak this plan."

"Did you notice, when we made our scout around the mountain, the many eagles nesting on the northern face?"

Little Horse and the others nodded.

"In the cliffs," Little Horse added, making it a flat reminder, not a question.

"In the cliffs. See Arrow Keeper's eagle-tail feather?" Touch the Sky stated.

"Eagles nest in cliffs," Tangle Hair said slowly, catching on but reluctant to accept it. "And eagles are symbols of warriors."

"You have seized my words before I shaped them, Tangle Hair. Words I am reluctant to speak. For I am nearly certain that Arrow Keeper is telling us there is only one way up Wendigo Mountain—by scaling those same cliffs that killed our ancients."

Less than one full sleep to the southeast, at Gray Thunder's camp, Wolf Who Hunts Smiling was up early, too. He and Medicine Flute had met in the common corral. Pretending to work their ponies, they could easily speak frank words without fear of unfriendly ears overhearing them.

"Brother," Wolf Who Hunts Smiling said. "In my haste not to get caught with the Arrows, I was a bit too quick to get rid of them."

Medicine Flute stood idle and watched his friend while he lunged his pure black pony, leading it in tight circles by a buffalo-hair rope tied to its hackamore. He ignored his own pony, a scrawny dun with flat withers. The dun's lack of muscle definition contrasted sharply with the black's. Bored by horses, the slender, sleepy-eyed youth instead played an eerie and toneless melody on his flute, made from a hollowed-out human leg bone. He pulled the instrument from his lips long enough to say, "Too quick to get rid of the Arrows? How so?"

"I was drunk at the prospect of finally possessing the means to kill White Man Runs Him. In two sleeps, that will be done. But even better if, after Touch the Sky's head is offered, the brave I chose as our only true shaman were to somehow magically return the Arrows after Sis-ki-dee refused."

"I like the sound of this," Medicine Flute said. "But tell me a thing. Do you believe this Sis-ki-dee ever planned to return them?"

Wolf Who Hunts Smiling flashed the lupine grin that had earned him his name.

"Your thoughts run with mine. I was a fool to think he would. But truly I would like to have that crazy-eyed Contrary Warrior in my battle camp, if possible. So I will talk about the matter with him. But I will also watch for a way to lay hands on those Arrows myself. The shaman whose magic returned them to our clan circles unsullied would rule over the tribe until his death."

"Yes," Medicine Flute agreed softly, "until his death."

Wolf Who Hunts Smiling saw the gleam of ambition in his companion's eyes. Good. It was ambition, and ambition alone, that could grasp the reins of leadership and drive an entire tribe. Medicine Flute was lazy, and if not an actual coward, he was certainly no warrior. But he was crafty enough to understand that an Indian blessed with big medicine never lacked for new moccasins and tender hump steaks.

As for Wolf Who Hunts Smiling, he was weary of this constant cat-and-mouse game. He and Touch the Sky had tested, tormented, and probed each other's vulnerable places while they waited for the right moment to close for the kill.

Wolf Who Hunts Smiling had powerful dreams of glory. When he was still a child playing war with willow-branch shields, he used to watch the chiefs and soldier-troop leaders ride at the head of the Sun Dance parades. Their war bonnets, heavy with coup feathers, trailed out behind them. And they held their faces stern and proud as the people pointed in awe—for were they not warriors who must maintain an aloof dignity around women and children?

Now, mere dreams of glory were no longer sufficient. There was a gnawing in his belly, a cankering need for power and respect.

"Brother," he said, gazing out toward the serried peaks of the Sans Arc range, "this Touch the Sky and his fawning admirers have cost me my coup feathers! When our women and children were seized during the hunt, his group rescued them and made mine look like squaw men.

"Recently, he has become the pet of many. They say he defeated the white buffalo hiders, using magic to make Uncle Pte stampede on them. They say that he restored our trade goods after killing a tyrant on the Cherokee reservation."

Wolf Who Hunts Smiling dropped his distant gaze to Medicine Flute's eyes.

# Wendigo Mountain

"All along I have swallowed this bitter bile, yet see how I still smile? For now he has lost our tribe's most sacred possession."

"As you say. And with Arrow Keeper gone, few are willing to pet this dog now."

Wolf Who Hunts Smiling nodded at this. "If Sis-ki-dee has not already killed him, it will happen soon enough by his own hand."

"He would fall on his own knife?"

Again Wolf Who Hunts Smiling nodded.

"I know this tall buck well. Once he fails to get those Arrows, his noble sense of 'honor' will drive him to it."

"Depriving you," Medicine Flute said, "of that pleasure."

"True it is, I would like the pleasure of gutting him. But this way I come out with a clean blade to show the Councillors, yet *he* will be dead."

# Chapter Eight

"They are leaving us alone," Touch the Sky said. "But they are like hawks who keep their prey in sight long before they swoop for the kill. They know by now that we have this camp in the foothills. They are watching it. So we will make it appear as if we were still here even after we have started our climb. With luck, we may throw them off a little."

Little Horse and the rest nodded. Leaving false camps behind had saved them before. While the afternoon sun blazed down from a seamless blue sky, they worked back out of sight of the sentry posts on the slope.

They built up fires that would burn far into the night. Limbs were stacked so that they would roll onto the fire as the smaller sticks holding them back were burned away, a crude system of time-released deception they had learned from the wily Comanche. They also left mounds near the fire to simulate the shapes of seated and sleeping bodies. The remounts were left there to graze.

As they moved closer to Wendigo Mountain, they kept back in the aspen and cedar groves so their motion wouldn't be detected by the sentries at their stations on the slope.

"I found a place up ahead to tether our ponies," Shoots the Bear said. He had ridden out earlier to scout for grazing land. "It is not far enough away to suit me. It is a short ride beyond the northern face. A small meadow bordered by a rill. Our ponies will not be safe from a scout, but they cannot be seen from the southern slope."

"It will have to do," Touch the Sky told him. "You found the best place you could."

A grim sense of purpose marked the faces of each brave. They had paid close attention to those daunting cliffs during their initial scout of the mountain. Now, as they slipped past them again on their way to the hidden meadow, Touch the Sky and the rest craned their necks to look upward.

The sheer, rugged, breathtaking beauty was wasted on these Cheyennes who would never see this place as a gift of the High Holy Ones. Bluff faces of stone stretched steeply upward, offering few shelves or ledges to provide rest for weary climbers. Back here, too, the white collar of steam ringed the mountain about halfway up. Nor could any of them deny the fear that lay in their bellies with a leaden heaviness, the strong tribal fear of this place where the Wendigo lay in wait to snare foolish Cheyennes.

"Two Twists," Touch the Sky warned the youngest brave. "Keep your pony to the trees. If a Blackfoot spots us back here and guesses our plan, we will be picked off the mountain like nits from a blanket."

"Better than dying like old women in our tipis," Two Twists shot back. "I am ready."

Little Horse grinned at this bravado. Two Twist's warlike attitude was starting to show.

Touch the Sky joined them in their grin. But he made sure Two Twists was listening when he replied, "Only fools rush to a quick death. An old woman who dies in her tipi has had a long life. A long life is nothing to scorn, so you keep your honor in the living of it."

But now they fell silent as they reached the hidden meadow and turned their ponies loose on long rawhide tethers. By the time they had rigged for battle and the long climb, their shadows had lengthened behind them. The final task was a careful inspection of the braided buffalo-hair ropes coiled around them like brassards. Weak spots were reinforced with tendon. A weak rope could mean disaster for all of them on that unholy cliff.

"We are as ready as we have time to be," Touch the Sky finally announced. "Only one thing remains."

# Wendigo Mountain

He pulled a blunt piece of charcoal from his parfleche and went around to each brave in turn, marking his face with bold black strokes—the symbol of joy in the death of an enemy.

"We have a hard climb ahead," he told them, "and most likely a bloody fight waits for us at the top. But you all know it as well as I. The fate of those Arrows is the fate of our tribe. This time there can be no turning back. So from here on out, let our thoughts be bloody and nothing else."

By the time Sister Sun had burned down to a dull orange ball on the western horizon, the five Powder River Cheyennes were up against it in the truest sense of the words.

They had sneaked up to the base of Wendigo Mountain's northern face, quickly hiding in the scree. Then began the arduous climb up those sheer cliffs.

The work was dangerous and exhausting, and at the beginning Touch the Sky—in spite of his bold words earlier—almost called off this crazy plan. But each time he thought of that, Little Horse's words returned to him, a hint from Arrow Keeper's medicine dream: *There will be trouble ahead for Touch the Sky, trouble behind for Honey Eater.* And the young warrior had learned one thing well by now: Trouble never went away on its own if you ran from it. You either had to take it by the horns or suffer a hard goring.

Progress was slow, every finger-length eked out

at the cost of much sweat and toil. Touch the Sky went up first, clawing for handholds, groping constantly for toeholds on the smooth limestone expanse. Each time he reached a spur or occasional stunted tree or bush, he carefully tested its strength. Then he secured a rope to it. Little Horse followed next, then Two Twists, Tangle Hair, and Shoots the Bear.

Salty, stinging sweat beaded up on his scalp and then rolled into his eyes. The fierce winds fanned the sweat, causing him to shake.

A few inches, another foot, and now the cliff face was so smooth it seemed as if further advance was impossible. But Touch the Sky refused to give up. Fingers and toes seeming to make their own holds, he somehow inched his way up that smooth stretch.

But Little Horse—not quite so agile of limb—was stuck, along with the others behind him.

Touch the Sky knew he had to get a rope snubbed to something or this mission was smoke behind them. A moment later, he realized things were even more desperate than that.

"Brother!" Little Horse called up to him, his voice sounding tiny in the immensity of the constant wind. "I am losing my hold!"

Touch the Sky glanced down and felt his blood go cold. Little Horse was literally hanging on by his last leg. From here, he was hunched up like a bug about to tumble.

"Can you move back down?" Touch the Sky called out.

"No! I fear I would slip and knock the others down, too!"

"You are a fighting Cheyenne, buck! Hold but a bit longer, brother, and I'll have a rope down to you."

Touch the Sky's mouth formed a grim, determined slit. Muscles straining like taut cables, he scrabbled for some kind of hold. Above, perhaps ten handbreadths away, he spotted a small rock spur. If only he could reach it in time! But his promise to Little Horse was proving easier to shout than to carry out.

"Brother!"

This time Little Horse's voice was strained with fear and effort. Touch the Sky risked another glance down. His friend desperately hugged the cliff face, but the increasing gusts of wind threatened at every moment to tear him loose and hurtle him to the basalt turrets far below.

"Brother!" he cried out again. "I fear this is it, my time to cross over is at hand. I can hold no longer. I will have to leap now to avoid hitting the others."

"Hold!" Touch the Sky shouted back. "I will have a rope down in a little."

Desperation welled up inside him. How many times had his loyal, sturdy little friend pulled him from the jaws of death? Even now, about to crash to a hard death, all Little Horse could worry about was protecting his brothers.

Touch the Sky grasped, clawed, somehow found holds where none existed. His fingernails had torn loose long ago. Spidery lines of blood spread from his fingertips all the way down his arms. But now the rock spur was just above him.

Then his bones turned to stone when he heard Little Horse chanting the death song!

Touch the Sky unlooped his rope, flung it up toward the spur, missed.

He wasn't even aware that he cursed in English. He threw the rope up again, snared the spur this time. Fingers working with desperate competence, he knotted the rope.

"Little Horse!" he shouted, dropping the rope toward his friend just before Little Horse lost his battle with the cliff. He flung himself back away from it, falling so he wouldn't strike the others on his way down.

The rope slapped Little Horse in mid-air just before he began to plummet. He instinctively grabbed at it, missed, grabbed again; a moment later it snapped taut, held, and Little Horse dangled safe though somewhat shaken from the impact when he swung back into the face of the cliff.

It was a slow, agonizing process getting him and the rest of them up. Each man in turn climbed to the level of the rock spur, then threw the rope down to the next man. When Shoots the Bear was safely up, Touch the Sky began covering the next expanse of cliff.

By now his arms trembled with weariness. The Cheyennes inched closer toward the belt of steam. Once again the nimble young brave covered a smooth expanse of cliff while his companions hung on for dear life and waited for the rope.

Touch the Sky reached a tiny ledge the width of perhaps three fingers. He hauled himself up, hugged the stone face, again snubbed his rope around a rock spur. He had partially completed the knot when disaster struck.

Touch the Sky had already noticed the slight cleft in the otherwise solid rock wall. But he didn't realize it was a falcon's nest until a startled bird flew out from the cleft and full into Touch the Sky's face—knocking him from his fragile foothold on the tiny ledge.

His four companions watched in wide-eyed shock as their battle leader began the long fall to his death.

"Easy now," Sis-ki-dee told Takes His Share. "With luck, we'll beard the lion in his own den."

Sis-ki-dee imitated the fluting warble of a wood thrush, and the battle group behind him stopped in their tracks. The sky was dark but star-shot, casting a soft glow like foxfire over the trees and scattered boulders dotting the Sans Arc foothills. Below them, perhaps a double stone's throw distant, was the Cheyenne camp.

"It has a bad feel to it," Takes His Share said. "I know these white-livered Cheyennes are superstitious about leaving their fires after darkness. But would *all* of them be sleeping?"

Sis-ki-dee's sinister grin showed well that he was ahead of Takes His Share on this point.

"And have you noticed there is no sentry?" he said. "When did Cheyennes ever neglect to post a night watch?"

They advanced quickly toward the fire.

"Only two horses," Takes His Share said.

"We'll throat-slash them," Sis-ki-dee said. "Look, they're only pack nags. Our Cheyennes have played the fox, stout bucks!"

Moments later, a bloodless takeover of the camp proved the Contrary Warrior's words.

"Kill the horses," he ordered his men. "Quickly! Then prepare to ride."

"Ride where, Contrary Warrior?"

Sis-ki-dee stared back toward the looming peak of Wendigo Mountain. Even as he stared, thin filaments of lightning flashed near the granite summit. They rivaled the insane sheen of his eyes.

"Only think, warrior. Why was this camp made?"

"To divert us, clearly."

"Clearly, indeed. But divert us from what?"

Takes His Share shed much brain sweat, but only ended up shaking his head.

"It puzzles me, I confess. They cannot be ascending the slope. Half our force is watching it."

"As you say. Half are on the slope, the other half wasting time at this camp. As for our little Cheyenne foxes, they are on the far side of that mountain, defying their own Wendigo in order to surprise our camp. Let us make a fast ride to those cliffs, buck, and see what surprises we may devise to outfox the foxes!"

As Touch the Sky hurtled earthward, he clung to the rope that had been only partially knotted before he fell.

There was a hard, fast snap as the rope tightened, and then a bright orange starburst inside his skull when his head slammed hard into the wall of stone. The blow didn't knock him unconscious nor cost him his grip, but Touch the Sky dangled helpless, on the feather edge of death, as his mind played cat-and-mouse with awareness.

*Brother! Can you hear me? Touch the Sky!*

He was on some kind of important quest, he knew that. But time and place and purpose got all mixed up in memory, and now he was again in the midst of his great vision quest to the Black Hills—the journey Arrow Keeper had sent him on to experience the same medicine dream the old shaman had once experienced.

*Touch the Sky! Wake to the living world, brother!*

But now the images and sounds came tumbling back, reminding him of his inescapable destiny.

The voice of Old Knobby, the hostler at the feed stable in Bighorn Falls: *The Injun figgers he belongs to the land. The white man figgers the land belongs to him. They ain't meant to live together.*

He heard John Hanchon, his adopted white father: *I've worked until I'm mule-tired, but I still go to bed scared every night.*

The words gave way to mind pictures from his vision at Medicine Lake. He saw horses rearing, their eyes huge with fright, while red warriors sang their battle cry. Rivers of blood flowed everywhere, cannons roared, steel clashed against steel. From across the vast plains red warriors streamed, flowing like the blood they must soon shed. One brave led them, his war bonnet streaming coup feathers.

Glimpses of the ice-shrouded lands to the north. He saw the faces of his enemies, Hiram Steele and Seth Carlson. He saw a long, ragged column of starving Cheyenne, again being led by the mysterious brave whose face he could not see.

This time the voice belonged to Honey Eater's dead father, Chief Yellow Bear, speaking from the Land of Ghosts:

*We who have crossed over know everything that will pass. I have seen you bounce your son on your knee, just as I have seen you shed blood for that son and his mother.*

A thundering crash that wasn't in memory. Abruptly Touch the Sky felt the burning in his palms as the rope slipped through them. He came fully awake just in time to grip hard and stop his fall.

"Brother!" Little Horse bellowed yet again above the angry shriek of the wind. "Can you hear me?"

"I hear you, buck!"

Another crack of thunder, ghostly white flashes

of lightning. The wind had taken on a raw knife-edge of cold now that Sister Sun was asleep.

Slowly, laboriously, every muscle crying out at the effort, Touch the Sky climbed back up to the rock spur. Heels biting into the small ledge, he finished the knot and tested it. Then he dropped the rope down to a relieved Little Horse.

Again, one by one, the braves made their way up to the tiny ledge.

"Only one last stretch!" Touch the Sky rallied them above the weather roar. By now his voice was hoarse from the effort. "Through the steam, and then we have a slope for footing the rest of the way."

His loose black locks swirled like living snakes in the tempest. They all watched as Shoots the Bear, the last and heaviest brave, climbed the rope to join them.

Touch the Sky and Little Horse both reached down to hoist him. His fingers met Touch the Sky's and started to close, and then a heartbeat later the rock spur snapped.

It was just a fast noise like a strong bone breaking. Touch the Sky closed his hand on thin air as Shoots the Bear's hideous death shriek melded with the wind.

# Chapter Nine

While the moon inched toward its zenith, Sis-ki-dee and his renegade band rode hard toward the northern face of Wendigo Mountain.

At first they noticed nothing unusual. No signs of enemy ponies or any camp. Nor, in the moonless night, could they see very far up those sheer cliffs.

"Perhaps my thoughts flew too quickly to the cliffs," Sis-ki-dee confided to Takes His Share. "But if that tall Cheyenne licker of white men's crotches is not coming up this way, then how? Will he sprout wings?"

"Certainly not by the southern slope," Takes His Share said with conviction. "Not one shot has been fired from that direction."

Sis-ki-dee's men had lit torches to scour the

rocks. Sis-ki-dee sat his big claybank, watching them and brooding. Eerie, flickering light reflected off the fancy silver trim of his stolen saddle. It also emphasized the numerous facial craters of his smallpox scars, the mad gleam to his eyes.

"Then how?" Sis-ki-dee repeated. "Where is he? For count upon it, that one will not hide in his tipi while his tribe's Sacred Arrows are in enemy hands."

Suddenly a shout went up from Sioux Killer, a brave searching in the heaps of scree in front of them.

"Contrary Warrior! Here is a thing you will want to see. Come quickly!"

The Blackfoot swung down and hobbled his horse's foreleg to rear. Then he picked his way over the scattered piles of rock, aiming for the flickering illumination of Sioux Killer's torch.

Abruptly, Sis-ki-dee pulled up short.

He stared at the place where Sioux Killer pointed. Then his jaw slacked open in surprise. But only moments later, a huge smile divided his face.

The torch clearly illuminated a short and narrow basalt turret which ended in a sharp point. And there, skewered through the vitals about sixteen handbreadths above the ground, was a Cheyenne warrior wearing a hideous death grimace.

"I was right," he said triumphantly. "They have decided to climb up from this side."

"But it is a fool's plan," Takes His Share said.

"Not so much foolish as desperate, brave. But that hardly matters. For as this one proves eloquently enough, those cliffs cannot be scaled."

"Not by most Indians, perhaps. But that Cheyenne does things other red men cannot."

Sis-ki-dee readily acknowledged the truth of this with a nod.

"He does, doesn't he? But even if he could make the climb, no one is in our camp. Turn it over all he will, he'll never find those Arrows."

Sis-ki-dee continued to stare at the grotesque dead man. The pain etched into his face defied description. Looking at it inspired Sis-ki-dee to mischief.

His strong white teeth flashed in the flickering light when the idea occurred to him. For Sis-ki-dee, defeating his enemies was not nearly enough retribution. Life was meant to be an entertainment; mere victory was boring. If at all possible, he preferred to terrorize his quarry before killing it. He turned to Takes His Share.

"Pick several strong braves and remove that body. Do not harm it. I want it left intact. Tie it to a horse."

"Why, Contrary Warrior?"

Again Sis-ki-dee flashed his crazy-by-thunder grin. He pointed to the dead Cheyenne.

"Do you think this one died hard? We will make his tall leader's life a hurting place. Quickly now! In case he does somehow survive the climb, we must have a surprise ready to welcome the Noble Red Man and his braves."

The night was well advanced, and to the north of the Powder River camp lightning crowned the Sans Arc mountain range. Black Elk, his cousin Wolf Who Hunts Smiling, and Medicine Flute sat around a small fire behind Black Elk's tipi.

Black Elk was plaiting a new bridle out of rawhide and horsehair. Medicine Flute had taken a rare break from the incessant piping on his leg-bone flute. Now he sat peeling a twig with his teeth, his sleepy, heavy-lidded gaze directed into the leaping flames while Wolf Who Hunts Smiling spoke.

"Cousin, fear has our tribe by the throat. Two sleeps from now Woman Face's head is due in payment for the Medicine Arrows. Yet, where is he? Many are starting to wonder a thing. What happens if this dog decides to tuck his tail and flee?"

Black Elk nodded.

"He is no coward. But neither is he loyal to the Cheyenne way. For all we know, he is rabbiting to safety even now. Meantime, we cannot attack for fear of endangering the Arrows."

"Never, not since the time when he was accused of helping the white miners steal our lands, has there been so much talk against him. I have been speaking with the people, telling them about Medicine Flute. How his medicine is strong along with his loyalty to the tribe."

Wolf Who Hunts Smiling paused, recalling some past slight that made him scowl.

"Now the people are saying, no more of this business with tolerating a shaman who was raised by hair faces. Arrow Keeper is gone, perhaps dead by now. True, I will not have the pleasure of using Touch the Sky's guts for tipi ropes. But we have finally had done with White Man Runs Him."

"Too early for a victory dance, buck. You have declared him dead more than once."

When he finished speaking, Black Elk's eyes cut toward his tipi. All was dark within. But was Honey Eater really asleep, or was she listening for news to send to her tall buck?

Let her listen, he decided angrily. Her blunt coldness with him, her brazen disrespect ever since Touch the Sky rode out, had worked him up to a murderous rage. How dare a mere woman lord it over a war leader! No woman turned Black Elk into a squaw man and lived to boast about it.

Again, as the anger bubbled up inside him, the thought cankered at him. Had Honey Eater let the tall dog lift her dress?

Wolf Who Hunts Smiling cast a furtive, sidelong glance at his cousin. He saw Black Elk scowling as he stared at the tipi.

"Cousin," Wolf Who Hunts Smiling said, "we spoke earlier on a certain matter. I have held council with several bucks. All reliable, all respected. They have agreed to come forward, if you give the sign. They will swear on the

Medicine Hat that they saw Touch the Sky hold"—
here he glanced at Medicine Flute and decided to
avoid Honey Eater's name—"a certain woman in
his blanket for love talk."

Black Elk said nothing to this, though he
took the meaning clearly enough. Something
else was troubling him. Lately he had expended
much brain sweat wondering how this Blackfoot
renegade named Sis-ki-dee had obtained those
Arrows. Touch the Sky would always carry the
white stink on him, truly. But in his secret heart of
hearts, Black Elk did not believe he was a traitor.
He had not voluntarily given those Arrows away.

How, then, did Sis-ki-dee get them?

He watched his sly, ambitious cousin in the
firelight. Would he place his dreams of glory
before the well-being of the entire tribe?

Wolf Who Hunts Smiling had already come
dangerously close to unpardonable treachery in
an earlier scheme with Medicine Flute. The two
had cleverly challenged Touch the Sky's right to
the title of shaman, engaging in deceptions and
lies unknown to the Council of Forty. Black Elk
had reluctantly gone along with it, hoping to
expose Touch the Sky as a pretend shaman. But
the resourceful brave used strong magic to defeat
the Comanche trick rider Big Tree, emerging with
even more supporters.

Truly Black Elk wanted this Touch the Sky,
this dog who might have rutted with his wife,
dead. Just as his jealous visions of Honey Eater
lying with Touch the Sky had finally driven him

to want her dead, too. But not at the terrible expense of the entire tribe's well-being. Black Elk would not go that far.

Even now the wily Wolf Who Hunts Smiling discerned some of these thoughts in his cousin's troubled frown. It was burning ambition versus stupid loyalty, and Wolf Who Hunts Smiling was confident that his ambition would win out. By goading Black Elk into killing Honey Eater, Wolf Who Hunts Smiling also strengthened his own position. For then he would have power over Black Elk. He would know a damaging secret about a truly dangerous man. If Black Elk could not be won over, then he must at least be knocked from his position of authority.

"Count upon it, cousin," Wolf Who Hunt Smiling said. "True it is, the loss of our Arrows is a great tragedy. We have yet to learn the terrible consequences of this loss. But every strong wind blows something good before it, too. This tragedy also marks the end for White Man Runs Him."

Shoots the Bear's unexpected death stunned the remaining Cheyennes into disbelieving silence.

For many heartbeats they clung where they were, four tiny specks of humanity pinned to the vast face of the treacherous and indifferent cliff. Thunder muttered, lightning flickered, the wind carried a cold promise of rain. Truly it was a bad death, the worst conceivable to a Cheyenne. Not only did their comrade die in a place fraught with evil medicine, but he died unclean, unable to sing his death song.

It was more than a bad death. It was also a bad omen, a serious warning to the rest of them.

But fear, Touch the Sky reminded himself, was no defense. Only action would save the rest of them—and, more important, the Arrows. He glanced up and noted the location of the Always Star to the north. The night was advancing, and so must they. Now he spoke, careful to avoid the dead brave's name.

"Brothers! The one who was our comrade died bad. But now *we* are up against it. More death will not save the one who has left us. Nor will it save the Sacred Arrows."

*Or Honey Eater*, a sere, gravelly voice remarkably like Arrow Keeper's whispered out of the howling wind.

"Now comes the last climb. Be strong, and take heart. From here the going is easier. There are more holds and places to rest. We will not even need the ropes."

"We are with you, Bear Caller!" Little Horse shouted above the shriek of savage winds.

He used the name terrified Pawnees gave Touch the Sky after a grizzly bear routed them and saved his life.

"Our brother died giving his all to the tribe," Little Horse added. "What better way can a Cheyenne die? We are pledged to the same sacrifice, if Maiyun wills it. As for me, I have no dream of a long life. Lead on, buck, for I am keen to grease Blackfoot bones with my war paint!"

Little Horse's brave words rallied his comrades. And Touch the Sky had spoken straight-arrow: from here the going was easier. Even the climb through the steamy mist was uneventful, even pleasant, as the tendrils of warm steam thawed their cold skin.

But Touch the Sky could not rid himself of the coppery taste of fear. For this was Wendigo Mountain, where any kind of bad medicine might happen. And in Sis-ki-dee, they were not just up against an enemy—this was a murdering, marauding, implacable beast who truly thrived on evil.

He had little luxury for thought, however, because now he was approaching the summit of the cliff. All seemed quiet enough up above. But what if Sis-ki-dee had discovered their bold plan? What if, even now, his battle-hardened renegades lay in wait to slaughter them?

He held up until his comrades flanked him just beneath the top of the sheer face. A line of rimrock was all that kept them from the rest of the talus-strewn northern face. One more open space to cross, and they would be on the opposite slope and above the Blackfoot camp.

Touch the Sky placed an arm over his comrades' shoulders, huddling them close. He spoke just loud enough to top the wind noise.

"Spread out wide, brothers. We will go over together on my signal. Tangle Hair, hand me that scalp on your sash."

Tangle Hair unknotted a rawhide whang and handed the Pawnee scalp to his battle leader. The others watched, quickly catching on, as Touch the Sky tied the scalp to the muzzle of his Sharps. Then, cautiously, he raised it above the rimrock. Only the dark hair showed. But no shots were lured.

"They are there or they are not," Touch the Sky said. "If they are there, make it one bullet for one enemy!"

He slung his rifle across his shoulders and crawled over the rimrock. The rest, spread out on either side, topped the cliff with him.

Touch the Sky believed he was prepared for anything. But nothing between this living world and the Land of Ghosts could have prepared any of these deeply spiritual Indians for the blood-curdling sight that greeted them. For just as they reached the top, a brilliant flash of lightning turned the night into clear daylight.

Young Two Twists cried out and fell to the ground, literally struck down by fear. The rest froze where they stood.

There, his accusing eyes wide open and staring at them, a gaping and bloody hole where his stomach once had been, stood Shoots the Bear!

# Chapter Ten

Absolute silence from the Cheyennes for the space of ten heartbeats. Their black locks flew about like wild sisal whips in the unrelenting wind. The bold black charcoal streaks on their faces could not offset the fear starched into their features.

Then, as realization set in, Touch the Sky felt his fear give way to hot rage.

"Stand up, Cheyenne," he told Two Twists sternly. "Be a man, for this has nothing to do with matters spiritual. Look there, and there."

Lightning flashes were almost constant now. He pointed to the rocks heaped around the legs, and to a cleverly disguised rope around the upper body, running to a hidden stake nearby. Both had been used to prop up and pose the body.

"The wily Red Peril and his murdering followers found our comrade and hauled him up here."

Touch the Sky's words made the rest overcome their fear enough to glance nervously about them. The Cheyennes had finally ascended the cliffs. But between them and the final summit of Wendigo Mountain stretched a final, rock-strewn slope. The rocks were easily big enough to hide ambushers.

"Sis-ki-dee has stooped to the basest form of sacrilege in defiling our dead this way," Touch the Sky said. "But we have more urgent matters to hand if our quest is for the Arrows. If they bothered to haul our dead comrade up here, clearly they knew we were on our way up.

"Cover down brothers, and quickly, for right now Sis-ki-dee must be hiding nearby and enjoying his laugh at us. When his amusement wears off, comes the fight!"

Even as he finished speaking, the hideous "shout that kills" erupted, the frightening battle cry Sis-ki-dee had taught to his men. It was a shrill, deep-chested scream designed to unnerve opponents. In one movement the Blackfoot renegades rose from hiding and rushed them.

There was neither time nor space for falling back. Touch the Sky and his companions leaped behind boulders even as the first volley of fire turned the air deadly all around them.

Fortunately their weapons had been loaded and ready to hand. And Cheyennes, like their Sioux cousins, were notorious bullet hoarders trained to make each shot count. Touch the Sky fired a quick snapshot from his Sharps, dropping an attacker. There were sharper cracks as Tangle Hair and Two Twists fired their sturdy British trade rifles, also scoring hits.

But at this range it was once again Little Horse's revolving-barrel scattergun that truly surprised their enemy and saved them. As good as his reckless boasts, courageously tempting death, Little Horse stood in the open and jeered at his enemy.

His barrels were adjusted for the widest shot pattern. As fast as he could revolve them, he unleashed all four loads at the attackers. Blackfoot warriors dropped as if a Bluecoat canister shell had landed in their midst.

This excellent marksmanship by all four Cheyennes bought just enough time for the beleaguered braves to finish taking hasty shelter so they could reload. Knowing his bow would be more deadly at this distance and afford him more shots than his rifle, Touch the Sky notched a fire-hardened arrow on his string. His left hand gripped several more at the ready, the shafts formed from dead pine for lightness and strength.

But for the moment targets were scarce. Their enemy, stung by the quick and effective Cheyenne response, had quickly learned respect. Now they were carefully hidden, not counting their dead comrades who now littered the slope.

Next came Sis-ki-dee's insane, mocking laughter. When he spoke, it was in the mixture

of Cheyenne and Sioux understood by many
Plains tribes.

"Noble Red Man! If you are truly so 'noble' as
you pretend, why risk your comrades like this? It
is *you* Sis-ki-dee wants. Surrender, and the rest
may go free. They may even take the Arrows with
them."

Touch the Sky's men had no intention of letting their friend negotiate his own death. It was
Tangle Hair who quickly answered, speaking for
all of them.

"We came up as one. We will either leave as
one or die as one. But if we die, we will fall on
Blackfoot bones!"

Again came Sis-ki-dee's mocking bray.

"More noble savages! The example of your tall
leader no doubt inspires you!"

"No doubt at all," Tangle Hair shot back. "He
inspires me, indeed!"

Sis-ki-dee flung out an arm toward the dead
Shoots the Bear.

"Is it even so? Then look on your noble and
dead brother there, another who was inspired
by the tall Ghost Warrior. Think carefully on my
offer. For your only other choice will be to die as
one! And I will personally make water on those
Arrows before I destroy them."

"Then come on, Death!" Little Horse bellowed.
"We are the Fighting Cheyenne! Our faces are
marked black in honor of the Black Warrior's
arrival!"

To taunt them, Little Horse ducked up out

of hiding for a moment and jeered at them. A second, intense volley of fire was the Blackfoot response.

Rock dust flew into Touch the Sky's eyes, bullets ricocheted around him with an ear-stinging whine. A raggedly cropped head appeared above a rock as a renegade drew a bead. Touch the Sky risked exposure long enough to loose another arrow. The fire-hardened point pierced the Blackfoot's right eye with such force it pushed gray brain-suds out the back of his skull.

"Good shot, brother!" Little Horse called over to him. "You just lightened the weight of his thoughts!"

Continuous lightning turned the battlefield into day. Sis-ki-dee's well-armed men maintained a withering field of lead. The Cheyennes could do little now but hunker down.

Desperate, but forcing himself to stay calm for the sake of his brothers, Touch the Sky signalled to Little Horse. Despite the danger, they could not stay pinned here. Retreat back down the cliff was out of the question. They must move forward and get some operating room. Otherwise, they would stay right where they were until their bullets and arrows gave out—at which time they would either join Shoots the Bear in this high-altitude grave, or die like their ancestors who had leaped off that cliff.

Touch the Sky said a brief prayer to Maiyun. Then, leading his braves in one of the most desperate and dangerous maneuvers of their young lives, he screamed the Cheyenne battle cry and broke from cover into the middle of a firestorm.

"Hi-ya! Hiii-*ya!*"

One by one, each covering the other, they advanced from rock to rock, leap-frogging through the deadly hail of bullets. Soon their faces were powder-blackened by the fierce rate of their own return fire. Repeated slaps of their rifle stocks had raised bruises on their cheekbones. Every inch of the shale-littered slope was gained at the expense of reckless valor.

Now and then Touch the Sky glimpsed Sis-ki-dee, easy to spot when lightning gleamed on his brassards or the huge brass rings in his ears. But every bullet or arrow sent toward him seemed to swerve wide as if loath to lodge in such a man-monster.

At first, despite being vastly outnumbered, the Cheyenne charge actually began to force the Blackfoot attackers into a slow retreat toward the summit. Then things began to come quickly apart like a wet rope unraveling.

Touch the Sky made occasional visual checks to make sure each of his comrades was all right. Now, just as his eyes flicked to his friend Little Horse, the plucky brave dropped his scattergun and clutched at his left shoulder. Blood spread from a new bullet hole.

Only an eyeblink later, Tangle Hair cried out as a round caught his momentarily exposed right thigh.

In the space of a breath, their firepower was cut

in half. Even though young Two Twists plugged gamely away, further advance was impossible. Only two of them were capable of moving now, and the fire from above was too deadly.

Touch the Sky saw that his companions were hastily binding their own wounds to stem the loss of blood with the strips of cloth they carried in their pouched breechclouts. Soon Tangle Hair again resumed fire, but at a slower rate than before. Little Horse, however, was unable to hold his weapons.

Two Blackfoot warriors, emboldened by this spectacle and eager to close for the kill, led a charge from the rocks. Touch the Sky shot one in the gut and left him writhing in agony; Two Twists only managed to wound the other. But it was enough to quell the assault.

For a moment there was a lull in the fierce fighting. The acrid stench of cordite hung thick in the night air. Another lightning flash, and Touch the Sky locked gazes with Sis-ki-dee.

The insane brave watched him, a triumphant sheen in his eyes. He said something to his men. Another volley of fire erupted. But this time no living man was the target. At least a dozen bullets thwapped into the body of Shoots the Bear. Held up by his props, the corpse twitched and leaped and seemed to perform a macabre dance.

"Look, contrary warriors!" Sis-ki-dee called out. "See how the Cheyenne dances to entertain us! A pity that he died without singing his death song. But little matter, for his entire tribe is soon doomed! One of them was careless, and now they have somehow misplaced their Sacred Arrows!"

Despite the desperate hopelessness of their situation, Touch the Sky felt his stomach roiling in anger. Desecration of the dead was the worst insult one tribe could heap on another. Another shot, and Shoots the Bear's head exploded like a clay pot.

Sis-ki-dee laughed long and hard.

"Settle in, Noble Cheyennes!" he called out. "We have plenty of time, ammunition, and food. Surrender the tall Ghost Warrior, and the Arrows are yours. Otherwise, first you die, then your tribe when I destroy the Arrows!"

Time dragged on. The rain held off as the sky gradually lightened toward dawn.

"Little Horse," Touch the Sky called over quietly. "How is your wound?"

The game little fighter was slow to answer. His weak tone belied the bravado of his words.

"What wound is that, brother? Do you mean this flea bite on my shoulder?"

"Tangle Hair?"

"A mere flesh wound, buck."

But his tone, too, was weak with loss of blood.

"You are both better fighters than liars," he told them.

For a moment, Touch the Sky felt the exhaustion of the long, hard climb followed by the adrenaline tension of combat. Black dots marched across his vision, and he wanted desperately to close his eyes. But, even a few moments sleep might mean sure death for all of them.

Frustrated, trying to master the weary riot of his thoughts, the tall brave carefully studied the area before him. It was littered not only with rocks and dead Blackfoot warriors but with stunted bushes twisted into grotesque shapes by the constant winds. Seeing those bushes gave him a desperate idea—foolishly desperate, a plan so risky it had almost no chance of working.

But what else was there for it? Arrow Keeper was not here to save him with magic. The situation had been dramatically altered when Little Horse and Tangle Hair were wounded. Two Twists could still move quickly, but the other two would need plenty of time to escape to safety.

Touch the Sky's warrior training and experience told him there was only one chance. He must sneak through the enemy position and somehow create an effective diversion in back of their camp, one that would flush them out long enough for his wounded comrades to gain safety.

Risking exposure several times in the almost constant glimmers of lightning, Touch the Sky used his knife to cut several of the short bushes loose. He planned to copy a trick from the Apaches to the south, masters of stealth and invisible movement.

He stripped to his clout. Slicing fringes from his buckskin leggings, he secured bushes to the back of his neck, over his buttocks, and to the back of each leg.

"Hold fast, brothers," he said quietly to the rest. "If you see your opportunity to move, seize it. Two Twists! I must leave my weapons behind. If you can, bring them when you escape."

"But where are you going?"

Ignoring their barrage of protests and curious questions, Touch the Sky inched slowly away from his position, armed only with his knife.

He hugged the ground close and moved torturously forward, trying to time his movements between lightning flashes and loud gusts of wind. Fear left his mouth feeling stuffed with cotton. But he continued to crawl forward.

It was a long, dangerous ordeal. At every moment he expected a bullet to send him across the Great Divide. He kept himself flat to the ground and made no unnecessary movements. At one point, his body drenched in nervous sweat, a swarm of gnats covered his face and almost choked him. But his lips formed their grim, determined slit and he refused to swat them.

He was unable to gauge his progress except by sound. Gradually, Blackfoot voices grew louder and louder, then softer and softer until he could hear them no longer. Then he knew that he had managed to slip past his enemy.

Touch the Sky rose cautiously just past the summit, his cramped muscles protesting.

He could see the Blackfoot stronghold below on the southern face of Wendigo Mountain.

Touch the Sky took heart when he saw that the camp was deserted. No doubt Sis-ki-dee had left another force further down this slope in case the Powder River Cheyennes tried to send a second force up.

He slipped quickly into the camp. As tempting as it was to search for the Arrows now, he resisted the urge. Every moment he delayed might mean death for his comrades—a risk he might take if the Cheyenne truly believed that Sis-ki-dee was foolish enough to hide the Medicine Arrows where they would be quickly found. But Touch the Sky knew better.

No, first things first. For now he needed a diversion. And he found one soon.

The Blackfoot stronghold was a tight cluster of tipis and curved wickiups with a common corral off to one side. A huge fire in the middle of camp had burned down to bright embers. Well back from the fire, in an area reserved for supplies, sat a case of 200 rifle cartridges.

Touch the Sky grabbed a glowing stick from the fire and raced among the tipis, setting fire where he landed. Then, moving swiftly, he upended the case of cartridges into the fire.

This move was dangerous, for he would have only a few seconds before those bullets started sending lead all around the area. He raced to a line of cedar trees below camp. Anyone spotting him at that moment might have quailed in fear: Touch the Sky still wore the bushes, which flapped like clumsy wings as he ran. And his charcoal-smeared face looked ferocious in the gathering light.

Just as he reached the shelter of the cedar brake, pandemonium broke out in the camp.

The air bristled with the sound of a fierce battle. Rounds sang through the trees, shattered branches, shredded through the tipis and wicki-ups. Several horses in the nearby common corral dropped, blood spuming from their wounds. Now it was finally light enough to see the black billows of smoke rise into the sky from the burning camp.

Despite his utter exhaustion, despite everything he still faced, Touch the Sky felt his lips easing into a grin. He had created a wonderful semblance of a massed attack. And sure enough, he could see Sis-ki-dee racing down the slope, North and Savage rifle at a high port, his men trailing out behind him.

"I have done my best, brothers," Touch the Sky said aloud, urging his comrades on. "Now do it!"

# Chapter Eleven

Honey Eater was mercifully unaware of the fierce battle that Touch the Sky and his comrades had fought during the night. Nonetheless, she had enough serious worries tangling her brain to ensure that she spent a sleepless night.

At the first pale glimmer of dawn, which was visible through the smokehole at the top of the tipi, an old grandmother sang the song to the rising sun. Honey Eater rolled out of her robes, naked save for her delicate bone choker. She slipped on a buckskin dress and stepped into her moccasins.

She didn't need to worry about waking Black Elk. Like most Indian braves, he was a late and heavy sleeper when he was in a peace camp. She could see him now, on the other side of the tipi's tall center pole. Pale light filtered through the smokehole and lay across his face. Even in his sleep, she noticed with a tiny shiver, he scowled as if riding into battle.

She stood there a moment and remembered a time when she had felt differently toward Black Elk. No, he had never made her smile inside as Touch the Sky did. He was covered with hard bark, cold and remote and obsessed with warfare and his warrior pride. This unreasoning pride had led to savage jealousy now turned murderous. But there had been a time when Black Elk had at least been fair, or had tried to be, toward Touch the Sky, just as there had once been a time when Black Elk would never have cut off her braid to shame her, or beat her with the bullwhip tucked into his sash.

But those days were long gone, a thing of smoke blown behind them. And now she and Black Elk no longer lived as man and wife. Though it was important to Black Elk's manly pride that they keep up outward appearances, he had lately taken to sleeping in his own robes on the opposite side of the tipi.

One of Honey Eater's cousins had whispered a thing in her ear, a story that Black Elk now rode out 'hunting' so often because he was topping a young widow from Straight Pine's Arapaho camp. If true, this was a great relief to Honey Eater. Black Elk considered a true man to be a volcano—he must regularly relieve the pressure between his legs or he would explode. And she could no longer abide his touch.

But truly, it also worried her. For lately, Black Elk had harbored a cold and menacing indifference toward her that somehow seemed more dangerous than his rages.

Something brutal was in the wind. She was sure of it. All these meetings lately out by the meat racks with Wolf Who Hunts Smiling and the rest of Black Elk's Bull Whip brothers—they could only mean trouble, and plenty of it. Trouble for Touch the Sky, certainly. But lately she sensed that Black Elk's wrath had finally begun to include her in his cold-blooded schemes of murder.

The slender girl slipped past the entrance flap, still braiding her hair, her face lost in troubled thought. Just then, glancing down toward the mist-covered river, she spotted a doe and fawn. The doe fondly nuzzled her offspring, and for a moment Honey Eater smiled.

Her offspring . . . it was common knowledge what Black Elk had said to some in his lodge. Things about how a squaw could harden her heart toward a man, thus denying his seed from fertilizing inside her. Many of the Bull Whips believed this and goaded him on. His bitterness at her inability—some called it a refusal—to give him a son was deep. It grew deeper as time passed and more and more jokes were made about Black Elk's manhood.

But abruptly she was startled out of her musing by the angry scolding of jays. Now, as she knelt to stir the embers under the cooking tripod, more immediate troubles came crowding back.

*One sleep.*

One sleep, and Touch the Sky's life was forfeit if he could not return those Sacred Arrows! Of course Honey Eater was frightened, like all the others in camp, by this threat to the Arrows. The fate of those Arrows shaped the destiny of the tribe.

But Touch the Sky did not, *would* not, cause their loss. She was sure of that. As sure as she was the daughter of one of the greatest chiefs in Cheyenne history. The treacherous Wolf Who Hunts Smiling was behind this terrible trouble. He and perhaps that sly, lazy 'shaman' with the grisly bone flute.

Honey Eater stoked up the flames, then went out back to the meat racks and selected an elk steak for Black Elk's breakfast. By the time she returned, a group of women were gathering in the middle of camp. It was the custom to go out in the cool of early morning. They would scoop ants from the anthills near the river, wash them, then crush them to a paste that would be made into a tasty soup.

This reminded her that life went on because it had to. The hunters rode out, the women gathered wild peas and onions, the children played at taking scalps and counting coups. But behind it all was a growing sense of panic and hopelessness. Where were the sacred Medicine Arrows? Many believed the end was at hand—and that

Touch the Sky had brought this destruction to the tribe.

*One sleep.*

Her desperate urgency scattered all other thoughts but that of Touch the Sky. She had meant what she told Black Elk recently: If Touch the Sky were killed, she would find some way to kill Wolf Who Hunts Smiling and any others involved in the sordid scheme. She had no fear of whatever Black Elk was planning against her—except the fear that she might die before avenging her tall brave, the one true love of her young life. A man she might be living with now had fate not marked him out for a hard destiny.

Was he still alive? Where was he? He had known nothing but trouble ever since joining the tribe. And now, with Arrow Keeper gone, she had no sympathetic ear to confide in. Even her aunt, Sharp Nosed Woman, who once had harbored secret admiration for the tall youth's courage, had turned her heart against him.

By now the elk steak was sizzling, dripping melted kidney fat just the way Black Elk liked it. Honey Eater turned it, fighting back hot tears as the thought again intruded itself like an urgent drumbeat:

*One sleep.*

"One sleep," Wolf Who Hunts Smiling said. "One sleep, and he has run his tether out. You must not show the white feather now, this close to the blooding."

# Wendigo Mountain

Sis-ki-dee frowned, a rare sign of annoyance replacing the usual crazy-brave grin. The four of them sat around a council fire smoking good tobacco: Wolf Who Hunts Smiling, Medicine Flute, Sis-ki-dee, and Takes His Share.

"Cheyenne, be warned. You are alive only because I have found it amusing to stay my men's hand. Speak once again about Sis-ki-dee showing the white feather, and I will have them flay your soles. Then you will be sent back to the Powder on foot."

He looked at the other Cheyenne. "As for this sleepy-eyed worm larva, if he puts that bone in his mouth one more time he will have to swallow it."

Medicine Flute hastily put his flute away after this threat. But Wolf Who Hunts Smiling felt a murderous bile erupt up his throat. This Blackfoot dog sat on Cheyenne land and spoke with the same masterly, arrogant tone of the whiteskins. Still, the men in his Panther Clan took great pride in not letting any feeling show in their faces.

"No need to rise on your hind legs, Contrary Warrior. I was not insulting your courage. Sis-ki-dee would face down the Wendigo himself, as would I. I only meant that this is no time to be discouraged. You have frustrated him thus far."

"I have, wily Wolf Who Hunts Smiling. But this battle last night cost me more braves killed and wounded. And now the Ghost Warrior has gained the mountain. Even now he is watching this camp."

"Have you flushed him?"

"Would *you* flush that one?"

Wolf Who Hunts Smiling conceded this with a nod. "You speak straight. I might flush out a silvertip bear first. But only think. If he killed more of your men, all the more reason to fasten your courage to the sticking-place. White Man Runs Him swore an oath before council. If those Arrows are not returned in one more sleep, he must submit to death."

Now Medicine Flute spoke up.

"Count upon it. I despise him as much as Wolf Who Hunts Smiling does. But certainly he is no coward. Nor would this licker of white crotches ever break his word. He has promised the tribe his own death. He will make good on that promise."

Sis-ki-dee's smallpox-scarred visage creased in another ugly frown.

"That he will keep his word is not at issue. Like most fools he places great value on the importance of a promise. The issue before us now is his skill as a warrior. Have you seen those cliffs he and his men climbed? I showed you the battlefield, the spent casings. These are willful Indians."

"They are Cheyennes."

Angrily, Sis-ki-dee gestured around them.

"Never mind your foolish pride in your tribe! Look at this ruined camp! My braves have been tempered in hard fights against blue-bloused soldiers and fierce mountain Utes. Yet this tall Cheyenne led a mere handful of warriors past us. Do you think he plans to stay in hiding like a turtle ducking into its shell?"

"Of course not. He will make his move. Only, tell me a thing. You once laughed when I warned you this brave was trouble. Now I see you frowning. Is the Red Peril, too, coming unstrung as all the rest did before they died?"

Sis-ki-dee saw the clear challenge to his courage. His evil and crazy-brave grin was back.

"You are right, this is no time to recite his coups. Only think. I and my men have wounded two of his men, perhaps seriously. Another is dead. That leaves only one healthy warrior besides him."

"I have ears for this," Wolf Who Hunts Smiling said. "This Touch the Sky, he is not a god."

"No, you are right. He walks the earth and has blood in his veins, for I have spilled it. But if a thing cuts wood, you may call it an axe. This brave certainly has the look of a god."

"A battle god," Wolf Who Hunts Smiling conceded with a nod. "But he will die if we both refuse to lose heart. As you say, he is probably watching us at this very moment. Would I allow him to see me here with you if I believed he would survive?"

Here Sis-ki-dee met his visitor's eye frankly.

"On this last point, I am curious. Knowing how dangerous it is, why have you risked another trip up here?"

Wolf Who Hunts Smiling glanced briefly at Medicine Flute before answering. *Look sharp!*

*Here comes the dangerous stretch of the trail,* that glance said.

"Because," he replied, "I have thought of a better plan than the one we agreed on."

Now it was Sis-ki-dee's turn to cast a sly glance at Takes His Share.

"Oh? And what is wrong with the plan we have already agreed on? Do you mean that we should *not* kill the tall dog?"

"Of course we will kill him. We both want that. That part remains unchanged. But only think, Contrary Warrior. As you have assured me, our Medicine Arrows mean nothing to you. Your only wish is to see the head of White Man Runs Him balanced on a stick. Do my words fly straight?"

Sis-ki-dee only nodded vaguely, waiting to hear more.

"Therefore," Wolf Who Hunts Smiling said, "we have come to suggest a change. Rather than returning the Arrows yourself, give them to us."

Sis-ki-dee's eyebrows shot up. His playful mood was returning now that the game was getting crafty again.

"Give them to you? There is a curious notion. Why should I do this thing?"

"Quite simple," Wolf Who Hunts Smiling said. "Our goal is to gain dominion over this territory, agreed?"

Again Sis-ki-dee nodded, but vaguely.

"That goal is best accomplished if my shaman here, Medicine Flute, receives credit for returning the Arrows. The Headmen would be turned into fawning dogs licking his hand."

"Indeed," Sis-ki-dee said contemptuously, thinking of his own tribe's headmen, "they are squaw men moved by such considerations. This would be a fine thing—for you."

"And you, buck! For we are together in this venture. What strengthens my hand also strengthens yours."

"Perhaps," Sis-ki-dee said. "Perhaps not. Never forget, I have seen how aptly you are named. A wolf who smiles while it is hunting is a dangerous beast indeed to trust."

"Granted, as is a man who calls himself the Contrary Warrior. I do not claim to be an honorable man of my word. Neither are you, and thus we can respect each other. Women and old men are 'honorable' only because they lack the strength and killing instinct to live like the eagles who boldly devour the lambs.

"But Contrary Warrior, only think on this! Even a wolf will honor an alliance that behooves his own interest. I need a brave of your cunning and strength, a brave whose thoughts fly on the same ambitious winds as mine."

Wolf Who Hunts Smiling had always prided himself on his persuasive speaking abilities. Now, as he watched the favorable impression his words created, he felt a tug of inner satisfaction.

Sis-ki-dee said, "Well spoken, Cheyenne. And I, too, can use a capable ally."

"Then you will give me the Arrows?"

"What? Now, buck?"

"Of course. It is a long ride to this place."

A grin played at Sis-ki-dee's lips.

"But wily wolf! The Noble Red Man is not yet sent under. I cannot risk returning those Arrows until he is."

"This is foolish. No one will know I have those Arrows. Nor will they until Woman Face has been separated from his head."

"I will not risk that," Sis-ki-dee insisted. "Those Arrows remain with me until the tall one's head is tendered in payment, just as we agreed."

Wolf Who Hunts Smiling watched the other closely now as he said, "May we look at the Arrows?"

If Sis-ki-dee was nonplussed by this, he hid it well.

"What? With him watching? Have you been wandering in the sun too long?"

"Very well, if there's nothing else for it. Why push when a thing won't move?"

Secretly, Wolf Who Hunts Smiling had expected just such a response. For he had guessed by now that Sis-ki-dee planned to doublecross him and either destroy those Arrows or hold them for additional ransom. But it had been necessary to go through this sham to keep up appearances. For truly, if Sis-ki-dee knew that he knew, he would kill both of them as casually as he might swat a fly.

*So that's the way it is,* Wolf Who Hunts Smiling thought. He would have to wait in hiding, work quickly, and somehow get those Arrows himself.

"As you say, Red Peril," Wolf Who Hunts Smiling said. "We will wait until Woman Face is worm fodder. After all, the important thing is that you do intend to return the Arrows."

Sis-ki-dee nodded, fighting back a smirk.

"Of course. What use have I for your pretty sticks?"

# Chapter Twelve

Fortunately for Touch the Sky's small and battered band of warriors, the Blackfoot renegades had been left shaken by the Cheyennes' fighting spirit.

Filled with a new respect, they decided the best plan was to fort up and protect their camp. The only protection against such fighters, they agreed, was numbers. Had they risked dividing up into search parties, they might have flushed out the Cheyenne hiding place in a small, cup-shaped hollow almost within shouting distance of the camp.

"There is all the proof needed of his treachery," Tangle Hair said bitterly. "How I wish I could hear their words."

He, Touch the Sky, Little Horse, and young

Two Twists were well hidden behind a dense spruce copse. From here they spied on the meeting between the two Blackfoot renegades and the two Cheyenne visitors. They had made soft beds of young boughs for the two wounded Cheyennes. Little Horse had been fortunate: the slug had passed through his shoulder and left a clean wound. Touch the Sky had packed it with gunpowder and balsam before wrapping it again.

Tangle Hair had not been so lucky. Touch the Sky and Two Twists had been forced to dig the slug out of the meaty portion of his thigh while Tangle Hair bit down hard on a strip of rawhide. The wound needed to be cauterized, but they could not risk a fire. So they settled for carefully wrapping it now.

Both men were weak, but Touch the Sky knew they were tough enough to survive. Unfortunately, further combat was out of the question for either until they rested and recovered some strength.

And this was hardly the place for resting. Touch the Sky knew they risked discovery at any time. Nor was all the danger posed by humans. He had noticed how the trees all around this spot had been clawed high up—the territorial markings of a grizzly. This was a place to leave as soon as possible.

As was this entire mountain.

But for now all of them could see Wolf Who Hunts Smiling and Medicine Flute in the

Blackfoot camp, counciling with the murdering dog Sis-ki-dee.

"Where are the Arrows?" Two Twists said again. "They have parleyed for a long time now. But no sign of the Arrows. What, are they trading their clan histories?"

His voice was tense with frustration. Like the others, he felt powerless to help—powerless to help his tribe secure their Arrows, powerless to help Touch the Sky, a warrior's warrior whom Two Twists admired to the very core of his being. Who had rallied Two Twists and the other junior warriors to a brilliant defense when Kiowas and Comanches had attempted to steal their women and children during the annual hunt? Two Twists had watched Touch the Sky, who stood all alone in the open, use himself as a human lure to draw the enemy into effective range. With bullets creasing his ears and fanning his locks, he had stood tall and defiant and never once flinched, all for the sake of his tribe.

"Where are the Arrows? I know not, little brother," Touch the Sky finally replied. "Better to ask me where the buffalo go to die. But we must watch for our clue. For as surely as my blood is red, our Arrows are in that camp."

Touch the Sky gave the entire area a sweeping gaze before adding, "Or somewhere near it."

"What is the meaning of this third painting?" Little Horse said from his bed of boughs. The brave was paler than normal from blood loss. He had been studying the pictograph Arrow Keeper had left behind, unable to see much in the old shaman's crude artwork.

"Divine that answer," Touch the Sky replied, "and this trail takes a new turn. Believe me, bucks, I have studied it hard and long."

"It could be many things," Little Horse said. "It is only a long, curving line."

"Many things," Two Twists agreed. "A path?"

"Perhaps a river?"

"Could it be a snake?"

"It could be all or any of those," Touch the Sky told his friends. "But I have shed brain sweat on this matter. Think how this mountain is hollow in places from underground springs and other openings. This painting could also indicate a cave or perhaps a tunnel."

Little Horse nodded.

"You may be right, brother. Yes, you just might be. But what of that? I have noticed no tunnel or cave entrance, though truly, we have hardly had a good chance to explore this place."

"Nor are we likely to get one," Touch the Sky said. "So we must take turns watching them constantly, especially Sis-ki-dee. If he—"

"Brothers!" Two Twists cut in. "Look! Wolf Who Hunts Smiling and Medicine Flute are leaving."

"So it would appear," Touch the Sky said, watching the two braves head toward the slope and their waiting ponies. "We dare not break cover to follow them, and we cannot spare a man anyway. Only two of us are able. Let us hope they are truly returning to the Powder River camp, not going to the place where the Arrows are hidden."

*One sleep*, he thought desperately. With sunset tomorrow, he must either surrender himself for execution or bear the responsibility for ruining his tribe—as well as breaking an oath made before council. Keeping his word was doubly hard because he knew that Sis-ki-dee would never keep his.

If all that weren't trouble enough for one brave's lifetime, there was more. His death would also mark Honey Eater out for some awful fate. Arrow Keeper had predicted these things, and not once had Touch the Sky known him to err concerning medicine visions.

But for now, exhaustion had him and Two Twists firmly in its grip. He looked at the youth's face. It had aged ten years since beginning that harrowing climb up the northern face of this bad-medicine mountain. And truly, when had the tough little brave last slept?

"Two Twists?"

"I have ears."

"And a stout heart, buck," Touch the Sky told him. "With braves like you surrounding him, a man could sleep in peace at night. And speaking of sleep, lie down now. Then I will do the same while you watch."

Two Twists was too exhausted to protest. He was dead to the world almost as soon as he closed his eyes.

Fighting back stone-heavy eyelids and dizzying

waves of exhaustion, Touch the Sky constantly monitored the camp below. Secure in their concentrated numbers, the Blackfoot marauders had not bothered to establish an outlying guard.

He watched them amuse themselves by gambling, running foot races through the camp, wrestling, drinking the cheap whiskey sold illegally to Indians at the trading post at Red Shale. Many lined up to arm-wrestle between circles of hot coals, the loser receiving a harsh burn when his strength gave out. But Sis-ki-dee went inside of his hide-covered lodge and spent most of his time there. Several times Touch the Sky saw him step outside to scan the surrounding area thoughtfully—much as the Cheyenne himself was doing.

Finally, black waves of weariness washing over his depleted body, Touch the Sky woke Two Twists. The two wounded braves had both slipped into a fitful sleep.

"Watch carefully, little brother, while I join our comrades. If you see any sign of our Arrows, wake me."

Two Twists nodded. His eyes lifted upward to the heavens, tracking the progress of Sister Sun. She was almost straight overhead now. Time was slipping away from them like water running through their fingers.

He met Touch the Sky's eyes and nodded. Like well-trained Cheyenne warriors, both braves kept their fear out of their faces. But their eyes said it clearly without words: *We are up against it now*.

*May Maiyun help our tribe, and soon, or Gray Thunder's Shaiyena people will be in a hurting place.*

Touch the Sky's last thought, as he tumbled down into blessed sleep, was of old Arrow Keeper.

That, and the vague awareness of a sound further up the mountain: the triumphant kill cry of a mountain lion.

He dreamed, but not just one dream. It was as if the entire, tumultuous history of his life was paraded before his mind's eye in fleeting images.

He saw Bighorn Falls, the sleepy river-bend town where he had grown up as Matthew Hanchon with his adopted white parents; Kristin Steele, her bottomless blue eyes smiling at him as they met in their secret copse; the long-jawed, malicious face of her father's wrangler, Boone Wilson, as he beat the 16-year-old senseless for daring to love a white woman.

He saw himself riding out alone from Bighorn Falls in the dead of night, bridle pointed toward Cheyenne country, after Lt. Seth Carlson's threat to ruin his parents' mercantile business if he remained in town. Then came images of all his struggles and battles as a Cheyenne: images of torture by fire and near-starvation and festering wounds and ferocious combat.

All of it was familiar, a dream litany of his

138

hard life as a warrior caught between two worlds, welcome in neither.

And then came the one brief image that didn't fit, that made no apparent sense. The ridiculous image of Arrow Keeper.

The old shaman was completely naked, a younger man now though clearly Arrow Keeper. He was riding down a steep mountainside, long hair streaming out behind him in the wind.

Only, he wasn't riding a pony—he was mounted on the back of a magnificent mountain lion!

*Brother.*
*Wake up, brother.*
*Touch the Sky!*

"Wake up!" Two Twists repeated urgently, giving Touch the Sky a hard shake.

Abruptly the tall warrior sat up.

"What is it?"

Sister Sun had tracked even further west. A deep, luminous gold sheen lay over Wendigo Mountain.

"Look," Two Twists said, pointing. "Sis-ki-dee has headed up toward the peak by himself."

Touch the Sky looked where the youth pointed. He watched the Blackfoot leader swing wide around a spot where a patch of trees had been obliterated by a rock slide. He was indeed picking his way toward the peak. For a moment the sun glinted off his brassards and the huge brass rings dangling from his ears.

Then Touch the Sky spotted something else,

and his pulse suddenly quickened.

It was a brief glimpse of a tawny hide streaking up toward the remote pinnacle. A mountain lion. Alerted by his strange vision, Touch the Sky knew this was no coincidence.

He watched the lion bound higher and higher before seeming to disappear suddenly near the peak. He was just able to distinguish a slight cleft in the gray expanse of rock—no doubt the entrance to its den.

No, this was no coincidence. Old Arrow Keeper was still protecting the Sacred Arrows. In the face of utter hopelessness, he had sent this vision as a goad to his young assistant's flagging determination.

"Look!" Two Twists said. "Sis-ki-dee has stopped again. What is he doing?"

Two Twists had not noticed the mountain lion. But Touch the Sky had seen Sis-ki-dee watching it. And now the Contrary Warrior abruptly turned around again and returned to his camp.

"Bucks," Touch the Sky said, for the other two Cheyennes were awake now, too. "I believe we have located the Medicine Arrows!"

The rest stared at him expectantly, waiting for more. But there was no time now for explanations.

"Wait here," he told Two Twists. When the youth started to object, he added, "It will be difficult enough for one man to remain hidden, let alone two. Do not feel slighted, young buck. You may yet get another ration of hard fighting, if your belly hungers for it. For now, banish all thoughts of glory and think only of the need to find those Arrows."

It was a dangerous journey, and with every heartbeat Touch the Sky expected shots to ring out.

Fixing the exact location of the den in his mind, Touch the Sky broke from cover and headed up. The most direct route, unfortunately, cut through the Blackfoot camp. Touch the Sky was forced to swing wide to the west to avoid it, then double back.

Even so, he was dangerously exposed when he raced from boulder to boulder, from stunted tree to the next low-lying swale. There was not enough time to do this thing correctly, an advance that, by rights, should have taken a better part of the day.

He kept a wary eye on the camp. But so far Sis-ki-dee had not come out again. Soon Touch the Sky had slipped close enough to hear the mewling of young lion cubs coming from just inside the cleft in the rocks. This area was well disguised from below, a rockslide having caused a massive deadfall of trees that served as a blind.

He stayed downwind from the den. A mountain lion with young to protect would be a formidable foe indeed. Touch the Sky knew it was foolish to attempt to get any closer. He had his Sharps to hand, a round behind the loading gate. But one shot would bring that entire camp swarming over him.

Impatiently, he settled behind a boulder and waited. Soon the hungry mother rewarded him by slipping back outside again. She was already stalking more food to strengthen her milk for the cubs.

Touch the Sky waited until she had disappeared behind a razorback ridge to the east. Then, moving quickly forward in a crouch, he made it to the entrance and slipped inside the lion's den.

# Chapter Thirteen

"I saw the she-bitch return a short time ago," Sis-ki-dee told Takes His Share. "So I turned back. I have no desire to kill such a valuable ally. But I have watched her habits closely. By now she will have gone back out to hunt. I am returning to her den."

The two Blackfoot renegades stood in the center of their now heavily guarded camp. Sentries along the southern slope would signal long before any surprise attack by additional braves from the Powder River camp would stand a chance.

The only risk, to Sis-ki-dee's mind, was that tall Ghost Warrior and his band.

"They are close," Sis-ki-dee told Takes His Share again. "Never doubt that. For there sinks the sun, sinking too the tall buck's chances as well as any hope for his tribe. Their boldness will increase with their desperation."

"My thoughts too, Contrary Warrior. Have I ever spoken any way but one about this Cheyenne devil? I fear him and freely admit it. Only. . . ."

Sis-ki-dee tossed back his cropped head and laughed.

" 'Only' what? Do not play the coy woman, buck! Spit your words out as if you have a set on you! Say it bold, what troubles you?"

"Only this. As you say, they are watching our camp. So why, having stopped them this long, reveal the hiding place of the Arrows now?"

"Because, buck, I plan to reveal more than the hiding place. I mean to reveal the Arrows to them."

Takes His Share gaped stupidly. "But, Sis-ki-dee, for what good reason?"

"Am I ever without a good reason, even when it is not always immediately clear? Did we not just agree that the Cheyennes' boldness will increase with their desperation?"

Takes His Share nodded. He watched his war leader check the load in his North and Savage. Then Sis-ki-dee slid the Bowie from its sheath and tested the edge with a thumb.

"And how many sleeps remain before they run out of time?"

"Only one."

"Only one, indeed," Sis-ki-dee agreed. "And soon, we are plunged into darkness when the sun goes down. Better if they make their move while we can see them. Even more important, *I* want to control this thing. Sis-ki-dee is no brave to sit in his tipi, waiting patiently, until he is called out to the fight."

Sis-ki-dee's eyes glinted as they narrowed to study the surrounding terrain. For several heart-beats they focused thoughtfully on the narrow entrance to the lion's den, a mere dark line against the blight caused by the rockslide.

"They are out there, buck. So I will fetch those Arrows into plain view now as a lure and a reminder. This Cheyenne blister has chafed at us long enough. Now it is time to pop it once and for all.

"Keep a close eye on things down here," he added.

A moment later he started up through the huge piles of scree, angling toward the mountain lion's den.

Touch the Sky paid scant attention to the mewling and whimpering of the cubs, squirming balls of fur in their soft bed to the left of the entrance. But he reminded himself to hurry. Few animals were more ferocious than a mountain lion protecting her young. And he had no idea how far away this one's hunting territory extended.

Fortunately, enough light remained to illuminate the cavern chamber. A quick, cursory look revealed nothing. But he hadn't really expected it to—Sis-ki-dee was not that careless.

Trying to quell the urgency inside him, Touch

the Sky began a more thorough search of the chamber. Occasionally, at first, he hurried to the entrance and glanced outside to make sure that nothing—on two legs or four—was approaching. But as he became more absorbed in searching the farther reaches of the stone cavern, he neglected to check as often.

He peered into every nook and cranny; he slipped his fingers into every cleft; he probed every possible opening. He felt the uneven rock floor for hiding places, ran his eye carefully overhead.

Nothing.

The desperation welled up inside him, but he fought it down the way a man overcomes a temptation. Desperation led to panic, and panic left a warrior useless. He thought of Arrow Keeper, and that thought calmed him.

He was sure now that the old shaman was with him, helping him even now, if only he could clear his mind and attend closer to his shaman senses. Had not the pictograph already proven valuable? Had Arrow Keeper not sent him medicine visions as clues?

Touch the Sky knew he had not ended up here purely by chance. The hand of the Good Supernatural—with Arrow Keeper's assistance— had guided him to this place. And those Arrows were close. He could feel the weight of their presence as a person can feel the weight of a hidden stare.

*As the twig is bent, so the tree shall grow,* the old

medicine man had told him long ago. This was during his first initiation into the Cheyenne way. And thanks in part to Arrow Keeper's wisdom, had this tree called Touch the Sky not grown straight and tall and strong? A tree to match its lofty name?

Deliberately, Touch the Sky brought his rapid, uneven breathing under calm control.

He willed his tense muscles to relax.

Despite the danger pressing in on him from all sides, he cleared his mind of all fear, of all 'thought.' He stood there in the center of the cavern, his eyes closed, his mind free but attentive.

Outside, the winds lashing Wendigo Mountain rose to a hollow, shrieking cry that sounded unmistakably human, the voices of those long-ago Cheyenne hunters whose souls were trapped in this most unholy of places. But Touch the Sky refused to let fear violate his quiet, motionless concentration.

The knowledge came to him all at once, certain and sure and beyond language. When he finally stirred himself again, his movements were sure and precise. He knew right where to go, the way beavers know where to build their dams.

Touch the Sky crossed to the back of the big chamber. He stepped behind an abutment of limestone and into the well-concealed tunnel he had missed the first time around. Several overhead airshafts sent light stabbing into the sunken tunnel.

Looking due north, Touch the Sky could see

that this was only one of a maze of several tunnels. They slanted down toward the cliffs at the backside of Wendigo Mountain. He wanted to explore them. But for now he was concerned with one spot just past the entrance of this first tunnel.

He propped his Sharps against the damp stone wall. Then, hand over hand, he climbed to the top of the tunnel and thrust one hand up into a narrow space near the cold stone ceiling.

He probed a fissure, and immediately his fingers brushed slick oilskin.

Elated, heart stomping against his ribs, Touch the Sky climbed quickly back down and stepped into a shaft of light. Carefully setting the bundle down, he knelt beside it. Heart hammering with apprehension and anticipation, he opened the slicker.

Fingers trembling, he opened the soft coyote-fur pouch inside. Then his grim lips eased into a wide smile—the first that had touched his face for some time.

There lay all four Medicine Arrows, sweet and clean as he was sworn to keep them.

Quickly, all business now, he wrapped the Arrows in their fur pouch again, then folded the slicker around them. He had just begun to stow them away when an angry snarl behind him turned his blood to ice.

Touch the Sky whirled and spotted his rifle, too far away to be any help now. But it would have been useless even if he had held it in his hands, because the very moment he turned to look behind him, the enraged mountain lion slammed into him like a blurry yellow missile and knocked him flat.

"Panther Clan, this scheme would be scanned," Medicine Flute said nervously. "This Sis-ki-dee is no brave to trifle with."

"Truer notes never crossed your lips, flute blower," Wolf Who Hunts Smiling replied. "He is no brave to trifle with, indeed. That is why we are here."

The wily Cheyenne nodded toward the Colt Model 1855 percussion rifle in his hands. It had been among the possessions stripped from Touch the Sky when he was still called Matthew Hanchon and wore white man's shoes. By now it had seen hard service. A strip of buckskin reinforced the cracked stock.

"I have no plans to trifle with him. I see now that it is useless to attempt sharing power with that one. I mean to get those Arrows and then kill him. Nothing trifling in that."

After failing, during his recent meeting with the Blackfoot, to secure the Medicine Arrows, Wolf Who Hunts Smiling decided on a bold and decisive plan of action. Instead of returning to their camp, he and Medicine Flute took up a position in a thicket to the south.

Clearly, the Cheyenne now realized, he had been a fool to give those Arrows to Sis-ki-dee. Once they were actually in his hands, Wolf Who

Hunts Smiling had nearly panicked. If his tribe ever caught him with them, no amount of sly talk would save him from a hard death. Thus he had shown bad judgment in trusting the Blackfoot renegade.

Now it only remained to figure out where those Arrows were hidden. Wolf Who Hunts Smiling had received his first valuable clue when Sis-ki-dee had started up toward that peak, then halted when he spotted the mountain lion.

Wolf Who Hunts Smiling couldn't see, from this altitude and angle, the precise spot where the she-bitch actually entered her den. Nor could he see very far west of this low-lying position—the direction from which Touch the Sky and the lion had approached and entered the den.

But he could clearly now see Sis-ki-dee starting back up toward the peak again. And a further stroke of luck: the braves in camp, bored by their constant vigilance, were placing bets on target plinking. One more shot might not be noticed among all the shots already echoing atop the mountain.

"Now we are close to owning the Arrows, buck," he assured Medicine Flute. "Sis-ki-dee is not climbing up there to relieve himself. If you know how to fire that rusted firestick of yours, be ready. For I am about to stir things up around here."

With that, Wolf Who Hunts Smiling broke from cover and made his way closer to the pinnacle of Wendigo Mountain.

# Wendigo Mountain

*    *    *

The mountain lion leaped on Touch the Sky so hard that the impact brought him down immediately.

He felt the sudden animal warmth of the contact, stared directly into those slavering jaws, felt fire erupt in his side as several claws raked bloody furrows. Gobbets of fresh meat still clung to the cat's deadly fangs.

The lithe killer had gone straight for his jugular. But the momentum of its powerful leap made it overshoot its human mark, claws raking on the stone behind him as the lion hit hard and quickly recovered for another leap.

But the delay gave Touch the Sky just enough time to snatch his obsidian knife from its sheath. He rolled hard to the right as the lion leaped again, missing him by inches.

The Cheyenne rose to his knees, then into a low squat. Powerful leg muscles bunching, he leaped on the cat.

The lion was an eyeblink quicker, managing to scuttle just enough to avert the killing blow; it was turned to a wound instead as the blade caught the cat just above the right forepaw.

A snarl of rage, an unbelievably fast spin, and the lion was on Touch the Sky.

The youth managed to get an arm up, protecting his face from the deadly fangs. He arched his back hard, tossing the cat. In a heartbeat it was up again and flying at him.

Once more molten fire poured over him as

the sharp claws ripped into his chest. But this time Touch the Sky managed one good thrust of his knife. The blade caught the lion in the soft underfold of its belly.

Desperate, knowing another wound would never stop this blood-lusting beast, Touch the Sky drove his knife clear to the hilt, then gave it the 'Spanish twist,' ripping deep and wide into warm vitals. He felt heat escape from the lion's punctured organs, felt the huge beast quiver violently, then unleash a fierce death cry. Finally it went slack, its wild blood mingled with the Cheyenne's.

For a moment Touch the Sky lay gasping under the dead beast, chest heaving as he got his breath back. Then, sore muscles protesting the effort, he threw the dead animal off him and staggered to his feet.

Touch the Sky limped across to the spot where he had left the Arrows. He gave silent thanks to Maiyun when he realized they had remained unscathed throughout his desperate struggle with the mountain lion.

"I did not choose to violate your home and leave your children orphans, cousin," he said quietly and with genuine regret at having been forced to kill this animal. After all, she had only been defending her young.

Below, in the camp, he heard the drunken cheers, the guns going off as the wild braves shot at targets. He was about to pick up the Arrows when a familiar laugh made his skin crawl.

"The Noble Red Man braves all to save his tribe's pretty-painted sticks! Then he cries over a dead lion. Better to cry for his own hide, for truly his days between the sky and the earth are now over!"

Touch the Sky whirled. Sis-ki-dee filled the opening of the den. The sun backlighted him in a bloody penumbra. His finger slid inside the trigger guard of his big North and Savage rifle.

"My mistake has been in always insisting on taking you alive. Each time you managed to somehow play the fox."

"Perhaps," Touch the Sky replied, merely sparring for time, "you are not so clever as you think."

"Perhaps not. But here I stand, rifle trained on you. And over there is your weapon. Use magic, shaman, and cause it to fly into your hands."

Suddenly Touch the Sky focused his eyes behind Sis-ki-dee, as if someone had appeared in the entrance behind him.

Sis-ki-dee laughed. "Truly, you are a game bird! Even now you pull tricks out of your parfleche."

With no warning, the mirth bled from Sis-ki-dee's face. His finger took up the trigger slack.

"Never mind skinning off your face while you are still alive to see it," he said. "It will impress my men just as much after you are dead."

Sis-ki-dee caressed the trigger.

"Take your last breath, Ghost Warrior! Sis-ki-dee never misses at this range. Nor will you turn this bullet to sand. It does not matter how loudly you sing your death song. This is Wendigo Mountain. Any Cheyenne who dies here dies unclean!"

# Chapter Fourteen

Sis-ki-dee's last word still hung in the air, mocking Touch the Sky on the threshold of death, when a rifle shot sounded above the moaning of the wind. But Touch the Sky knew that a man never hears the shot that kills him—*this* bullet wasn't meant to send him over.

Even as his battle-savvy brain registered this fact, he watched a round rip through Sis-ki-dee's leather shirt. It had been fired by someone outside the entrance to the den. Had Two Twists disobeyed orders, Touch the Sky wondered, and broken from cover?

Touch the Sky gave thanks for insubordinate junior warriors, for evidently Two Twists had just saved his life. But all this flashed through the Cheyenne's mind in an eyeblink. Even as his brain grappled with events, his body sprang into action.

Sis-ki-dee had leaped to the floor upon feeling the tug of a bullet rip through his shirt. Certain he was being attacked by the rest of the Cheyennes, he scrambled to his feet and lunged toward the secret escape tunnels. His rifle came up to the ready as he charged at the Cheyenne intruder.

Instinctively, Touch the Sky's first move was to scoop up the Sacred Arrows. Sis-ki-dee was rising as he leaped over the dead mountain lion. Touch the Sky lunged for his Sharps, still propped against the wall of the cavern. He only had time to swing the rifle up and snap off a round without aiming.

He missed. Luckily, so did Sis-ki-dee. But the Blackfoot's round struck rock only inches from Touch the Sky's eyes and flung powder into them, temporarily blinding him.

Reflexively, Touch the Sky dropped the oilskin pouch as his hand flew to his eyes. By the time he could open them again, blurry now with tears, he saw Sis-ki-dee disappearing around an elbow turn in the main tunnel—and the yellow oilskin was clutched close to his side!

It was not Two Twists who fired the bullet that saved Touch the Sky's life.

Unaware that he was in fact saving his worst enemy in the world, Wolf Who Hunts Smiling had only meant to kill this renegade Blackfoot who meant to play the fox with him. For surely the Arrows were inside that den. And Wolf Who Hunts Smiling wanted to seize this moment for the kill, when a volley of shots from camp covered the noise of his own shot.

But in his eager haste he had felt himself jerk his trigger at the last moment, throwing off his aim.

Had he at least wounded the Blackfoot? It was hard to tell from here. But shots had been fired inside the cave, too. Hope welled inside Wolf Who Hunts Smiling. Had one of those shots, fired after his own, finally snuffed the life of White Man Runs Him?

Now he quickly reloaded. Staying out of sight of those below, he scrambled up toward that entrance. He avoided the great golden splashes of light made by the day's late sunlight.

He must lay hands on those Arrows! Never mind whether or not they meant anything spiritually. With them safely stored in Medicine Flute's tipi, Wolf Who Hunts Smiling would bend the people to his own purposes. Soon would begin a great war of extermination against all the whiteskin invaders.

But even now, caught flush in the excitement of danger, two questions nagged at him: Where was Sis-ki-dee, and where was Touch the Sky?

As Sis-ki-dee disappeared from view, his insane, mocking laughter taunted Touch the Sky and dared him to follow.

Follow the Cheyenne did, although this maze of tunnels was unfamiliar to him. Just enough light filtered down through the airshafts to illuminate the tunnels in a grainy sort of twilight.

First he paused to reload. Going mostly by touch in the stingy light, he fished a paper cartridge from his parfleche. He chewed off one end, shook the powder into his charger, seated the ball. Then he thumbed a primer cap behind the loading gate.

When he'd finished, Touch the Sky stood stone silent, stone still, and listened.

The noises from camp receded behind him now, but not the mournful howling of the wind. It chased itself in and out of the numerous airshafts, reminding Touch the Sky of the noise the wind used to make in the stovepipes back at his childhood home in Bighorn Falls.

Beyond the mournful sound of the wind, he heard something else: faint footsteps, moving out ahead of him. He started toward them, but soon he halted. His brow wrinkled in confusion.

For now the footsteps seemed to come from his right. He took the next tunnel that jogged in that direction. But as soon as he did so, the noise of someone running seemed to shift to his left.

Again Touch the Sky stopped, confused and disoriented.

Then, clear as a rattler's warning in still morning air, he heard it: Sis-ki-dee's high-pitched, insane, mocking laughter. Much closer than he expected.

And then a pebble bounced off his back, and Touch the Sky flinched violently. He whirled and drew a bead—on empty air.

The crazy laughter rose an octave, blending into the steady shriek of the wind.

Takes His Share grew impatient.

The Contrary Warrior had told him to keep an eye on things. But only Sis-ki-dee could truly control these braves when they were becoming wild. And now, as the liquor flowed, they were indeed wild.

A group, faces flushed with drunkenness, had gathered around a campfire. Now they tossed cartridges into the flames and waited for the round to detonate, risking their lives merely for the thrill of it. If Sis-ki-dee was gone much longer, there wouldn't be any camp to return to.

Takes His Share slipped his big-bore Lancaster under his arm and headed up the slope. The last of the day's sun blazed in its full glory now, throwing the Sans Arcs peaks into dark silhouette.

He picked his way carefully across the blighted area caused by the rockslide, his rifle at the ready in case the cat was inside. Then he stuck his head into the narrow cleft.

"Contrary Warrior? Are you in there? Can you hear me?"

Nothing. But he thought he heard a faint noise within.

Cautiously he stuck his head inside.

Cold steel kissed his temple, and then a bright

explosion of orange sent Takes His Share across when Wolf Who Hunts Smiling blew his brains all over the rock wall beside him.

"I know what he said," Two Twists said impatiently to Little Horse. "But he has been gone far too long now."

Little Horse winced as he rolled to a sitting position and glanced up the slope in the direction Touch the Sky had gone.

"I agree, little brother. But let me go."

"You! Here, aim this."

The younger brave handed his British trade rifle to Little Horse. But his left arm had stiffened so badly he could not even lift it to aim.

"See? Tangle Hair cannot walk, and you cannot shoot. It comes down to me. If it were up to you, you would have gone to check on Touch the Sky by now."

Little Horse was forced to nod at this.

"Then go. But move carefully, buck, and keep an eye on your back-trail. Hear them in that camp? If they catch you, count upon it, your screams will provide the night's entertainment."

Two Twists nodded, nervous sweat beading on his upper lip. Holding his rifle at a high port, he moved out through the piles of scree.

Wolf Who Hunts Smiling could not puzzle this situation out.

He had found no blood on the rocks, so evidently his shot had missed Sis-ki-dee. And this dead lion explained the shots he had heard after his own. But where was Sis-ki-dee?

He had made a quick search of the cavern, missing the hidden tunnel entrance at the back. And then that fool Takes His Share had come sniffing after his own death.

Now what? Wolf Who Hunts Smiling had searched this entire cavern and found no sign of the Arrows. He couldn't remain here much longer. Soon someone from below would miss Sis-ki-dee or Takes His Share.

Frustrated, but knowing there was nothing else for it, he stepped over the dead Indian and left the cavern.

Deep in the maze of hidden tunnels, the deadly cat-and-mouse game went on.

Touch the Sky could not be sure if he was the pursuer or the pursued. At one moment he would hear footsteps out ahead of him. The next, he heard the steps coming up from behind him. But always, when he whirled around, there was nothing there. At least, nothing he could see in the smoky lighting.

It was a war of nerves, and no one was better than Sis-ki-dee at waging this style of fight. The Blackfoot knew these tunnels and thus had a distinct advantage over the Cheyenne. Touch the Sky had no idea, when he first had plunged into the maze, just how extensive the tunnels were.

They turned and twisted, took sharp dog-leg turns that sent him back over ground he had just covered. Occasionally, in the confusing dimness ahead, he would glimpse what he thought was a figure. When he had a clear shot, he took it. Now and then his enemy fired back, and Touch the Sky heard the protracted whine as bullets ricocheted from wall to wall along the tunnels.

"Ghost Warrior!" a voice rang out, and Touch the Sky instinctively crouched, unable to pinpoint its location.

"Ghost Warrior! I have one of your Arrows in my hand now! Listen! I am going to break your pretty stick!"

There was indeed a sharp sound of wood snapping. Touch the Sky winced as if he'd been kicked in the groin.

"Here! Stick this in your parfleche!"

Something struck the stone wall out in front of him. Touch the Sky groped ahead, stooped to feel the floor of the tunnel. His heart thumped as if he had just run hard up a long hill.

His groping fingers felt broken wood, and his heart sank.

Then he pulled it into a shaft of light and saw it was only a normal flint-tipped arrow of the type used by the Blackfoot tribe.

The mocking laughter again, seeming to come from all around him in this place without directions.

Two Twists looked just as puzzled as Wolf Who Hunts Smiling had.

He saw the dead lion, the dead Blackfoot. And

like Wolf Who Hunts Smiling, he failed to find any secret tunnel entrance at the back of this big cavern. Clearly some lively sport had taken place here. At least that was not Touch the Sky lying dead there near the entrance. Would that it were Sis-ki-dee instead of just his lieutenant.

He was about to back out of the cavern and look elsewhere when he remembered.

He remembered how he had fallen to his knees, speechless with fright, when he climbed over the cliff to confront the dead Shoots the Bear standing over them in that ghastly lightning. And he remembered his hot anger when he realized what the murdering renegades had done to Cheyenne dead.

His face grim with sudden resolution, he set his rifle aside and squatted beside the dead brave. Turnabout was fair play. He slipped both hands under the arms of the corpse and began tugging it to its feet.

Sis-ki-dee had stashed plenty of ropes at the end of the tunnels where they debouched out of the face of the cliffs. But he had no intention of making that long climb down except as a last resort. By now, any Cheyennes who had come into the cavern after him should be gone. Better to simply kill this tall dog in the tunnels, then return to the lion's den.

So far it had been child's play to track his movements. Sis-ki-dee knew all the places where he could cross to a new tunnel and thus slip behind the confused Cheyenne. True, he had not yet gotten a clear shot at him. But as soon as he did, all playing would be over.

He stopped for a moment, listening for any noises that did not belong to the wind. A smile divided his face as he heard stealthy movements just ahead, where two tunnels formed an intersection. The Ghost Warrior would have to emerge from one or the other.

He squatted back in the shadows and set the oilskin bundle down. His index finger eased inside the trigger guard and took up the slack.

Touch the Sky stopped just back from the opening ahead of him. A cool breeze licked his face and told him he was crossing another tunnel.

But his shaman sense felt something else—the familiar cool prickle of impending danger.

He moved another step closer, hugging the cool stone wall. Now he sensed the menace in the air.

Another step, and the fine hairs on his nape stood up.

He waited, took a long breath, expelled it.

*Now*, whispered Arrow Keeper's voice, *charge him quick while he's expecting you to crawl to your death. Now, tall warrior!*

"Hii-ya! Hii-*ya!*"

Touch the Sky leaped from the tunnel, saw his surprised quarry squatting in an adjacent tunnel, raised his Sharps, and fired. The bullet hit Sis-ki-dee square in the tough brass rings of his brassards, ricocheting off. But the tough Blackfoot renegade had the reflexes of a wolverine. In an instant he was gone, his mocking laughter taunting the Cheyenne.

Now Sis-ki-dee depended on his knowledge of the tunnels to lead his quarry a merry chase. It was run and duck and shoot as Touch the Sky chased his enemy down for the final kill. When Sis-ki-dee was sure the Cheyenne was lost deep in the bowels of the maze, he made straight for the cavern again, Medicine Arrows clutched tightly under one arm.

Outside, the sun was finally saying good-bye in a last glorious burst of flaring gold. Sis-ki-dee, chest heaving from his exertions, broke into the main cavern again. A fast glance told him no enemies were lurking about.

Then he glimpsed a figure standing near the entrance, waiting.

His rifle was instantly tucked into his shoulder socket. Then he grinned by way of greeting as he recognized the figure: It was only Takes His Share.

"Quickly, buck!" he told his lackey. "Outside the cave! I hear him coming. We'll wait for our rabbit to poke his nose out, then let daylight into his soul!"

Takes His Share said nothing, only stood there staring at him. Now Sis-ki-dee squinted in confusion. He moved closer, stared even harder. Then the bold warrior who did not believe in spirits realized with a cold shudder that was not foam coming out of Takes His Share's ear, it was his brains!

His dead companion stood in the entrance, staring at him. How could this thing be?

"No," Sis-ki-dee said, backing away as fright turned his calves to water. "I never harmed you, leave me alone!"

Now there was nothing else for it. He faced a walking dead man before him, a superb Cheyenne warrior behind. His only chance was to duck back into those tunnels and escape down the cliffs.

Caught in a bone-numbing panic, Sis-ki-dee never even noticed that he had dropped the Medicine Arrows to the floor of the cavern. Only concerned to get away from this evil spirit and the blood-lusting Cheyenne, he spun on his heel and raced back into the network of tunnels.

# Chapter Fifteen

An angry but nervous Sis-ki-dee lowered himself down the precarious northern face of Wendigo Mountain, forced into a hard climb that wiped the arrogant grin from his face. Only a few stone throws away, separated from him by the rock shell of the mountain, Touch the Sky continued his fruitless search of the tunnels.

The shaman senses soon convinced him he was alone in the confusing maze. But where was Sis-ki-dee, and from which direction had he left? So far Touch the Sky had been unable to find the point where the tunnels debouched at the cliff. Perhaps he was wrong, perhaps they did not provide another way out. Maybe Sis-ki-dee had merely doubled past him in the dark maze and left by the entrance on the southern slope.

Frustrated, he worked his way back to the main chamber, mainly guided by the increased lighting at that end of the tunnel. It was nearly dark now. Wandering around would only get him killed when Sis-ki-dee returned to his camp and alerted the men—assuming he hadn't done so already. They might be grouped out there right now, rifles trained on that opening.

Thus preoccupied, Touch the Sky almost tripped over the Medicine Arrows.

He had just eased out from behind the limestone outcropping that hid the tunnel entrance. His moccasin brushed something that rustled. When he glanced down and recognized the yellow oilskin glimmering in the stingy light, his heart missed a beat.

Afraid to look closer, yet knowing he must, Touch the Sky squatted lower. He unwrapped the slicker, then the coyote fur, and peered close in the weak light. All the while his face showed nothing.

Then a wide smile eased onto his face as he realized that all four Arrows were there, all whole and all sweet and all clean.

But it seemed too easy. How did they just happen to be lying there for the taking? Where was Sis-ki-dee? Touch the Sky glanced toward the front of the chamber and, squinting in the half-light, spotted a figure waiting.

Too late his tired mind warned him: *It's a trap!*

He drew the Arrows close, about to tuck and roll back into the darkling tunnels. But then the realization struck him, more a feeling than any visual evidence: Whoever it was, he wasn't moving. And something about the perfect lack of motion told him he would never move again.

He rose, took a step closer, took a few more. Now, near the body, he recognized Sis-ki-dee's favorite. He could also see the rocks propped around the feet and ankles. And he recognized the familiar braiding pattern of the buffalo-hair rope that he could see kept the upper-body weight from falling.

The sturdy braid used by Two Twists' clan, famous for their strong ropes.

Suddenly Touch the Sky understood what must have happened to Sis-ki-dee.

Elation tingled his blood. But this was hardly a moment for celebrating. He still had to get those Arrows out of this enemy stronghold and safely back to the Powder River camp.

His face wrinkled in distaste as he cut the rope that held up Takes His Share. The dead Blackfoot slumped heavily down, and Touch the Sky stepped over him—averting his eyes in case the dead man's ghost tried to enter him that way. He ducked for cover in the same movement that brought him outside.

"Brother! Is it you? I almost shot you for Sis-ki-dee!"

"Am I that ugly, Two Twists?" He made out the shadowy mass of his young friend, ensconced in the rocks.

"Not only is it I, stout buck," he added, "but

thanks to your grisly handiwork inside, look what I carry!"

"Our Arrows!"

Even in the weak light Touch the Sky could make out the youth's wide smile.

"But how did *I* get them back?" Two Twists demanded. "I have been out here hiding, useless as a cowering rabbit."

"A rabbit, then, worth five braves! Tell me, rabbit, did Sis-ki-dee come out this way?"

"If he had, brother, either he or I would lie here dead."

Touch the Sky nodded. "As I thought. Your little puppet show with the dead scared the big Indian witless. He dropped the Arrows and ran. I would wager a new blanket that he is on the cliff even now."

"Then Maiyun grant that he be dashed to a pulp on the turrets!"

Touch the Sky nodded toward the main camp below.

"Save your oaths for later, buck. We must slip past the rest of them, and quickly. Soon the dogs will miss their master."

"But how, without ponies? Tangle Hair cannot walk, and Little Horse cannot easily climb over all the scree we must cross."

Touch the Sky watched the huge bonfires down in camp. Their tall flames threw a flickering, lurid glow over everything, distorting shapes and shadows. Though the low-lying camp was sheltered from the winds, the noise still shrieked in the air all around them.

"Their corral is past one end of camp. We could get to it quickly from here. But too many Blackfoot devils are clustered nearby. We need a diversion to clear them out."

"What type of diversion, brother? Shots fired on them?"

"No, muzzle flash would give us away."

As he spoke, Touch the Sky had been watching a lone pony that grazed, untethered, in the sporadic clumps of grass between this position and the camp below. It was a broken-down nag, obviously kept around for packwork. But such horses often became friendly with humans.

He glanced back over his shoulder toward the cave entrance where the dead Blackfoot lay.

"If it worked once, and with *him*," Touch the Sky mused out loud, "perhaps it would work again down below."

"Brother, I am slow with riddles. What do you mean?"

"You will see soon enough. For now, hie down that slope and talk sweet words to that pony. Grab its halter and lead it up here. But be careful not to show yourself."

While Two Twists did as he was told, Touch the Sky stepped back into the den and hauled the dead Blackfoot outside. By the time Two Twists showed up, leading the pony, Touch the Sky had cut the buffalo-hair rope into several shorter lengths.

"Time for this one to make one last ride,"

Touch the Sky said grimly. "Here, help me get this reluctant rider mounted. Then be ready to seize the moment, Cheyenne."

Both Cheyennes averted their nostrils when they breathed so the ghost wouldn't enter them. Once the dead man was mounted and tied into place, Two Twists dug into his parfleche.

"Wait," he said, "one more touch."

Touch the Sky let Two Twists add his macabre detail. Then he led the pony closer to the west end of camp, the end nearest the corral. When he had gone as close as he dared, he slapped the pony's rump and turned it loose.

Touch the Sky crouched behind a rock and watched. The obedient, docile mount walked slowly into the huge-glowing circle of the bonfires. At first a few men, busy drinking and cavorting, only raised a careless hand in greeting.

Then the pony stopped right beside the biggest fire.

Someone pointed, shouted something. Suddenly the rest nearby fell silent and stared at Takes His Share.

His face grinned foolishly in death. A piece of gray brain matter oozed from a hole over his ear—and yet, only look! He sat his saddle! And thanks to the crowning touch added by Two Twists, a hunk of half-eaten venison protruded from his mouth!

A hideous shriek of terror was taken up by many others. Braves ran fleeing toward the far end of camp. In the ensuing confusion, the two

Cheyennes slipped quickly down into the corral and cut out four strong ponies.

"Brothers!" Little Horse greeted them back at the hidden copse, relief evident in his voice. "It sounds as if they have all lost their wits! We were sure you were both dead and the Wendigo was working his way around to us!"

"I paused to pluck these from their camp," Touch the Sky said with casual bravado, handing Little Horse the Medicine Arrows as if they were a mere afterthought. "Now tuck those away safely and prepare to ride, warrior. We still have a fight ahead with the sentries on that slope!"

"Cheyenne Headmen! You know why we have been called into special council. Arrow Keeper has left us. No man knows if he is dead or alive. Until we have proof of either, his name may be spoken. But none dispute that he is gone. And now we must choose a new shaman and Keeper of the Arrows."

Chief Gray Thunder paused. It was so still in the council lodge that Touch the Sky could hear the bent-sapling frame creaking. Gray Thunder sat near the center pole, the Sacred Arrows in their coyote-fur bundle at his side. He had been entrusted with their care since the joyous moment when Touch the Sky's band had ridden into camp.

"We have heard words spoken for and against Touch the Sky. We have heard words spoken for and against Medicine Flute. We have heard all the old accusations hurled between Touch the Sky and Wolf Who Hunts Smiling, along with some new ones as each proves how he out-hates the other.

"I am weary of it. The red men have enough enemies without, we need not war within. Now, all who have earned the right to speak have done so. It is time to give over with words and let the stones speak."

Touch the Sky sat in the portion of the council lodge reserved for warriors who could speak but not yet vote. The voting Headmen filled the other part. It had been a bitter council. It was as if the departure of Arrow Keeper had signaled a new era in tribal history, an era doomed to be marked by divisive factional loyalties and a fierce struggle for control of tribal destiny.

Gray Thunder passed a rawhide pouch among the Headmen. Each of the Councillors possessed a white moonstone and a black agate. Those voting for Touch the Sky placed a white stone inside the pouch; a black stone indicated a preference for Medicine Flute.

For a moment, as the pouch was finally handed back to Gray Thunder, Touch the Sky met the eyes of Wolf Who Hunts Smiling. Both braves were equally apprehensive. Each knew that this vote today meant more than just a new shaman. It would shape the very mission and destiny of the tribe.

Touch the Sky's gut tensed as he watched his chief open the pouch and hold it over the robe underneath him, preparing to spill out the contents. Again the young brave felt the weight of his loneliness as he wished, yet again, that Arrow Keeper could still be here.

Gray Thunder spilled out the stones, counted them into two piles. Then he nodded as if inwardly satisfied that justice had been done.

He looked up at the others.

"The stones have spoken," he announced. "And this place hears me when I say the tribe has spoken with one voice. From this day forth, Cheyenne law and title are clear. Touch the Sky is our new shaman and Keeper of the Arrows!"

Little Horse, Two Twists, and Tangle Hair—still walking with a hickory cane—rose as one, raising a mighty shout of triumph and support. Other members of the Bow String Soldier troop also cheered, as did various admirers of the tall Cheyenne.

But clearly Touch the Sky's enemies had been ready for this moment. And Chief Gray Thunder's conciliatory words about speaking in one voice had been wasted on them. the division in the tribe's future power struggle was made clear when, to the last man, the Bull Whip troopers stood up and silently walked out, following their leader, Lone Bear.

Every Cheyenne remaining in the lodge knew there could be no stronger gesture of contempt for the proceedings short of taking over the village by raw power. For the protestors had walked out without the final prayer or smoking to the

Four Directions. In effect, they were saying the council never took place and would not be recognized.

"Congratulations, brother," Little Horse told him later that morning. "Arrow Keeper picked you out long ago to be our medicine man. Now his choice finally has the sanction of council on it."

Touch the Sky nodded. He had just finished moving his tipi to the empty hummock where Arrow Keeper's had once stood—the custom when a new shaman took over. But he nodded across the central camp clearing. Black Elk and Wolf Who Hunts Smiling stood in the doorway of the Bull Whip lodge, watching him. Medicine Flute slouched there, too, bone flute dangling from his mouth.

"It has the sanction of council, truly. But the elders voted out of respect for Arrow Keeper's wishes, not out of love for me. Not only is Siski-dee still out there somewhere, plotting more schemes from the black heart of his sickness, but my enemies right here still dream of stringing their new bows with my guts."

"Let them dream," Little Horse scoffed. "The man who uses your gut for bowstring would have a long-flying arrow indeed."

"I would rather have my gut."

Still, his friend's words rallied the troubled Touch the Sky. He glanced at Black Elk's tipi and again heard Arrow Keeper's words: *There will be trouble ahead for you, trouble behind for Honey Eater.*

Then let the fight come, he vowed. For her sake, he was ready. A man might quickly tire of struggling for his own life but for Honey Eater he would die a thousand times and call those deaths better than one long life without her.

Touch the Sky looked at his friend. "Let us go work our ponies, brother. The next fight is coming, and we have been promised a share in it."

Little Horse grinned at this show of spirit. But then, he had come to expect such mettle from this tall brave who was marked out for trouble.

"As you say, shaman."

# DEATH CAMP

# Prologue

Though he sat behind few men in council, the tall Cheyenne brave called Touch the Sky faced a future as uncertain as his past.

His original Cheyenne name was lost forever after a bluecoat ambush near the North Platte killed his father and mother. The lone Indian survivor of the bloody battle, the squalling infant was taken back to the Wyoming river-bend settlement of Bighorn Falls near Fort Bates.

He was adopted by John Hanchon and his barren young wife Sarah. Owners of the town's thriving mercantile store, the Hanchons named the boy Matthew and raised him as their own blood. But their love couldn't protect him from the hostility and fear of other white settlers—especially when, at 16, he fell in love with Kristen, daughter of the wealthy and hidebound rancher Hiram Steele.

Steele had Matthew savagely beaten when he caught the Cheyenne youth and Kristen in their secret meeting place. The rancher also warned the boy to stay away from his daughter or face certain death. Frightened for Matthew's life, Kristen lied and told him she never wanted to see him again. Still, Matthew's love for his parents and Kristen kept him in Bighorn Falls.

But Seth Carlson, an arrogant young cavalry lieutenant from Fort Bates, was also in love with Kristen. Either Matthew pulled up stakes for good, he warned, or his parents would lose their lucrative contract with Fort Bates—the lifeblood of their business.

His heart saddened but determined, Matthew Hanchon set out for Cheyenne territory in the up-country of the Powder River. He was immediately captured by braves from Chief Yellow Bear's Northern Cheyenne camp. Declared a spy for the white-skin soldiers, he was tortured and sentenced to die. But just as a young brave named Wolf Who Hunts Smiling was about to gut him, old Arrow Keeper intervened.

The tribe shaman and protector of the sacred medicine arrows, Arrow Keeper had recently experienced an epic vision. His vision foretold that the long-lost son of a great Cheyenne chief would return to his people—and that this youth would lead his people in one last, great victory against their enemies. This youth would be known by the distinctive mark of the warrior, the same birthmark Arrow Keeper spotted buried past the youth's hairline: a mulberry-colored arrowhead.

Keeping all this information to himself to protect the youth from jealous tribal enemies, Arrow Keeper used his influence to spare the prisoner's life. This action infuriated two braves: the cunning Wolf Who Hunts Smiling and his fierce older cousin Black Elk.

Black Elk, the tribe's war leader despite his youth, was jealous of the glances cast at the tall young stranger by Honey Eater, daughter of Chief Yellow Bear. And Wolf Who Hunts Smiling, proudly ambitious, had turned his heart to stone against all whites without exception. This stranger, to him, was only a make-believe Cheyenne who wore white men's shoes, spoke the paleface tongue, and showed his emotions in his face like the woman-hearted white men. He insisted on calling the new arrival Woman Face and White Man Runs Him.

Arrow Keeper, however, buried Matthew's white name forever and named him Touch the Sky. But acceptance did not come with that new name. As he trained to become a warrior, Touch the Sky was humiliated at every turn. And his enemies within the tribe did not cease their relentless campaign to prove he was a spy for the hair faces.

Through sheer determination to find his place,

assisted now and then by the cunning he had learned from white men, Touch the Sky became one of the greatest warriors of the *Shaiyena* nation. His fighting skill and courage won him more and more followers, including the ever loyal braves Little Horse, Two Twists, and Tangle Hair. Under Arrow Keeper's careful eye, Touch the Sky also made great progress in the shamanic arts.

With each victory, however, his enemies managed to turn appearances against him and to suggest that he still carried the white man's stink, which brought the tribe bad luck and scared off the buffalo. Although the entire tribe knew that Touch the Sky and Honey Eater were desperately in love, Honey Eater was forced into a loveless marriage with Black Elk, who chafed in a jealous, murderous wrath, plotting revenge against Touch the Sky.

Arrow Keeper, well into his frosted years, eventually realized he must leave the tribe before Touch the Sky could assume the role of shaman and Arrow Keeper. He departed to build a death wickiup, disappearing and thus leaving the question of his life or death a mystery to the others.

Now Touch the Sky is challenged at every turn by Black Elk and his cousin Wolf Who Hunts Smiling, who argue he cannot be trusted to protect the sacred arrows. Unknown to everyone except the false shaman named Medicine Flute, the ambitious Wolf Who Hunts Smiling is on the brink of taking over the entire Cheyenne nation.

## Death Camp

He then plans to join his secret renegade allies in a war of extermination against the white-skin settlers.

Only one man can thwart his bloody scheme: the tall brave named Touch the Sky.

# Chapter One

Despite the warm spring sun and the hopeful singing of the meadowlarks, Touch the Sky wore a deep frown. All around him, the Cheyenne summer camp of Chief Gray Thunder's band was joyously alive with preparations for the annual spring dance. Young boys shouted from the common corral, where they were tying bright strips of red flannel to the ponies' tails, readying them for the parades. Merry singing and laughter livened the women's sewing lodge, where the unmarried girls were embroidering dance shawls and sewing the moccasins widely recognized for the best beadwork on the plains. Warriors stood in the doorways of their clan lodges, plaiting new rawhide bridles and clipping bright ceremonial feathers with the distinctive endmarks of their clan or soldier troop.

Another hard winter was behind the tribe. The valleys were no longer locked by ice; soon game would once again be plentiful on the hunting ranges the Cheyenne shared with their Sioux cousins. The rivers and creeks were swollen with crystal-clear snow runoff from the mountains. The new grass was green and lush, already well above the ponies' hocks. Soon the far-flung Cheyenne bands, ten in all, would unite as one for the dance festival.

For all these reasons, hope filled the tribe's collective soul like rain falling on parched earth. But for three sleeps in a row, Touch the Sky had experienced a vision, but it was not just the normal kind of troubling vision. This was an omen that warned of grave danger.

Had the omen concerned him alone, he would hardly have granted it a moment's thought. Truly, danger was the ridge he had lived on since his arrival in camp several winters ago. But this latest omen foretold that he would not be suffering alone. For if this was a true vision, the entire tribe would soon be in a hurting place.

"Brother," a voice said, scattering his thoughts like cottonwood fluff in the wind, "I would ask you a thing."

Touch the Sky glanced up from the mountain-lion skin he was supposed to be adorning with elk's teeth and brightly dyed feathers. He sat cross-legged before the entrance flap of his tipi.

His abode stood on a lone hummock between the nearby Powder River and the rest of the tipis, which were arranged in clan circles.

Although the shaman's lodge, like the chief's, always stood off by itself, Touch the Sky had never lived in a clan circle. His original clan was lost to that elusive thing the white men called history. However, the entrance to his tipi, like that of every Cheyenne tipi on the plains, faced east toward the source of all life—Sister Sun, the day maker. His past may have died in that bluecoat raid 20 winters earlier; but not his need to belong.

Touch the Sky forced his attention back to his visitor. The youth was wiry and somber looking; his hair hung in two braids instead of the loose locks or single braid preferred by most Cheyenne braves.

"Two Twists," Touch the Sky replied, holding his face stern, "when fellow warriors parley in a peace camp, they do not simply spit words at each other like rude white men. Words between friends are important. Sit. Grab a coal from the firepit and light this."

For a moment, surprise glinted in Two Twists' eyes. He was not old enough yet to join a soldier troop. Yet Touch the Sky was offering his best clay pipe, telling the junior warrior that, in Touch the Sky's eyes, he was an equal despite having barely 17 winters behind him.

"Little brother," Touch the Sky said, "why do you gawk like a surprised newborn at a dry dug?

Did you not climb the cliffs of Wendigo Mountain beside me? I mean to be answered, buck! Did you?"

"I did," Two Twists said hastily, a bit of Touch the Sky's proud boasting tone seeping into his own voice.

"When the mad renegade Sis-ki-dee unleashed fifty braves against the five of us, did you cower behind any man?"

"No, shaman, I did not!"

"No, indeed, for you fought like ten men as did your Cheyenne brothers, and we evened the battle for them! I was there; I saw you lift your clout at them to show your contempt. Now I call you a full warrior and my brother, worthy to wear the medicine hat into battle. Now sit and smoke."

Proud elation swelled Two Twists' chest like a deep breath. But only squaws and white men showed their private feelings in their faces for all to see. He held his face impassive as a stone mask. Nor did he thank Touch the Sky. True warriors knew they had earned any praise they got, and thus they owed no man gratitude.

Quietly, content in each other's company, the two braves followed the ancient custom. They smoked to the four directions, at first speaking only of inconsequential matters. Finally Touch the Sky placed the pipe on the ground between them, the signal that serious talk could begin.

"Brother," Two Twists said, "I have just come from a visit at the lodge of the Bow String troopers. The talk went round to past spring dances. Then it touched on a certain topic."

"I am called a shaman by some," Touch the Sky said, "though others call me White Man Runs Him. Still, I know of no magic for cutting sign on the human breast. I would rather a man tell me his thoughts freely than force me to read them like a hidden blood spoor. Speak plain, buck."

"I have known you to make greater medicine than thought reading," Two Twists said. "But I will not make you resort to magic. My question, plainly, is this. May we still pronounce the name of the one who was our shaman before you? I ask this thing because some of the Bow Strings said that he has now crossed over to the Land of Ghosts, that we may never say his name again."

"His name, Cheyenne, is Arrow Keeper. I speak it freely because his fate remains unknown. You may speak it too."

"But he left to build a death wickiup."

Touch the Sky nodded. "So he said, and perhaps he did. But from the moment of birth, puzzled one, we all begin heading toward death. Though Arrow Keeper always speaks truth, sometimes the shaft of his words flies indirectly to the target."

Not all of this answer made clear sense to the youth. But his respect for this tall Cheyenne brave gave Touch the Sky's own words a credence beyond their apparent meaning.

Two Twists watched his friend's nimble fingers deftly work the crude bone awl and buffalo-sinew thread, attaching an elk tooth to the beautiful mountain-lion skin, which had been Arrow Keeper's parting gift to Touch the Sky. The skin marked an important transition in the younger brave's life. For with Arrow Keeper's secret departure from the tribe, Touch the Sky was left his chosen successor. After a sharply divided Council of 40 barely approved him, he became tribal shaman and keeper of the sacred medicine arrows.

Touch the Sky realized full well that both titles were a great honor, so great that many in the tribe refused to grant him the right to them, in their hearts if not openly. But with every honor came grave responsibility. This new omen might perhaps have been sent to Touch the Sky by Arrow Keeper. After all, it was he who had first warned Touch the Sky about the omen, he who had first explained how this particular dream vision foretold great disaster for the tribe as one.

But what, Touch the Sky wondered yet again, was he supposed to do? Seek another vision to learn more? Offer a penance to the high holy ones? As he knew from experience, visions often raised more questions than they answered. At best, they were half-glimpsed shapes in a dense fog. They offered only a frustrating hint, never a clear answer.

"Look here, brother!" a hearty voice called out. "Our ponies grow fatter, the service berries are plump with juice, and these two jays sit with glum winter faces. The cold moons are over, bucks!

Soon our trade goods arrive from the miners; soon we trail the buffalo herds!"

The speaker was the sturdy warrior named Little Horse. He was accompanied by Tangle Hair, a Bow String trooper. Like young Two Twists, both braves had made many mortal enemies within the tribe when they swore their loyalty, their very lives, to Touch the Sky. Little Horse and Touch the Sky had faced death together so often that a strong, easy fellowship bound them.

"Hear the first drums?" Little Horse asked. "Soon the Cheyenne nation will dance, and Touch the Sky will lead us!"

All four braves had recently traded their leggings and knee-length fur moccasins for breechclouts and lighter elkskin moccasins. The tallest of them, Touch the Sky was wide in the shoulders, lean from the hard winter but well muscled for a red man. He had a strong, hawk nose, and he wore his dark hair long and loose. But it was cut high over his eyes to leave his vision clear.

Touch the Sky opened his mouth to reply to his friend. But he bit back his words when yet another familiar pair passed within hearing: Wolf Who Hunts Smiling and his new shadow Medicine Flute.

Tangle Hair spoke in a low voice. "There go two who would eat their own young!"

"Straight words," Little Horse said grimly. "And see how they stare toward us goading."

Wolf Who Hunts Smiling was aptly named.

# Death Camp

Even now his sly face was divided by a wolf grin while his swift-as-minnow eyes mocked them across the clearing. Medicine Flute shared his companion's cunning, but not his battle-hardened body. He was slender limbed, with heavy-lidded eyes in a lazy face. As always, he played the monotonous, atonal tune on the human-leg-bone flute for which he was named.

"They look," Touch the Sky said, "but have you noticed a thing, brothers? Wolf Who Hunts Smiling seldom taunts any of us. This new silence is dangerous. His cousin Black Elk mimics him in this. They have finally decided to let deeds speak for them, and they have had a long winter to scheme new treachery."

"As you say," Little Horse said. "More and more within the tribe are beginning to believe Wolf Who Hunts Smiling's bent words about Medicine Flute's big medicine. He goes about playing the big Indian, saying, 'But everyone saw how Medicine Flute first predicted he would burn up a star, then did it before the entire tribe. Let White Man Runs Him match this.'"

Touch the Sky nodded. His lips formed a grim, determined slit as he recalled how that burning star had sent many into hysterics. Most of the tribesmen had never heard of a comet or knew—as Medicine Flute had learned—that white men could predict their passing.

"I have watched Wolf Who Hunts Smiling closely," Touch the Sky said. "His ambition is like

17

a sapling that grows too rapidly and crowds out the growth around it. There was a time when he would hesitate to sully the arrows by shedding Cheyenne blood. That time is long past. Now we four know what no one else in our camp suspects. We have seen proof that he has made private treaties with red enemies of our tribe. His plans are as clear as blood in new snow. He means to kill me and set Medicine Flute up as tribe shaman and arrow keeper. He who controls a tribe's medicine controls its destiny."

Little Horse nodded. "Truly, his ambition is no secret. He preaches to the junior warriors and tells them the red man must launch a war of extermination against the *Mah-ish-ta-shee-da*. He tells them that you are one of their spies, that you work from within to steal our homelands for your white masters."

Little Horse had used the Cheyenne name for whites. It meant yellow eyes, because the first white men the Cheyenne had ever seen were severely jaundiced mountain men.

Even now Wolf Who Hunts Smiling's cunning eyes met Touch the Sky's gaze. They gave Touch the Sky a cold, mocking promise of a hard death soon to come.

"He is reminding you, brother," Tangle Hair said, "that he once walked between you and the campfire. By thus publicly announcing his intention to someday kill you, he is forced to either match word to deed or become a laughingstock."

# Death Camp

"He is trouble anytime," Touch the Sky said. "I never take him or his cousin Black Elk lightly. Both would use my guts for tipi ropes. But, brothers, I fear more trouble approaches like rain on top a flood. I have had an omen."

At these words, all three of his companions looked sharply at him. An omen was always important. But when experienced by a brave with the third eye of a shaman, it became crucial.

"What omen, brother?" Little Horse demanded.

"A brief medicine vision was placed over my eyes. I dreamed the entire tribe was riding a high ridge at dawn. And just as Sister Sun rose from her birthplace in the east, a full moon descended in the west. I saw both at once."

All three braves understood the awful significance of this. They stared at him, wordless. Then Touch the Sky heard again the gravelly voice of old Arrow Keeper, drifting back like a memory smell: *Heed any vision in which the sun and a full moon share the sky at once. For such a sign means much pain and suffering ahead for your tribe—perhaps even its destruction.*

Dust hazed the valley of the Little Bighorn, a light golden fog in the slanting rays of late afternoon sun. The river tracked like a looping brown ribbon, winding through lush natural meadows bright with new wildflowers. At the head of a long redrock bluff overlooking the valley, Capt. Seth Carlson sat his big 17-hand cavalry sorrel.

"Yonder comes the bull train," he said to the civilian beside him. "Just like I told you. Twice a year, regular as Big Ben, the miners pack in trade goods for the red Arabs at the Powder River camp. It's a peace price, payment for the right to haul ore out over Cheyenne grantland."

Hiram Steele nodded impatiently. "I've always had a keen grasp of the obvious, Soldier Blue. I once had the contract to supply those goods, remember? Why in the hell do you think I wrote to you and went to all this trouble—for my health?

"That damn Matthew Hanchon and his partner did the hurt dance on me down in Kansas. It was them who got the Cherokees on the warpath against me. By the time the territorial court was done with me, I was lucky I had a pot left to piss in. Now I plan to give as good as I got. And if I can't get Hanchon direct, I'll get him through his tribe."

Steele's flint-gray eyes squinted out from a big, angular face. He sat a dark cream stallion with a black mane and tail. Satisfaction oozed from the hard creases of his face as he watched the long column of pack animals below. Their panniers and pack saddles were filled with badly needed contract goods for the Cheyennes: powder and lead, flour, meat, coffee, sugar, tobacco, cloth, and blankets.

Indians were highly partial to blankets, Steele told himself again. His lips eased back from his teeth in a smile. He tugged one rein until his horse turned around. Well back from the two men, a

lone Crow Indian held the lead line of a pack-
horse. It was piled high with new wool blankets,
bright red ones, like the old Hudson's Bay blankets that Indians prized.

"That Crow know what he's handling?" Steele
said.

Carlson nodded. "He got the vaccine in time to
survive. Once you've had the disease, you can't
catch it again. He's the one who wrapped the dead
bodies in the blankets."

"You're sure this will do it?"

Again Carlson nodded. "We lost plenty of men
at Fort Bates from mountain fever until Washington finally sent out the vaccine," he said. "It's
rough. You get the ague and the shakes real bad.
Then you just burn and burn with fever till you
dehydrate. It took out an entire Blackfoot village
up north."

Steele met the younger man's eyes. "You getting
snow in your boots? Maybe you've been listening
to the Indian-loving Quakers?"

Carlson snorted. "Stuff! I got as much right as
you to hate Hanchon, maybe more. He's only cost
you money. He's cost me promotions and your
daughter."

Steele said nothing. It was true that Kristen had
once been in love with the Cheyenne—a source of
shame that Steele would never live down. However, he also knew that Carlson was wrong about
one thing. Kristen had never been the officer's girl
and never would be. But let Carlson think what

he wanted to because he too longed to kill Hanchon with a desire as powerful as hell thirst. Such an ally was useful.

"You say you know the lead bull whacker?" Steele said.

"Know him real good. Name's Orrick. He hangs out at the sutler's store at the fort."

"You think he can be persuaded?"

Carlson laughed, strong white teeth flashing from a weathered face. "Can he be persuaded? Would a cow lick Lot's wife? Show him that highgrade you got in your saddlebag, he'll nail his colors to our mast. He'll go blind long enough for us to slip those blankets into the load."

Steele nodded and his eyes puckered in satisfaction. He turned again and nodded at the Crow. Then all three men chucked up their horses, leading their load of death down into the valley.

# Chapter Two

"Aunt?"

Honey Eater was busy sewing an embroidered hem on her little niece's calico dress. Without glancing up, she said, "Yes? What is it, little one?"

Laughing Brook watched her favorite aunt closely. She was glad that mean Uncle Black Elk was not here. Now she could spend precious time alone with Honey Eater. The child agreed with the general camp opinion that Honey Eater was the prettiest woman in Gray Thunder's tribe, and no Cheyenne tribe was ever short of beauties.

"Why did all the people shout and cheer when True Brave flashed mirror signals from Bald Mountain?"

"Because his signals meant welcome news. Our trade goods are coming."

"Trade goods?" Laughing Brook, like more and more young girls in camp, had taken to braiding white columbine petals in her long hair, copying Honey Eater.

"Yes, trade goods," Honey Eater said. "This calico cloth we used to make your pretty festival dress. The sugar you like to stir in your yarrow tea. Do you like the crisp meat that sizzles and curls, the fragrant meat called bacon?"

Laughing Brook nodded solemnly. "I like it better than buffalo."

"Well, then, bacon, too, arrives soon with our goods. Child, stop fidgeting so. I'll be done soon!"

"But, Aunt? Who sends these fine presents?"

"They are not presents, little one. They are paid to us by the paleface miners."

"But why? Palefaces hate us. They kill us and hurt our ponies."

"Yes," Honey Eater said with patient sadness, "many do, but not all of them. Some try to speak one way to the Indian, to treat us as their friends. The miner's chief Caleb Riley is a man of honor. He promised that we would share their wealth with them so long as they use our land."

Late morning sunlight slanted through the huge tipi's smokehole. It highlighted the flawless topaz skin of both aunt and niece.

"Aunt?" Laughing Brook's eyes cut shyly away. "Medicine Flute has been speaking about the palefaces. He says they are all our enemies. He said that—"

# Death Camp

"He said what, little one?"

"He said that Touch the Sky grew up among white skins. He said Touch the Sky carries the stink that scares off the buffalo herds. He said that Touch the Sky leaves messages hidden in trees for bluecoats, that he is our enemy."

Sparks snapped in Honey Eater's dark almond-shaped eyes. She ignored her work, taking the girl's frail shoulders in her slim, strong hands.

"Child, have ears for your aunt, who loves you as much as she loves life itself. I am about to speak words you must place close to your heart forever. Do you understand?"

Solemnly, Laughing Brook nodded, and Honey Eater said, "Little one, we Cheyenne do indeed have many enemies. And it is true that Touch the Sky has friends among the white skins who raised him. But never believe that Touch the Sky is your enemy. This Medicine Flute, who blows hollow notes from a grisly bone—not once has this one ever shouted the war cry in defense of his tribe.

"But Touch the Sky? All of us—every woman, child, and grandparent in this camp—are alive today because of his bravery and suffering. Do you remember the buffalo hunt to the south when Kiowas and Comanches stole us?"

"Yes, we were hungry, and they hurt us."

"They did, child. But Touch the Sky saved us. These goods about to arrive—with only the help of his brave friend Little Horse, Touch the Sky earned them for us. At great risk, he helped the white skins build their road for the iron horse."

"Does Touch the Sky make you smile inside?" Laughing Brook asked with the candid curiosity of youth.

Honey Eater swallowed audibly. Her throat swelled shut so all she could do was nod.

Laughing Brook looked confused. "But you are married to Uncle Black Elk?"

Again Honey Eater nodded, her face a study in misery. She glanced around her comfortable home and realized it was really two lodges, and the center pole had become the boundary line. She was married to a brave whom once she had respected, but had come to loathe with all her being. His jealous and angry decision to quit lying with her was the only welcome thing he ever did for her. His belligerent accusations had turned to a quiet, dangerous hatred.

Laughing Brook was quiet for a long time, thinking. Then she sighed, unable to comprehend the mysterious ways of adults. Suddenly, from outside, came the voice of the excited camp crier as he rode up and down the village paths: "The pack train is in sight! The pack train is in sight! Soon our goods arrive!"

Letting loose an exclamation of joy, Laughing Brook spun around and ran outside. Honey Eater knew that she too should feel elation. The winter had been long and hard, and most in the tribe had spent it huddled over their firepits. The arrival of this pack train meant welcome diversion from many moons of monotony and suffering.

So why, she wondered, did it feel like a cold fist of ice had replaced her stomach?

Touch the Sky hoped to catch a glimpse of Honey Eater in all the confusion and excitement of the bull train's arrival. But only young Laughing Brook emerged from Honey Eater's tipi. The girl's long braid streamed out behind her as she raced across the central clearing to join Chief Gray Thunder and the throng in front of the council lodge.

The pack animals had been formed up in a circle for the initial inspection and unloading. River of Winds, one of the most trusted braves in camp, was in charge of this duty, assisted by several of his fellow Bow String troopers. The Bow String troopers were the most popular soldiers because of their leader Spotted Tail's firm belief that negotiation was the best way to solve conflicts.

River of Winds moved from animal to animal, checking each load, then nodding his approval to the lead bull whacker. Once before, as the result of Hiram Steele's duplicity, cleverly disguised shoddy goods had been delivered. So River of Winds meticulously inspected each load, looking for flat stones in the slabs of bacon, making sure the salt pork was not marked condemned for troop use. Patiently, the Bow Strings kept the excited people back so the unloading could proceed.

"Brother," Little Horse said close to Touch the

Sky's ear, "look. Wolf Who Hunts Smiling and Black Elk call Caleb Riley's miners your white masters. They named you White Man Runs Him after you helped them. They swore to never touch these goods. Now see how they are poised to make the first grab! It's every Indian for himself, and the Wendigo take the hindmost."

Touch the Sky glanced toward the little stand of willows, where the Bull Whips had gathered. Even as his attention sought them out, Black Elk looked over at him. Like angry stags about to clash over territory, they aggressively held the stare, a long measure of their mutual contempt and hatred.

Black Elk had been the tribe's war leader for as long as Touch the Sky could remember, and a good choice, at that. When the war cry sounded, there was no soft place left in Black Elk's breast, nor could fear touch him. And at first, though as hard as white man's tempered steel, he had tried to be fair to Touch the Sky.

But by now all the people knew about the great love between Touch the Sky and Honey Eater, they knew that she would never have accepted Black Elk's bride price if she had not believed, with all her heart, that Touch the Sky had chosen a white woman over her and deserted the tribe forever. Too late, she found out she was mistaken.

"Yes," Touch the Sky finally replied, still watching Black Elk, "they will take more than their share, meantime demanding the blood of all white men."

"From the look of him, brother," Little Horse said, "Black Elk is keen for Cheyenne blood—yours."

The Bull Whips forced their way closer through the crowd, cracking their highly feared knotted-thong whips to make room. Touch the Sky could clearly see Black Elk with his dark scowl and his fierce eyes like black agates. Most noticeable, however, was the dead flap of his left ear. It had been severed in battle by a bluecoat saber. After Black Elk killed the soldier, he had sewn his own ear back on with buckskin thread. It hung there lopsided, as wrinkled and dry as overtanned leather.

The inspection was finally over. The Bow Strings were heaping the goods for distribution by clans. The white bull whackers were recruiting their animals for the long ride out.

Abruptly, Touch the Sky felt a cool insect prickle moving up his spine, lifting the fine hairs on the back of his neck. He sensed danger the way a burro senses a snake before seeing it. By now he was long familiar with the subtle warnings of his shaman sense.

"What is it, Cheyenne?" Little Horse demanded. He watched storm clouds gather on his friend's brow. But Touch the Sky said nothing. His eyes had locked with those of the lead bullwhacker.

The man was typical of his companions in this

trade—string bean thin, tough as sinew, his filthy hair tied in a heavy knot on the back of his neck. An 18-inch Bowie protruded from his sash, as did a cap-and-ball dragoon pistol. All the men were so filthy that Touch the Sky could see fleas leaping from them.

However, close calls in the past had taught the men some manners with the Indians. They wisely removed the scalps from their sashes before arriving, and they made sure to give the peace sign when riding into camp. Cheyennes were not cold-blooded, and few would fire without being attacked first. But if whites offended the Cheyenne chief or the wrong warrior, they might leave camp minus their topknots.

But Touch the Sky read none of this in the bull whacker's look. It wasn't fear he read there. Instead, oddly enough, he read a quick hint of furtive guilt. The face of a man about to do something he hadn't quite accepted in his heart. But what? This was a hard man who would not easily feel the prick of conscience.

However, before Touch the Sky could puzzle it out further, the white skin turned away, and the men were kneeling to untie the animals' hobbles, preparing to ride out.

"Brother," Little Horse said again, "what have you felt or seen?"

Touch the Sky shook his head. He watched the clan headmen lining up for their distribution of goods. "Something," he replied miserably.

# Death Camp

"Enough to worry, too little to act. But I suspect we will have our answer soon enough, and we will be sorry to have it."

Touch the Sky was right: Trouble was seldom bashful about announcing itself. After all, he was poised for its arrival, fully warned by his medicine dream and his premonition when the goods were unloaded. Even so, when the enemy came, it was as unexpected as it was devastating. And it was an enemy that rendered a warrior's skill useless.

After the distribution of the goods, one sleep passed without incident. The first far-flung bands of the Northern Cheyenne were due to arrive at any time for the spring dance. Anticipation of their arrival, plus the holiday mood caused by the pack train's windfall, left Gray Thunder's camp in high spirits.

The clan and lodge fires shot orange spear tips into the air all night long. Younger braves gambled on foot and pony races. Older braves sneaked behind their lodges to drink weak corn beer and recite their coups to any who cared to listen. The women hovered near the cooking pits to roast elk and antelope meat for the dance feast, meantime exclaiming over the fine quality of the cloth sent by the miners. The children ran wild everywhere, playing at taking scalps and counting coups. Stirred up by all the unusual activity, the camp dogs howled and barked as if moon crazy.

Then, on the second morning after the pack

train departed, a woman's sudden scream of grief and terror split the predawn stillness. In a heartbeat, his warrior's body responding even before his mind woke up, Touch the Sky was out of his robes and groping for his Sharps percussion rifle. Eyes still clogged with the cobwebs of slumber, he stumbled out of his tipi into the grainy chill.

Other braves also assumed the camp was under attack. Many rushed out of their tipis still naked. Whoever the invaders, it was the warriors' first responsibility to form a line of defense behind which the women, children, and elders could escape by hidden trails. But there was no attack. Instead, there was a flurry of activity around one of the tipis of the Broken Lance Clan.

"What has happened, brother?" Little Horse called out, meeting up with Touch the Sky in the gathering throng.

Touch the Sky shook his head. A horrible feeling of doom had settled deep into his bones. They watched young Two Twists, who had reached the tipi before most of the others. He turned and fought his way through the curious people, anxious to reach his friends.

Even limited to the light of a full moon and a few dying camp fires, Touch the Sky could see that Two Twists' face was urgent with worry.

"What passes?" Little Horse demanded. Even as he spoke, several old grandmothers began keening in grief. The cry was taken up by others.

"The little one who was Dancing Woman's baby

has gone under! And brothers, three more children are dying!"

This terrible news struck the two braves with the force of bluecoat canister shot. Cheyennes, like Apaches, valued their children over all else. Even the stern warriors cried openly at the funeral scaffold of a child. To Cheyennes, every adult in camp was the parent of every child.

"Gone under?" Touch the Sky said woodenly. "But how? From what?"

It cost Two Twists a physical effort to speak the dreaded words. "From mountain fever," he replied, and Touch the Sky felt his face drain cold.

# Chapter Three

Mountain fever! The words struck as much fear in Touch the Sky as might the sentry's wolf howl of alarm. How many Indian camps had been wiped out or nearly destroyed by this mysterious and dreaded disease? Touch the Sky knew that a Pawnee attack would have been a kindness compared to this.

Nor could there be any mistaking the disease. It always ravaged children more quickly than it did adults. It literally burned the life out of them, killing them rapidly from total dehydration—as Dancing Woman's child had died, as more were dying even now.

The urgency of the situation meant they could not wait for the usual Council of 40. Chief Gray Thunder, through the camp crier, announced a council of the warriors to take place as soon as emergency measures could be taken for dealing with the crisis.

Strips of black cloth were tied to the tipis where infections had broken out. A few elders and women began constructing a hasty pest lodge. The infected would be moved in together and tended by a few Cheyennes who had beaten incredible odds and survived the illness, thus becoming immune.

How many more would be struck down? Touch the Sky saw that very question in the eyes of everyone he met. Even as the pest lodge took shape, additional chilling news flew through camp. The first adult was sick, a grandfather in the Rattlesnake Clan. Touch the Sky's eyes flew constantly to Black Elk's tipi, hoping for a reassuring glimpse at Honey Eater.

"Brother," Little Horse said, "the talk grows ugly over near the Bull Whip lodge. Black Elk and Wolf Who Hunts Smiling are working their brothers up to a frenzy against you. They say the white freighters brought this disease. They say that it was deliberate and that it could never have happened if you did not gnaw the bones thrown to you by palefaces. I fear they have some plan afoot and mean to make your life a hurting place at the council."

"No doubt they do, buck. When have they ever missed a chance to fan the fires against me? Let them. Here I stand, a living man despite all their efforts. The first one of them foolish enough to bridge the gap will be dead before he hits the ground."

Although his boast was sincere enough, Touch the Sky spoke it absently. He was still thinking about Little Horse's words and glancing uneasily at Black Elk's tipi, wondering and fearing. He wished with all his might that Arrow Keeper were still there; his wisdom was always as reassuring as the lee of a mesa in a windstorm.

"I fear they are right about one thing," Touch the Sky said, forcing his eyes back to Little Horse. "It was the freighters who brought the disease to us."

Little Horse nodded glumly. "It is no fault of yours, warrior. But I fear you have truth firmly by the tail. If so, then I too share the blame. For did I not help you sight the path through for the iron horse?"

"Never mind blame. Though the cause may be secret, the effect is known. But it was the freighters."

"Them," Little Horse said, "or something they left has this bad medicine clinging to it."

Others too had come to this conclusion. As the day's new sun tracked higher across the sky, more and more in the tribe fell ill. And finally, the mystery was explained as the one telltale pattern emerged clearly. The afflicted Cheyennes shared one fact in common: They had worn or slept in one of the recently delivered blankets.

A survivor of an earlier clash with the disease

was sent round to gather every single blanket that had been distributed. Huge clouds of black smoke billowed into the sky as the wool blankets were burned in the camp clearing. The moment Touch the Sky learned of this, he hurried to River of Winds' tipi.

His agitation was great. Not every clan received blankets from each consignment of goods. Had Honey Eater or Black Elk acquired one this time? River of Winds had distributed the goods; he would know which clans had received them. Touch the Sky suddenly pulled up short when he saw black flannel tied to the elkskin entrance flap of River of Winds' tipi.

Of course the brave would be sick, Touch the Sky realized. Had River of Winds not touched all the goods, blankets included? The pest lodge was not yet completed, so River of Winds should still be inside alone, since his own wife and child had been killed one winter earlier by the yellow vomit.

"River of Winds? It is Touch the Sky. Can you hear me, brother?"

"I hear you," came the weak reply from inside. "But come no closer unless you are eager to feed the worms."

Touch the Sky winced. The brave's voice was already drawn tight with pain and suffering. "Brother, I am sorry for your illness. Indeed, it comes upon the heels of hard fortune for you. But be strong. You and the other sick ones are neither forgotten nor gone from this life. We are Cheyennes. We take care of our own. Soon we will move you to the pest lodge, and the cure songs will be sung over you night and day. Only will you tell me a thing"

"As for cure songs, tell the old women to sing away. I do not wish to die alone in silence. For, brother, I am gone, and so are the others. Better to build our scaffolds and sew us new moccasins for this final journey. But speak. What thing would you have me tell you?"

Again Touch the Sky's troubled brow wrinkled. The pain must be great, for River of Winds was not given to easy pessimism. "Were blankets distributed to the Panthers or the Antelope?"

There was a long excruciating silence while Touch the Sky nerved himself for bad news.

"Neither clan received blankets this time," River of Winds finally answered. And because he understood why Touch the Sky had asked, he added, "I envy you this love, for now that I am dying nothing else matters but death. Still, rest easy on one score at least. Unless she becomes careless, Honey Eater will survive."

A heavy stone was lifted from Touch the Sky's chest by River of Winds' words. But as his fear for Honey Eater lessened, his concern for the afflicted increased.

The pest lodge—a large structure made from bent saplings covered with hides—was completed. Though the danger of infection was great,

# Death Camp

Touch the Sky knew he must risk a visit. If the people could not count on the strength of their shaman, what was left to them? Had Arrow Keeper ever cowered in his tipi when smallpox or the red-speckled cough ravaged the camp?

The emergency council was set to begin soon. Touch the Sky would have just enough time to sing a brief prayer to bless the new lodge with good medicine.

Solemnly he prepared. First he visited the sweat lodge to meditate while cleansing his pores in hot steam. After drying himself with clumps of sage, he donned his best beaded leggings, leather shirt, and crow-feather warbonnet. Then, leaving all his weapons in his tipi, he walked to the pest lodge.

Worried loved ones formed a ring around the lodge. A second baby had died, and mourning cries filled the camp. Several of the people cleared a path as Touch the Sky headed for the entrance. Some of them looked grateful for the visit. Several others, influenced by Wolf Who Hunts Smiling and the clever shaman Medicine Flute, shot resentful glances at him.

As Touch the Sky's hand gripped the hide flap, he again felt a warning moving like a cool feather along the bumps of his spine. He threw back the flap. Immediately the fragrant smoke of sweetgrass and dogwood incense wafted into his nostrils. It was dim within, the air strident with the sound of painful and labored breathing. Above the sweet tang of the incense hung the musty stench of serious illness. Somewhere a child whimpered.

Black Elk and Wolf Who Hunts Smiling never showed pity in their faces. But Touch the Sky knew that compassion, when it was due, was the mark of a true warrior. His deep concern for these innocent sufferers who shared his blood made him vow to face the Wendigo himself, if he must, to save them. And again he silently thanked Maiyun that Honey Eater had been spared. Deep in his heart of hearts he knew, if she should die before he did, he would not want to live.

The sick Cheyennes—including men, women, and children—were scattered about on heaps of robes. Touch the Sky spotted Sharp Nosed Woman, Honey Eater's aunt and a rare survivor of mountain fever, moving from one victim to the next. She held a gourd filled with cool water to the patients' dry lips and patted their burning faces with wet cloths. The moment she spotted Touch the Sky, her jaw fell slack. She shot him a beseeching look, as if she were suffering from some terrible guilt.

"Touch the Sky, can you forgive me? I am truly sorry. Indeed, if we lose her, my grief will cry out to heaven alongside yours. But how could I have known? How?"

Touch the Sky shook his head, baffled. "Forgive you? Sharp Nosed Woman, if a better Cheyenne woman than you lives in our camp, I have yet to meet her. Speak words I can carry off in my sash.

If we lose whom? How could you have known what?"

It was her turn to frown in puzzlement. "Two Twists did not tell you?"

"Tell me what, sister?"

"He did not tell you how I received one of the new blankets? How I traded it for a shawl she embroidered?"

But suddenly Touch the Sky heard nothing else. His world was spinning round like a leaf trapped in a whirling dervish. He had just spotted the young woman lying near the back wall of the pest lodge—or rather he spotted the soft white blur of the columbine petals braided through Honey Eater's hair.

"The filthy dogs who brought this sickness were lured to our camp by White Man Runs Him! It was he who helped the white skins build their iron road over our land. It was he who drank devil water with them at the trading post, he who deserted his tribe to fight for whites. Will a fish leave the river and live in the trees with birds? He is a pretend Cheyenne, sent among us by bluecoats to work their malevolent plans from within!"

Rarely had the fiery-tempered Wolf Who Hunts Smiling been in better speaking form. At his words, Black Elk's fist shot into the air and a shout of support exploded throughout the council lodge.

"This White Man Runs Him," Wolf Who Hunts Smiling said, "has far more in his parfleche than our doting elders suspect. He wears two faces, and he wears them well. I say again he is involved in a scheme to take our hunting ranges! He will help to kill us off, then share the profits with his soldier brothers."

But before the eloquent speaker could whip himself to an even higher pitch, Little Horse was on his feet. Normally, Touch the Sky could hold his own with any man in council. But Little Horse knew his friend was devastated.

"Listen to this wily wolf! Lies and treachery come so naturally to him that it is like breathing. Ask him about his private treaties with our enemies Sis-ki-dee and Big Tree. And still he rails against Caleb Riley and his miners. Yet see that twine-handled knife in his sheath? The fat tobacco pouch on his sash? I saw him drinking coffee this morning, cramming his greedy and lying face with hot bacon—he who mourns so for our sick and dying. He speaks from both sides of his mouth, and neither side speaks straight."

"They cannot," Tangle Hair said, "for he is too busy chewing white man's bacon."

At this remark, many Bow String troopers roared with laughter. Even Gray Thunder grinned in spite of himself. Never, Touch the Sky thought through his numbness, had he seen the council so sharply divided. Indeed, despite this momentary levity, this new tragedy was pushing the tribe to the brink of internal war. Chief Gray Thunder seemed to have aged ten winters in the last two sleeps. The tribe was pulling two ways despite his best efforts to keep them unified as one people.

Gray Thunder folded his arms until the lodge had quieted again. "Cheyenne people, have ears. No more jokes while our loved ones lie dying! More and more are falling ill. I have been forced to send word bringers out to warn our fellow *Shaiyenas* they must not enter our camp. The spring dance cannot be held. We all know that Wolf Who Hunts Smiling and Touch the Sky would gladly feed each other's liver to the dogs. This is no time for them to strut and make the he-bear talk. Our loved ones come first."

Touch the Sky's voice joined the chorus of approval for these words. Only one image dominated his troubled mind: Honey Eater lying in that pest lodge, her life ebbing away.

"Therefore," Gray Thunder said, "I will let both sides state their plan. No matter how some may feel, Touch the Sky is our official shaman. Arrow Keeper selected him, and no man on the entire plains has greater wisdom or stronger medicine than Arrow Keeper. Therefore, Touch the Sky will speak first."

The council lodge was as quiet as a sleeping camp at dawn. Touch the Sky rose. He saw Black Elk and Wolf Who Hunts Smiling glowering at him. Touch the Sky held his face impassive.

"My council will not be well received. But like our chief, I care not for brave talk and scowls, only to save our people."

"To save one of them," Black Elk said, "for he is keen to rut on her! The rest he does not value at a gnat's breath."

"This dead-eared braggart says I do not value our people. Yet look at his shame! His good wife lies dying; two children have just crossed over. Has grief moved him to compassion or the decency to work calmly with his tribe to fight this new trouble? No! He does dirt on a good woman and seizes her tragedy as one more reason to shed tribal blood and sully our sacred arrows!"

Gray Thunder had dreaded this turn of events. Violence lay thick in the air, and rage blazed in Black Elk's face. Several of the Bull Whips were forced to restrain him.

"Just what does White Man Runs Him have in mind?" Wolf Who Hunts Smiling demanded scornfully. "More cooperation with bluecoats?"

"Yes," Touch the Sky said without hesitation. His defiant answer hung in the air like the echo of a rifle shot. Even his friends looked surprised. "Our goal is to save the people. The peace road is the quickest route to that goal. The only ones who possess the magic called vaccine are the blue-bloused soldiers at Fort Bates. They have medicine men called doctors and know how to shoot this vaccine into the sick ones. I speak their tongue. I will approach them under a truce flag."

"No!" Wolf Who Hunts Smiling leapt to his feet. "This plan has the white man's stink all over it! I still say it was white soldiers who caused this disease to be among us, and perhaps this woman-faced pretend Cheyenne has helped them. Now he means to pretend to seek help from them, thus giving this mountain fever time to kill us off. We must take hostages and force white skins to help us!"

Pandemonium broke out when the wily young brave quit speaking. Only after he was forced to shout could Gray Thunder quiet the others enough to speak. Known for his even temper, he spoke with impatience straining his voice.

"Brothers! Will we shed blood at our very council, as do the barbaric Comanches? Enough of this bitter fighting. I am weary from it. The headmen will vote with their stones. White stones back Touch the Sky; black stones favor Wolf Who Hunts Smiling's plan. Whatever the stones decide will be final."

Each voting headman carried two stones in his parfleche: a white moonstone and a black agate. Gray Thunder started passing round the chamois pouch used for voting. Keeping his choice hidden in his hand, each headman slipped a stone inside.

As the pouch made its rounds, Touch the Sky's agitation was deep. Finally, the pouch was passed back to Gray Thunder, and he was on the verge of spilling the stones out onto the robes beneath him.

But now Touch the Sky reminded himself that Honey Eater was dying! Abruptly, agonizingly trapped between his love for Honey Eater and his duty to the Cheyenne way, Touch the Sky rebelled.

He seized the pouch from Gray Thunder before the stones could be spilled out. Gray Thunder's jaw slacked open in surprise.

"I am following only one plan," Touch the Sky announced boldly. "My own. Maiyun have mercy on any brave who attempts to stop me."

"This is open treason!" Wolf Who Hunts Smiling shouted. In a blink he was on his feet again, his knife in his hand. Black Elk and several other Bull Whips rose up with him. "Now he dies!"

But just as quickly, Little Horse, Tangle Hair, and Two Twists formed a ring around their leader. They too had weapons in hand.

"Come, then," Little Horse said softly, "and let the battle be bloody or nothing else!"

But no one moved. No ten braves in the tribe could have touched the tall shaman now—not through that ring of fighting Cheyennes. Bloodshed was barely avoided for the moment.

Gray Thunder shook his head in disgust. "Only look on this spectacle of shame. Our tribe's shaman makes a mockery of the headmen's vote. Our tribe's war leader and his cousin stand ready to kill a fellow Cheyenne in front of their peace chief. All this while death ravages our camp. I have lived too long to see a chief reduced to a squaw by his own people."

Gray Thunder rose, signifying that the council was over. "I am ashamed of these proceedings. I will not light the common pipe again and touch it with my lips, for I cannot sanction these events."

# Death Camp

He stared at Touch the Sky. "But I confess, buck, I voted for your plan and still back it. You have today disgraced the Cheyenne laws. I will consider your wrongdoing redeemed, however, if you bring this doctor and magic vaccine back in time to help our people."

Black Elk spoke next. "They will be brought back, indeed." His murderous stare knifed into Touch the Sky. "I am this tribe's war leader, and I decide our plan of battle—not even Gray Thunder can override me. And it is my wife who lies dying, not Woman Face's. So I spit his words back into his face. Maiyun have mercy on any brave who attempts to stop me."

# Chapter Four

"We'll bivouac here for the night," Capt. Seth Carlson told his platoon sergeant. "Looks like rain later, so tell the men to snap their shelter halves together before they bed down. Full bandoliers and every swinging dick is to have a light-marching pack ready at all times. If we engage these hostiles, we'll be covering plenty of landscape."

"That we will, sir," Sgt. Nolan Reece said, "assuming you mean Injin hostiles. I've never met the Injun yet who liked to fort up for a battle. The sneaking red devils fight from horseback and skirmish from behind rocks."

The two soldiers sat their mounts in the long shadow of a huge granite headland known as Lookout Bluff. The Shoshone River lay out of sight to the north, the rim of its shallow valley marked by the occasional clump of wind-twisted cottonwoods. Off and on for 20 years, since establishing the lonely remount post of Fort Bates in the southeast Wyoming Territory, the army had used this spot as an observation post and mirror station. Lookout Bluff commanded an impressive view of the territory's vulnerable northern approach, which was ranged by several hostile tribes and especially prone to raiding by the fierce Sioux and their equally fierce Cheyenne cousins. Behind the two soldiers, a 40-man platoon of cavalry and dragoon sharpshooters held double columns at wide intervals.

"Set up picket outposts," Carlson said. "Two-hour watches. We'll graze the horses farther out while it's still light, then bring them close to camp at dark."

"Yes, sir." Reece glanced discreetly away, out over the vast brown onsweep of short-grass prairie to the north. Any Indians heading south toward the fort or Bighorn Falls would have to cross it. "I understand, sir, that we're currently at peace with all the tribes in this sector and that we have standing orders to avoid them completely except for defensive actions if attacked."

He spoke casually, keeping any note of disapproval out of his tone. Reece liked duty under his new company commander. For like him, Carlson hated Indians with a passion that bordered on the fanatical. Sgt. Reece had once led a scouting patrol on a private mission to sack an Apache camp down in Ojo Caliente while their men were off hunting. But he didn't understand then how fiercely Indian women and children would fight for their homes. A stone-headed war club had shattered his right knee and left him limping badly for life.

Carlson knew his platoon sergeant was only hinting for information, not rebelling at this mysterious new training exercise.

"Except for defensive actions if attacked," Carlson repeated. "Law-abiding soldiers have a right to defend themselves. Don't you agree, Sergeant?"

"Speak the truth and shame the devil, sir."

"And let's just say the head of one of the Indians who attack us happened to be worth two thousand dollars to a certain merchant I happen to know. Now, if the Indians were attacking us anyway, killing him would only sweeten the victory a little."

"That it would, sir. It most certainly would, for a fact."

"Personally, I'd be more than willing to share that two thousand dollars with a fellow soldier, especially if he was to use his influence with the men and persuade them not to contradict our field reports back in garrison."

Reece grinned. Broken teeth flashed under a long teamster's mustache. "Sir, my hand to God, they're good lads all. Fine soldiers who 'preciate a pint of cool beer or a glass of Knockum Stiff. You point 'em, Cap'n. I'll make sure they peddle lead to the right red customers."

Carlson nodded. Most of his big bluff face lay in shadow under the snap brim of his officer's hat.

"You fairly certain, are you, sir, that the hostiles you have in mind will be riding this way?"

Carlson thought about that question. Only a miracle could have protected Matthew Hanchon's tribe from infection. With luck, the tall, trouble-making buck would catch the disease and die. If not, he would surely take it on himself to approach Fort Bates for help. Probably knew about the vaccine and the contract surgeons the fort kept around.

Carlson also thought about all the damn good reasons he had for sending this red son across the Great Divide. Chief among many that rankled at him was that humiliating business with Hiram Steele's daughter Kristen. It still made Carlson blush pink clear to his ear lobes to realize that she had preferred a full-blooded Cheyenne buck over him, a white man. She chose to kiss the lips of a filthy, gut-eating savage rather than those of a graduate of West Point, the scion of a Virginia senator!

"If I know this buck like I think I do," Carlson finally replied, "he'll be riding this way. But I'll warn you right now: Killing him will be a rough piece of work."

Reece reached down to massage his sore right knee. Each winter it stiffened up bad and made walking or mounting a horse harder and harder.

Soon the army would have to cashier his lame carcass, and Reece was fit for no other calling.

"Two thousand dollars?" he said.

Carlson nodded. "In double eagle gold pieces."

Reece flashed his broken teeth again, glancing back down the double columns. "Rough work is the only kind I know, sir," he finally replied. "You know what they say about Injuns. 'Injuns are only nits, but nits make lice.' I say let's kill some nits."

Touch the Sky's worst enemy was a familiar one: time. He did not know exactly how long Honey Eater or the rest had left before it would be too late for the white man's medicine—assuming he ever got any. Certainly not long. Perhaps the strongest of them might last a few sleeps. Riding hard and eating on horseback, they could reach Fort Bates in one-and-a-half sleeps. So even if everything went right, help could not be had in less than three days. And truly, Touch the Sky asked himself, when had everything ever gone right?

"Brother," Little Horse said soon after the nearly fatal council meeting, "I know who is riding with Black Elk. I saw them cutting their ponies out of the common corral. Not surprisingly, the white-livered Medicine Flute will remain in camp. He is to work medicine over our sick."

"Add his medicine to your empty quiver," Tangle Hair said, "and you are out of arrows."

"Straight enough," Little Horse said. He aimed

a searching glance at Touch the Sky. "But there are some whose medicine is real and strong. I only wonder why do they not use their powers more often during trouble?"

"Perhaps the medicine uses the man," Touch the Sky said evasively, "and picks the occasion. A shaman who could use magic at his whim would not be a man but a god. He must impress the high holy ones first and prove that he is worthy of help."

The same three comrades who protected Touch the Sky in council were preparing to ride out with him. All four braves had joined the rest of the adult males in cropping short their hair in sympathy for their dead. It was tacitly agreed among them that Touch the Sky was their leader in any crisis. Once they had wondered why the young buck did not join a warrior society—the Bow Strings, in particular, since he admired them and their leader Spotted Tail. But now they understood Touch the Sky was marked out for a far greater destiny—destiny in which he would lead his own vast faction. He was meant to lead, not join.

"Medicine Flute is staying back," Little Horse said. "Riding with Black Elk are Wolf Who Hunts Smiling, the Bull Whip named Stone Mountain, and Swift Canoe, who has recently been initiated as a Bull Whip."

"Four warriors who equal ten," Touch the Sky said glumly. "Swift Canoe is a feather brain, but I have seen even that one cleave a Pawnee in half."

As he finished rigging his calico pony for the hard ride south, his eyes kept cutting to the isolated spot where the pest lodge stood.

Two Twists saw him. "Brother, Tangle Hair and I will need a bit more time to ready our battle rigs. You have heard that Trains the Hawk, my favorite uncle, is among the afflicted. It would mean a great deal to him if our shaman visited the pest lodge and said a brief prayer before he left."

Trains the Hawk was indeed ill. But Tangle Hair was also the unofficial word bringer between Touch the Sky and Honey Eater, as well as Honey Eater's only trusted confidant on the subject of Touch the Sky. He knew full well that Touch the Sky longed to see Honey Eater once more—perhaps for the last time—before he rode out.

Little Horse aided the effort. "Certainly Black Elk will be no problem. He has made it clear that he is indifferent to his wife's fate. Though he hotly declares that she is still his property, and he prates about in her name, huffing out his chest and making brags, he will not visit the lodge."

They were right. Touch the Sky handed his pony's buffalo-hair reins to Two Twists. Then, his throat constricting with nervous anticipation, he crossed to the pest lodge.

Despite his concern for Honey Eater, his feet grew heavy for the last few steps. He could smell the sweet, fragrant incense and hear the children softly crying. Another victim had died, an elder from the silvertip clan. Again, grasping for any straws of hope, Touch the Sky reminded himself that young adults fought the disease longest. And Honey Eater was strong, descended as she was from a long line of great Cheyenne chiefs.

But then he lifted the entrance flap aside. And his hope died when he spotted the woman he loved with all his life. She lay where he had last seen her. But the cruel ravages of mountain fever had already begun to draw the skin of her face tight like green rawhide shrinking in the sun.

Honey Eater was alert, and she recognized him. Her eyes widened in gladness at seeing him. His own heart formed a tight fist of compassionate response when she moved her slim arms over her robe, crossing them at the wrists over her heart—Cheyenne sign talk for love. He quickly crossed his too. But Touch the Sky and Honey Eater both knew this was no place or time for a visit between them alone.

And yet, how much had passed between them! A whole secret life and love patched together in stolen moments and glances, brief exchanges of passionate, and pent-up feelings. Although they had not yet sealed their love's bond by merging their flesh, Honey Eater had finally told him that despite reciting the squaw-taking vows with Black Elk and accepting his bride price, she considered Touch the Sky her only husband. She would violate Cheyenne law and her own great pride and come to him as his wife if he ever sent for her.

But that he would not do, not so long as the

jealous, murderous Black Elk and his spies watched both of them night and day. Touch the Sky scorned any fear for himself. Neither Black Elk nor any other brave would readily close the gap against him. But Honey Eater had already suffered too much because of this love neither one of them could help. And so the two of them suffered on in silence and lived for their secret love, hobbled as it was by cruel reality.

Touch the Sky smiled again at Honey Eater. Then, stepping aside to speak briefly with Sharp Nosed Woman, he reached into his parfleche.

"For Honey Eater," he said. "She cannot pick any fresh ones, and they mean much to her."

He handed Sharp Nosed Woman several clumps of fresh white columbine gently pressed between broad wet leaves.

For a few heartbeats, the weary lines softened in the older woman's face. She nodded and smiled. "I will braid them through her hair myself. Do you know, Touch the Sky, that I once called her a fool for placing little flowers in her hair? If Honey Eater survives this, I will never tease her for it again."

She spoke bravely. But Touch the Sky read the desperation in her tone. Clearly, in her secret heart of hearts, she expected the worst. But hope was a waking dream. As Touch the Sky moved to turn away and say a brief prayer for all, Sharp Nosed Woman laid a hand on his arm.

"Hurry, Touch the Sky," she whispered, "I know

why she loves you, and I approve. I was there when you stood tall and saved the hunt camp from Kiowa and Comanche who meant to steal us for slaves. I watched you swing from the pole without complaint rather than call an addled old grandmother a liar when Wolf Who Hunts Smiling bribed her into a vision against you.

"Some say you once lost our medicine arrows. But if so, did you not scale the cliffs of Wendigo Mountain to get them back? Touch the Sky, if any brave in our tribe can save these dying Cheyennes, it is you. Ride on the wind, tall warrior, and may the high holy ones ride with you. Save them!"

"They have left camp, cousin," Wolf Who Hunts Smiling said, "and they are riding hard. They should reach the Shoshone River before Sister Sun goes to bed."

The young brave had dropped behind to watch their backtrail from a spine of rimrock.

"They had best not plan on passing us," Black Elk said grimly. "That was outright treason during council, bucks. All four of them are enemies of our tribe and our law. Armed enemies."

"Redrock canyons lie ahead," Swift Canoe said. "Perhaps we could hide and kill them there."

Black Elk seemed to consider this plan. But it was Wolf Who Hunts Smiling who spoke up. Some scheme blazed in his wily eyes—one better than Swift Canoe's pale suggestion.

"Never mind such stupid white-skin tricks. How

many times have they failed against this one? And every brave with him is worthy to wear the medicine hat in battle, even young Two Twists. No, never mind the white man's ambush. Better to heap the trouble on them when nature already has them distracted."

Black Elk scowled. "Cousin, you have not one coward's bone in your body. But why do you never speak straight? Take the short way to your meaning. I am a warrior, not a tongue-wagging old squaw."

Wolf Who Hunts Smiling grinned. "As you say, cousin. Well, is this plain enough? I recently scouted this very trail for our hunters. The Shoshone is swollen with runoff and badly flooded. The ford at Crying Horse Bend is fast and dangerous. We must make our move when they are trying to ford the river."

# Chapter Five

Touch the Sky's band pushed their mounts hard, bearing south along the ancient trace first blazed by plains hunters and warriors. They knew every water hole in the area and paused only briefly to let their ponies drink at rills and creeks. Luckily their winter-starved horses, after growing weak from nibbling cottonwood bark and old grass trapped under the snow, were in good fettle again from browsing the lush new grass and clover.

The Cheyennes knew that the Shoshone River was often troublesome to ford. Long after the Laramie, the Lodgepole, and other area rivers had receded to their meandering summer levels, the Shoshone still churned white foam well beyond its normal banks. But never had Touch the Sky seen the river so swollen.

"Brothers," Little Horse said as the four braves surveyed the ford at Crying Horse Bend, "can you even tell this was once a wading ford? Last time we crossed here, the water barely trickled over our ponies' fetlocks."

He was forced to shout above the booming roar of the Shoshone. Drift logs, sometimes entire trees, flashed by like a herd of swift animals. The water, muddied by mountain soil, churned and boiled. A huge sawyer had formed in midstream, a vast obstruction of limbs and driftwood and other debris that sawed back and forth in the current.

"Clearly," Tangle Hair said as Touch the Sky dismounted and began searching for sign along the bank, "the river will not be going down any time soon."

"This is the best ford along this stretch of the river," Two Twists said. "There is a better one at Elbow Bend—a sandbar ford that is much easier even in flood weather. But it is a half sleep's ride west of here, well out of our way."

"Unless appearances are dishonest," Touch the Sky said with some wonder in his voice, "then, out of the way or not, Black Elk's band chose Elbow Bend."

Little Horse had been reading the sign too. Now he nodded agreement.

"See here," Touch the Sky said, pointing. "Four ponies rode up to this spot. These many overlapping prints are where they stood. One set of prints goes off to the east. We could follow it to see how far the rider looked for a crossing. But why bother? Here his prints come back again. Nothing was found."

"Nothing," Little Horse said, "and then see where four riders rode west toward Elbow Bend. No prints return. And there is no other place to cross between here and Elbow Bend. So unless they ride back, they will have to cross there."

"They did not cross here," Touch the Sky said. "No prints enter the water."

Little Horse grinned. "Brother, why do you frown? This is an opportunity to be seized. True it is, Cousin River is out for blood. It will be a brisk bit of sport to cross here, no job for children. But I, for one, have no desire to die of old age in my tipi. I am for it. It will give us a good head start."

Despite this bravado, every brave present could not help realizing that drowning was an especially unlucky death for an Indian. A drowning victim's soul remained trapped in the water forever and became a lonely river spirit unable to cross over to the Land of Ghosts.

Touch the Sky glanced around suspiciously at the surrounding terrain: a few low hummocks, a thicket here and there, not much natural cover. But a well-trained Cheyenne who wanted to hide would not need much.

"That is what troubles me," he said. "It will indeed give us a good head start. And who here among us knows either Black Elk or Wolf Who Hunts Smiling to be timid? Black Elk is not as reckless as his cousin, but is it like either of them to avoid this ford?"

Little Horse's grin faded. He caught the drift of his friend's thinking and nodded. "No," he replied. "Neither one of them is such a close friend with caution."

"Not a bit," Tangle Hair said. "Not Black Elk and certainly not Wolf Who Hunts Smiling. But despite his name, Swift Canoe cannot swim, and Stone Mountain's pony is as timid as Stone Mountain is stupid."

Knowing he could not afford to lose a man, Black Elk might well indeed have chosen the safe crossing at Elbow Bend—especially, thought Touch the Sky, if a marksman or two had been left behind to kill their rivals once they entered the river. After all, it was Black Elk who taught young braves in the tribe to shoot game when it was thigh deep in water and could not flee quickly.

A decision had to be made. Touch the Sky's three companions were watching him and waiting. Worse, Honey Eater lay dying while he stood there like a dazed calf, indecisive. But he was reluctant to order this fording. Even the strongest swimmer could drown if he became separated from his mount in that raging current. It was not the Indian way to make important decisions without adequate discussion.

But again Touch the Sky saw Honey Eater

crossing her wrists over her breast. Again he heard the soft whimpers of the sick children. There was no time for long discussions.

"Check your rigs," he said. "Make sure your powder will not get wet, for we may need to burn it soon."

"Cousin River!" Little Horse shouted. "Here come four Cheyennes who never did you harm and always crossed you respectfully. This is for letting us live to see your far bank."

Little Horse had been saving some fine white man's tobacco in his parfleche. He shredded it into the boiling waters as an offering. Tangle Hair tossed in several delicious horehound candies he had traded from a Sioux. Two Twists threw in the last of his coffee beans.

Touch the Sky tossed in his ration of sugar. But he shot a secret glance at Little Horse, wondering if his friend had deliberately not mentioned one more fact that Touch the Sky had gleaned from those prints he'd read: One set of retreating prints was not as deep as the others. Meaning there was no rider on the pony because one brave stayed behind. Touch the Sky had little doubt who that skulking Indian was.

"All right, Cheyennes," he said finally. "Now we ride."

Wolf Who Hunts Smiling waited until the last rider, Tangle Hair, had entered the thundering river. Then, his face divided by the wily smile that was his namesake, he rose up from the shallow pit he had dug behind a spoil bank.

He had been right in his hunch: White Man Runs Him and his band had indeed opted for this dangerous crossing. The brave had convinced Black Elk and the others to cross at Elbow Bend—convinced them, in part, by assuring them he would remain behind to lessen Touch the Sky's numbers and perhaps even kill him. Besides, Stone Mountain's pony refused to enter the water there. And though Stone Mountain did not lack courage to try, he was stupid enough to end up drowning. Black Elk might need him for combat.

Wolf Who Hunts Smiling told the others to lead his mount and leave it hobbled out of sight for him. Now he checked the primer cap in his Colt 1855 rifle. Crouched low, keeping the spoil bank between himself and the river, he held the Colt across his chest and angled toward the raging water.

At first Touch the Sky attempted to keep an eye on the bank behind him as he entered the water. But the current quickly became a powerful foe trying to tear his pony out from under him. It was impossible to fight the river and pay attention to their backtrail.

The four braves formed a wedge, Touch the Sky at the apex. All four spoke to their mounts above the roar, trying to calm and encourage them. But it was all the ponies could do to keep from being sucked under.

In an eyeblink a huge log was bouncing and skipping toward Touch the Sky. The weight and speed of it and the jagged point caused by a break had turned it into a deadly weapon strong enough to pierce the pony's flank.

In a heartbeat Touch the Sky slid hard to one side and jerked hard on one rein, leading the hurtling log by putting his pony at the current's mercy. They floundered, but the maneuver slowed the deadly log's onward thrust just enough for Touch the Sky to hook it with one foot and send it veering. But now he was well downstream from the more narrow spot at the ford. He could glance to the right and spot his three friends—and further behind them Wolf Who Hunts Smiling!

Shock slammed into Touch the Sky even more brutally than the river. The brave on the bank had dropped to one knee and popped the rifle into his shoulder socket, drawing a bead. Somehow, in all the excitement, he must have lost track of the moment when Touch the Sky was swept downstream. Not once did he glance his way—perhaps, thought Touch the Sky, he believed his foe had drowned.

The struggling Cheyenne opened his mouth to shout a warning to his friends. But it was useless against the sustained roar of the Shoshone. He decided to fire a warning shot when, abruptly, the calico was sucked under and Touch the Sky found himself staying afloat with one arm while the other desperately tried to hold his Sharps up out of the water. His pony fought her way to the surface, and Touch the Sky managed to remain on her back.

"Brothers!" he screamed. "Behind you!"

But again his voice was lost to the flood-raging river, and now it was too late. The Colt coughed, and Touch the Sky's heart turned over when Tangle Hair's pony suddenly went under in a spray of white foam and blood. A moment later, Two Twists cried out as blood blossomed just above his left elbow. He too plunged into the maelstrom of the river.

The conniving brave on the bank had paused to charge his rifle again. Desperately trying to stay astride his floundering pony, Touch the Sky snapped off a wild shot at his enemy. The bullet kicked up a geyser of dirt near Wolf Who Hunts Smiling, and he flinched violently. He still hadn't spotted his drifting adversary to his left. Concluding a marksman must be hidden somewhere on land, he broke upstream at a run, heading for his hidden pony.

But Touch the Sky grimly realized that the ambitious schemer had inflicted serious damage. Fortunately, Little Horse had been near when Tangle Hair's pony was killed. Little Horse had grabbed for the other brave's arm and gained a purchase. Arms linked over the withers of Little

Horse's pony, they were about to reach the safety of the bank.

The wounded Two Twists, however, was not so fortunate. And even before Touch the Sky could think to act, the youth tumbled past him like a hayseed in the wind. Touch the Sky managed to heave his rifle over to the far bank. But river spray blinded him, and his pony began to wash out from under him. He struck one arm out, felt human flesh, and hung on for dear life. He and Two Twists went under in a tangled confusion of limbs.

Like Touch the Sky's calico, they were on their own. His face taut with the incredible effort, Touch the Sky kicked with his powerful long legs and swam with his free arm. Two Twists made a valiant effort too in spite of his wound.

Just when Touch the Sky feared his strength would give out, hands as strong as an eagle's talons gripped him. Little Horse and Tangle Hair pulled their two friends onto the grassy hump of bank. For some time all four braves lay there, catching their breath. It was Tangle Hair who spoke first. His voice was bitter with rage and loss.

"My best pony dead, already washed out of sight! So is my rifle, my rig."

Touch the Sky took a good look at the Two Twists' wound. "The bullet went through. Soon it will be stiff. But all this cold water slowed the bleeding. If we pack it with balsam and black powder, it will heal well."

Since his friends were safe, rage was settling

into Little Horse's normally placid features. "Did you see him, brothers? Did you? It was Wolf Who Hunts Smiling! He and Black Elk spoke of our treason, yet now they have just shed the blood of their own. Even the thought of the arrows did not hold them back! If he would sully our medicine arrows so boldly, there is no treachery beneath him."

Touch the Sky nodded. His lips were set in a grim, determined slit. "You have caught truth firmly by the tail, buck. There was a time when Black Elk, at least, would not shed tribal blood. But he authorized this attempt at cold-blooded murder."

"As he did, brother," Little Horse said, "when you sojourned at Medicine Lake in quest of your vision."

"Now we know just how it is," Tangle Hair said. "They are murderers, not fellow Cheyennes."

Touch the Sky knew he was right. Black Elk's band were no better than declared enemies to be killed on sight. But despite his anger, Touch the Sky's fear for Honey Eater's life determined his thoughts. Would he ever, he kept wondering with a sharp tug at his stomach, see her alive again?

But their duty lay all before them. And time, like a bird, was on the wing.

"Tangle Hair will take turns riding with all of us," Touch the Sky said. "Check your weapons and prepare to ride."

# Chapter Six

Shortly after sunup on the second day after Touch the Sky's band rode out, Seth Carlson spotted a mirror signal from the north.

"It's Trooper Nielson, sir, " Sgt. Reece said. "I posted him out halfway between here and the Shoshone River, at the old freight road station."

"Quiet," Carlson said impatiently. "I'm translating the Morse code." His eyes puckered as he read the quick flashes and the pauses between, spelling out the words. "Four riders coming from river on three horses. Cheyennes. One wounded. Flying truce flag."

Reece laughed a short, hard, derisive bark. "Four riders on three horses! Damn, I'm shittin' my scivvies in fright, sir, my hand to God! And one already wounded for us! This'll be a bird's nest on the ground."

Far less sanguine, Carlson said nothing. He had no proof yet that Matthew Hanchon would be among the approaching Indians. But he knew the Cheyenne's full measure, and in his heart he was convinced Hanchon would make an appeal to Fort Bates. The Indian had yet to discover, however, that his old nemesis Seth Carlson had once again been posted to Fort Bates.

And if Hanchon was coming, Reece was in for some unpleasant lessons about Indian warfare. Carlson hated Hanchon with a passion hotter than hell. But he was also quick to admit the buck had no peer as a fighter.

"Don't dance on his grave too soon," Carlson said.

Once again he glanced carefully about them. The sharpshooters, 40 strong, had taken up positions in two long files, forming a gauntlet between the granite headland of Lookout Bluff and a long, parallel ridge about a hundred yards to the east. The Indian trace passed by below, offering precious little cover as it funnelled into the narrow pass. The terrain hereabouts was too pocked with sand blights and dangerous prairie-dog holes. The Cheyennes would be extremely unlikely to stray wide or ride any other trail.

"I savvy which way you're grazing, sir," Reece said, rubbing a knuckle across his long teamster's mustache. "The Cheyenne—now they're pony-crazy. Almost all their combat training is based on the running skirmish. They run hard and make their opponents chase them until the pursuers' horses founder. Then they turn quick and attack."

Reece grinned. "But the thing of it is, forty marksmen can make the air hum with lead. We're gunna force 'em to hunker down in a fixed position."

Carlson nodded. "Exactly. But that's assuming we don't kill them before they take cover. The men are well within maximum effective range. If they hold and squeeze, the initial surprise volley should do it. I'll bust the first cap as soon as they hit that square clearing where the draw opens out."

As Touch the Sky found himself doing more and more lately, he felt the truth of yet another of Arrow Keeper's favorite sayings: *We must pass through the bitter water before we reach the sweet.* Wolf Who Hunts Smiling's failure to completely stop them at Crying Horse Bend had its good consequences. Surviving that gutsy ford gave the four braves a considerable time advantage over Black Elk's band.

Touch the Sky had made the briefest of pauses to rest the nearly exhausted ponies and their own muscle-strained bodies. By the time Sister Sun had streaked the eastern sky pink, they were again pushing their mounts hard to the south. They were forced to stop more often so that Tangle Hair could leap up behind a new rider. Though Two Twists never once complained, Touch the Sky knew that such a hard pace severely punished his wound.

"There it is, bucks," Little Horse said at that moment, lifting one hand to point ahead in the gathering light of morning. "The ancient headland we call Medicine Mound and the white-skins call Lookout Bluff. Say that name in English, brother."

Touch the Sky did, even as his eyes cut to the white truce flag tied to his lance. Every Cheyenne present knew what he, living among whites as Matthew Hanchon, had learned long ago. By any name, Medicine Mound had long been an observation post for the pony soldiers of Fort Bates. If it was presently manned, he would get a chance to practice his English very soon, assuming a bullet didn't end this mission in a heartbeat.

And it was presently manned. His shaman sense convinced him of that. It hinted at more than that, but he had no luxury to weigh the warning. Was trouble ahead? Trouble was ahead, lurking around the next dogleg bend, ready to pounce. Touch the Sky had no choice. Honey Eater and many more lay dying, while Black Elk and his band were closing in to make more trouble.

Touch the Sky signaled to his comrades, and they dropped back behind him. Again Touch the Sky regretted there was no time to look before they waded in so deep.

# Death Camp

As the sun burned off the last mist, the huge granite bluff rose up out of the plains before them. Touch the Sky lifted his lance, peace flag snapping, as the Cheyennes entered the narrow draw between the bluff and the neighboring ridge.

Capt. Seth Carlson's military career had struck some snags these late years, thanks to Matthew Hanchon. But no one in the army denied that Carlson was a seasoned and effective Indian fighter known for molding his troops into crack Indian killers. Units under his command had achieved notable victories against Sioux, Blackfeet, Crow, and Assiniboin. But Hanchon had somehow led a ragtag group of mostly unarmed Cheyennes to a stunning victory over Carlson's mountain regiment in the Bear Paw Mountains.

Carlson's men showed their remarkable discipline as the Cheyennes approached below. Not one broke cover or allowed a piece of brass to glint in the sun. All signals were relayed by hand. And Carlson knew that not one of them would crack a cap until he fired.

The muzzle of his Spencer carbine, well blackened to cut reflection, lay across a low rock in front of him. He had been waiting for the Cheyennes to ride close enough to finally discover if Steele's play with the infected blankets had lured Hanchon.

He raised a pair of field glasses, adjusted the focus, and studied the lead Indian carrying the truce flag. Even from there, with the naked eye, the buck's shoulders looked wide indeed. But with one twist of the focus, Carlson was staring at the face of the man he hated worst of all in the world.

He glanced over at Reece. "Here he comes," he said triumphantly. "It's Hanchon!"

"All due respect, sir, but you're wrong for a fact. It ain't Hanchon. It's two thousand dollars!"

Sharp Nosed Woman was too exhausted, too frustrated, for more tears. She had cried her eyes dry. Her face a frozen mask of resignation, she moved to the entrance of the pest lodge. Her eyes met those of an anxious-looking young mother named Sun Road. Sharp Nosed Woman shook her head. Instantly, Sun Road cried out in overwhelming grief and fell to the ground in a fit of crazy pain.

Just as quickly, following the ancient custom at such times, the women of her clan formed a ring around her for her own protection. No one tried to stop her when she groped in the dirt for a sharp flint and gouged her own arms with it. Even when scarlet ribbons of her blood stained the earth, they did not stop her.

Death was important. Sun Road's infant son had just crossed over, dead from the dreaded fever, and it was right that she marked her terrible loss with pain. The child's life had mattered, and his final agony must be shared. But they would watch her for the next few sleeps, not once letting her lay hands on a more dangerous weapon of self-destruction.

Sharp Nosed Woman turned away and returned to the gloomy interior of the morbid death chamber. The stench of serious illness was powerful, hanging dank in the air like a wet fog. Children cried softly. The older sufferers groaned and begged for water, yet could not hold it down once it was given.

Sharp Nosed Woman stopped and knelt beside Honey Eater. A smaller bundle lay beside her— Honey Eater's little niece Laughing Brook. The child was going rapidly. The pretty little girl's face was drawn as tight as the skin over a knuckle. Like Honey Eater, she had eyes fervid with the destructive fever heat blazing inside them.

"Look," Sharp Nosed Woman said to Honey Eater. "He brought these for you."

She held out the broad leaves with the fresh white columbine petals pressed between them. For a moment, despite the numbing death grip of mountain fever, a surge of joy lessened the suffering in Honey Eater's face.

"Shall I braid them in your hair, charmer? They are always so pretty there."

Honey Eater nodded. When she spoke, her exhausted voice was like a whisper from the spirit world. "But save a few."

She nodded toward little Laughing Brook, who had slipped into unconsciousness. Like her favorite aunt, whom she adored, the little one had several faded columbine petals in her hair.

"The dear little one," Sharp Nosed Woman said, but now a sharp lance of pain broke through her armor of numbness. A sob hitched in her breast and choked off the rest of her words.

Oh, hurry, Touch the Sky, Sharp Nosed Woman prayed silently, watching Honey Eater's wan face. Hurry! Never mind this columbine. Much longer and we will lose the fairest flowers in all the fields.

The morning sun was almost straight overhead when Touch the Sky's band edged into the wide apron of shadow cast by Lookout Bluff. His sense of impending danger was strong. They never should have approached the draw without scouting it first. But urgency made such precautions impossible. The fat was in the fire and it was too late to pull it out. Even so, he stopped his braves for a cautious moment. He had just heard a familiar clicking noise from the edge of the trail.

"I have already heard it, brother," Little Horse said grimly.

All four braves had heard it, and their eyes met in silence. The noises were made by the burrowing of wood-eating insects called deathwatch beetles. Hearing them was a strong omen of impending death.

"Brothers," Little Horse said, craning his neck to stare up above them, "we are not at war with any blue blouses, nor could Black Elk's band have gotten here before us."

## Death Camp

He spoke uncertainly, watching Touch the Sky. Little Horse was known for possessing the sharpest senses in the tribe. On a sudden impulse, Touch the Sky said, "Brother, sniff the winds good and tell us what you think."

The rest of them glanced oddly at Touch the Sky. But Little Horse only rode out ahead to a slight rise. He threw back his head, breathed deeply through his nose as he faced the four directions. Then, his face troubled, he rode back to join his friends.

"Earlier I told you I am no reader of thoughts," Touch the Sky said before his friend could speak. "But you smell horses, do you not? Many horses, probably well hidden nearby and muzzled with full grain bags to keep them still."

"Indeed I do, brother," Little Horse replied. "I smell horses rubbed with the stinky liniment used by soldiers."

"They are watching us now, perhaps through bead sights," Touch the Sky said calmly, openly scanning the bluff overhead.

"What about our truce flag?" Tangle Hair said from his spot on the back of Two Twists' pony.

"No one lurks in ambush and hides his horse to show respect to a truce flag," Touch the Sky said. "These tactics mean the attack is coming. They are only waiting for us to clear these shadows and enter that clearing ahead."

"Do we flee back north?" Tangle Hair said.

That seemed the only sane choice. And yet, sane

or not, it also meant sure death for Honey Eater and the rest. For the braves had to pass this point to reach Fort Bates.

Little Horse too realized this fact. "The best way to stop a charging bull is to throw him by the horns. Besides, I would rather be knocked out from under my feather by a bluecoat bullet than swim that angry river again."

Despite their looming threat, Touch the Sky felt a smile tugging at his lips. "Brother," he said fondly, "I believe you are bold enough to count coup on the Wendigo."

"The Wendigo?" Tangle Hair scoffed. "I once borrowed his flint and still have not returned it."

"That is why he killed your pony," Two Twists said, and all four braves tossed back their heads and laughed.

Thus the Cheyennes showed their contempt for the terrible death threat they faced. But it was also the beginning of Touch the Sky's strategy for surviving this trap without retreating.

"All right, bucks," he said. "Break out pemmican and venison. Enjoy your food as we let our ponies set their own pace into the clearing. But watch me and move when I move. Do you see past the clearing to that jumble of scree? We must reach it and cover down until darkness. But from now on, do not look overhead and show no sign that you are anything but hungry. Good luck, brothers, and may the high holy ones ride with us now!"

# Chapter Seven

Ever since the tribe learned of the infected blankets, a nubbin of suspicion had been planted in Touch the Sky's mind: As he led his comrades forward toward a hail of lead at any moment, that suspicion was growing into a certainty.

The soldiers hid in ambush above them. Touch the Sky knew full well the entire Cheyenne Nation was at peace with the Great White Father and his Council in Washington. True, isolated bands of the Southern Cheyenne Dog Soldiers were raiding against white-skins. But the Northern Cheyennes had lately suffered only minor run-ins with white settlers and soldiers.

It was a serious violation of the army's standing order, he knew, to attack a peace movement like this. And why would any field commander risk such a serious charge merely to kill four braves riding under a white flag? Even as he asked the question, he knew his old enemy Seth Carlson was back.

"Brothers," he said in a low but clear voice, "a shaman must follow the voices in the wind. Little Horse, are you ready for sport?"

"Is a she-bear with cubs ready for meat?"

"Stout buck! I am going to halt my pony. You continue to ride toward the rocks. Tangle Hair, you and Two Twists follow. Your ponies have all been trained to lie down when commanded. The moment you can do so, get behind the rocks."

Touch the Sky knew his comrades did not approve of his stopping in the sights of many bluecoat guns. But appealing to Little Horse in the name of shamanic power always commanded instant obedience to any order. Little Horse would question no order if Touch the Sky commanded it in the name of higher powers.

"As you say, brother," Little Horse replied in the same low tone. "But I tell you freely, today is not a good day to die. Meet us in the scree."

"I intend nothing else, buck. I have yet to bounce my child upon my knee."

By now all three of his friends had trotted past Touch the Sky. Their hoofclops were echoing down the draw when Touch the Sky shouted overhead in clear English, "Seth Carlson! Before you kill me, I have a message from Kristen Steele!"

Fear of death sent the blood hammering into his

temples. But Touch the Sky sat his calico pony calmly, only squinting a bit to counter the brilliant light of the westering sun. And even through his fear, the anticipation of what he was about to do tempted a grin onto his grim features.

He deliberately waited, watching his friends ease closer to the jumble of scree beside the trail. He was sure he was right about Carlson's being back. Indeed, he could feel the man's surprised indecision, his morbid curiosity, his eagerness to kill his worst enemy in the world held in abeyance by his obsession with the beautiful Kristen Steele. The woman had shamed Carlson forever in his own eyes by preferring an Indian over him.

When Little Horse was almost abreast of the scree, an impatient shout came from above. "Speak your piece quick, Hanchon. The buzzards are gettin' hungry!"

Touch the Sky knew the order to fire was about to come. It was now or never. He must time his words just right.

"Yes, sir, Capt. Bluecoat, sir," he replied, his tone openly mocking. "She told me to tell you that any decent white woman would chose to mate with a Cheyenne dog before she'd kiss your filthy lips! Jump, bucks!" he added in Cheyenne.

Carlson had been expecting nothing like this. He was so hot and weak with unbelieving rage that he couldn't see through the red haze of his anger. That rage swelled his throat shut, and no order came out immediately, only an empty swallow. The momentary delay was costly to the soldiers. Below, the three Cheyennes in the lead suddenly slid to the ground and whacked their ponies on the rump, sending them into the scree.

At the same moment, Touch the Sky dug sharply at his pony's flanks, surging forward. Simultaneously, he slid forward and down, into the famous Cheyenne defensive riding posture. He clung low on the pony's neck, swinging much of his body behind the horse.

"Fire!" Carlson finally managed, his own Spencer kicking into his shoulder as he wildly jerked the trigger, anger making him waste the round.

The calico was trained to flee in zigzagging patterns at the sound of gunfire. Carlson had failed to direct his men's fire toward Hanchon. Since Hanchon was clearly dead meat, most of them instead took desperate shots at the braves who were disappearing into the rocks.

Touch the Sky clung on for dear life as his pony surged toward cover. Bullets thwacked into the ground all around him, but not as many as he'd feared. He could hear Carlson cursing at his men, redirecting their fire.

Then, his jaw dropping in astonishment, Touch the Sky saw Two Twists leap back out from the cover of the scree. With a shout of utter disdain, the young brave stood in the open and lifted his clout at the bluecoats—an Indian gesture of pure contempt which always infuriated hair-face soldiers. Ignoring their C.O., many took aim at the gutsy youth.

Then Touch the Sky reached the jumble of scree. Little Horse leapt out, grabbed Two Twists, and tugged him back to cover. Touch the Sky bounced to the ground, came up on his feet, and whacked his pony on the rump. Then the same momentum that let him succeed in his strategy finally threw him to a hard landing among the scree.

"Welcome, Cheyenne!" Little Horse greeted him. Pride clear in his tone, he added, "Did you see young Two Twists here? I will personally add another feather to his bonnet. That was the finest coup I have seen in many moons. Either he is courageous or soft brained!"

"Crazy or brave," Touch the Sky shouted above the whang of ricocheting bullets, "either one will do for a warrior!"

Despite the warriors' bravado, however, Touch the Sky knew they were truly up against it this time. Hours of daylight remained. The soldiers held the valuable high ground. The Cheyennes were pinned down, trapped, forced to fight the way they hated to.

They were well enough protected for the moment, but only if they hugged the scree tight and stayed out of sight. The least glimpse at one of them from above sent bullets hurtling into their position.

Seth Carlson! Touch the Sky tasted bitter bile at the thought of locking horns with his old enemy when time was of the essence and Honey Eater and many more lay dying. Black Elk and Wolf Who Hunts Smiling were obstacles enough for any man. Now his most deadly paleface enemy was tossed into the potlatch.

Now and then, without warning or pattern, the soldiers would unleash another volley from overhead. In a lull between volleys, Touch the Sky saw Little Horse frown. All of them lay hugging the ground. That was why Touch the Sky soon felt it too—the faint vibration of riders passing.

"Brothers!" Little Horse said, barely lifting his head to peer toward the east. "Black Elk and his band have been warned by the bluecoat rifles. There they go, bearing toward Fort Bates!"

This only increased Touch the Sky's desperation. For if allowed to carry out his reckless plan to take hostages, Black Elk would ruin any chance for a mercy appeal to the fort. The sick ones back at camp were surely doomed then.

"What do we do?" Tangle Hair said. "It is a standoff now. We cannot move, nor can the soldiers come down off the bluff without giving us clear shots at them on an uncovered slope. They could rush us, but many would die."

"They will not rush us," Touch the Sky said. "Such a foolish move would leave many widows and orphans back east of the Great Waters. No, they plan to wait. They have food enough for many sleeps. We have only what is in our sashes and parfleches."

Little Horse nodded. "As you say, they plan to wait. What do we plan to do, shaman?"

"The only thing left for us to do," Touch the Sky said glumly. "We wait until Sister Sun has gone to rest. The white skins will send men down. Let them. We are going to slip past them in the darkness."

As soon as the last glow of day bled from the western horizon, both the soldiers and the Cheyennes went into action. Fortunately for the Indians, it was a cloudy night with no moon or stars visible. Despite the soldiers' caution, Touch the Sky could hear their equipment noises as they deployed on foot down off the bluff. Moving quickly, the four Cheyennes dropped farther back into the scree and recruited their ponies. They muzzled them with their sashes, wrapped their hoofs in rawhide. The braves had darkened their own bodies by rubbing dirt into saliva to make a mud paste.

Prior to sunset, they had wrapped their eyes tight and remained in total darkness for a long time. This forced them to be especially vigilant with their ears to detect movement from above. But it also gave them excellent night vision once they unwrapped their eyes. Now they could make out shapes at distances they never could have managed normally.

Thus giving themselves a tiny advantage, they led their ponies step by agonizing step through the rocks. Now and then Touch the Sky made out the vague shape of a soldier who could not see him. It was a harrowing exodus, every breath capable of warning their enemy.

But Maiyun smiled on his red children that night. After what seemed a tense eternity, they had outflanked the baffled soldiers and even discovered their hidden rope corral. They stole a sturdy roan for Tangle Hair and resumed their desperate ride toward Fort Bates.

There could be little elation at thus eluding the soldiers because Black Elk's lead was daunting. Touch the Sky was desperate for any plan that might cut that lead. The possible solution presented itself when they broke over the crest of a ridge and spotted a well-lit camp below.

It was more bluecoats, a large work detail of log cutters. Several huge squad fires were burning, flames sawing in the wind and illuminating small groups of soldiers everywhere. A railroad spur track ended at the camp. Several flatbed cars were piled high with fresh-cut pine logs.

But something else caught and held Touch the Sky's eye: two mobile wagons, loaded with wires and equipment, which the army called a Flying Telegraph Train. These contained the equipment, including an electromagnetic generator, for the portable telegraph system known as the Beardslee Telegraph. Touch the Sky had learned of them during his last days among the whites when the machines were first introduced. The mobile unit could splice into any telegraph wire, and several passed through this area. But his companions knew none of this.

"Here is more trouble," Little Horse said. "We must circle wide around them. More time out of our way."

"Not at all," Touch the Sky said promptly. "These blue blouses are timely met. You three are going to rest here a moment with the ponies. I am riding down to counsel with their soldier chief."

"Brother," Tangle Hair said, "lately you make great sport of presenting yourself as a target for bluecoats."

"Truly," Little Horse said. "I thought you were keen to catch Black Elk's group before they ruin our mission?"

"Just so." Touch the Sky nodded down toward the Flying Telegraph, clearly outlined in the ample orange-yellow glow from camp. "Those are not freight wagons. The soldiers can use them to send words through the talking wire."

"This talking wire," Two Twists said dubiously. "I have heard the lines humming like spring bees. But surely such powerful magic is not real?"

"As real as that bullet Wolf Who Hunts Smiling sent through your arm, buck. With luck, the talking wire will stop Black Elk long before we could. Wait here, brothers, and only hope these soldiers follow a better leader than Seth Carlson."

Touch the Sky let his pony walk closer. The soldiers were too numerous—and too well armed—to fear attacks, so no sentries had been posted. When the brave was perhaps a double stone's throw away from the camp circle, he called out from the trees, "Hello, the camp! Friend approaching with a message. Permission to enter your camp?"

The talking and singing ceased; a banjo fell silent. A lieutenant stepped out of a wedge tent, his blouse unbuttoned.

"Civilian or soldier?" the officer called out.

After the slightest hesitation, Touch the Sky replied, "Soldier, sir."

"Advance and be recognized, trooper!"

Touch the Sky swallowed the nervous lump in his throat. He nudged the calico with his knees, speaking quietly in her ear to calm her at all these new sights and smells. They moved into the dim edge of the firelit circle, then farther and farther into the light.

Exclamations followed them like dominoes falling.

"Holy Saint Francis!"

"Well, I'll be go to hell!"

"Injuns!"

"Mebbe it's a trick and we're being attacked!"

"Hold your damn horses," Touch the Sky said. "You boys got the eyeballs God gave you? This is a truce flag, not a wiping patch. How many wild savages do you know who palaver English like I'm doing right now? I've got three comrades sitting back there behind me, tired and hungry. Even if you don't give a hoot in hell for our red asses, I'm asking for mercy in the name of our women and children."

"You men!" the lieutenant barked. "Stack those rifles before you shoot somebody, you damned fools! I don't know what this red son is up to. Even if he's trying to bamboozle some grub out of us, he's no hostile. A fool, maybe, but no hostile. Who's your message from?"

"It's not from anybody. It's going to Fort Bates. You need to send a telegram, sir. Right now a band of marauding Cheyennes are heading that way along the old Sioux Trace. They plan to take hostages from among the settlers, then force Fort Bates to cooperate."

"If that's straight goods, then they're fools. Col. Neusbaum is one hard case. He barely negotiates a point with Washington, let alone hostile Indians." The officer looked at Touch the Sky askance. "You're a Cheyenne too, aren't you?"

When Touch the Sky nodded, he said, "I've seen the Apaches sell out their own for tobacco and such. I thought Cheyennes were tighter than that."

"We are. It is not easy for even the most errant Cheyenne to lose his place with us, so reluctant are we to forsake our own. Even some murderers may live among us, though in shame forever. But one crime we will not forgive is treason against the People. Some of the men in this group are traitors who have killed their own merely to acquire power."

Quickly, Touch the Sky explained the emergency back at the Powder River camp. At the mention of mountain fever, the front ring of troopers crowded back away from this new arrival.

"Don't worry," Touch the Sky said. "I'll stay back. But if these Cheyenne traitors strike first, I lose all chance for any help from the fort. You could not only warn the fort about this attack. You could also tell them that I helped you and that I'm on the way for help myself."

The young officer looked unsure. "The thing of it is, I got no kick if you're telling the straight. But I ain't putting paid to any deal before I got a little more information. How come your English is so good? You didn't learn that English at a reservation school."

"No, my name was once Matthew Hanchon. I grew up in Big Horn Falls."

"Hanchon? John Hanchon's adopted boy?"

When Touch the Sky nodded, somebody spoke up from the circle of gawking soldiers. "By Godfrey! It is Matthew Hanchon!"

A sergeant with ample folds of belly drooping over his blue kersey trousers stepped into the light. "Good God, you've put on some growth, tadpole! Collected you some fine battle scars too, I see. You recollect my ugly face? Use to was, I'd buy you a licorice stick from the sutler every time

90

you brought a load out to the fort from your folks' store."

"Tosh Blackford!" Touch the Sky said promptly. "You used to make plenty of money getting the troopers to bet on fights between red and black ants."

"Hell, he still robs us that way, the damn piker!" a trooper groused.

"Shut your gob, Peyton," Blackford said affably. He turned to the officer. "Lt. Westphal, I'll vouch for this lad, Injun or no. He's straight grain, clear through."

"Good enough for me, Sergeant. I was convinced when I found out he's John Hanchon's boy. If there's a better man in Bighorn Falls, I've yet to meet him. Trooper Crawford!"

"Sir!"

"Put that scouse down. You can feed your face later. Right now, go fire that Beardslee up."

"Yes, sir!"

Lt. Westphal looked at Touch the Sky. "I know Indians don't like saying their names in front of palefaces, so I'll just call you Matthew. Quick, now, tell me more about the Indians ahead of you."

# Chapter Eight

"There it is, Panther Clan," Wolf Who Hunts Smiling said to Black Elk. "One of those paleface lodges below is where Woman Face grew up wearing shoes."

"I have been here," Swift Canoe boasted. "I spied on White Man Runs Him when he played the fox alongside his white-skin soldier brothers. If River of Winds had not stopped me, I would have sent him across."

"Many would have done so," Black Elk scoffed. "You two have failed. Remember this. I alone have not yet closed for the kill against him. We two have locked horns, yes, but always the thought of the arrows held us back. Now it no longer matters. For he has the arrows, and thus they are no longer clean. And when I do close to kill him, there will be no would about it. It will be done and soon."

"I already know you as a war leader, cousin," Wolf Who Hunts Smiling said. "Now I know you as a speaker too. I have placed your words in my sash for they have weight and importance."

While he said this, the younger brave held his face impassive and gazed with the others down from the rimrock at the moonlit river valley. But inside he smiled in elation at Black Elk's deeply bitter tone. The insidious worm of jealousy had burrowed deep into Black Elk's heart, poisoning it, turning him from a hard but fair warrior into one obsessed by a murderous rage against Touch the Sky—and perhaps Honey Eater too. Wolf Who Hunts Smiling had worked tirelessly, often secretly, to nurture that evil, gnawing worm inside Black Elk.

Black Elk had to be ruined, for he was loyal to Chief Gray Thunder and too strong to be ignored. In his own way, he was nearly as dangerous to Wolf Who Hunts Smiling's ambition as was Touch the Sky himself. Both would die a hard death. With the Comanche Big Tree and the Blackfoot Sis-ki-dee joining their renegade bands with him, no fort would stop them. Then the lush green grass of the plains would be awash in paleface blood when the war to exterminate them began.

Black Elk had lost some of his lusty vigor as a leader; he had become an intense brooder as his hatred deepened. Like the cowardly women he often berated, he had lately begun to express his hatred more in words against his enemy.

"Had we time enough," he said, "I would learn which lodge was his and steal the white fools who raised him. After they had served as hostages, I would kill them anyway. We owe it to them. In keeping Woman Face alive, they dealt death to our tribe.

"However, with luck Woman Face is worm fodder by now. Those blue blouses had him pinned like a snake under a wheel. As for us, we must settle for the first white skins who are for the taking."

"Indeed," Swift Canoe said, "any will do. Once the long knives know Indians have seized even one of their dogs, they will go to Wendigo in their wrath."

"You speak straight arrow," Stone Mountain said. His flat buffalo-hide saddle creaked when the huge Indian shifted to look at the others. "Whites do not suffer such treatment lightly."

Black Elk's face twisted in rage and contempt. He stared at both the speakers. "What? Would these two quivering maidens rather be gathering onions and nuts with the women? This is a warrior's mission, bucks."

"I have never picked onions," Swift Canoe said resentfully.

"Nor I," Stone Mountain said. "True it is, I once helped the women stretch meat onto the drying racks, but—"

"You tangle-brained fools!" Wolf Who Hunts

Smiling said. "A rabbit could not find a full brain between you."

"Leave it alone, cousin," Black Elk said with disgust. "You are right, but why lecture rabbits?"

But something had caught Black Elk's sharp eyes even as he spoke. His wary attention alerted the others. He pointed to a narrow defile in a ridge to the east. A squad of soldiers debouched, racing toward the Cheyenne position. The cloud cover had blown off recently, and they were clear enough in the silver-white moonwash.

"And look there!" Swift Canoe added, pointing to the cluster of frame buildings comprising Bighorn Falls. Suddenly the main street swarmed with shadows—no doubt more mounted soldiers.

"They have somehow been warned of our arrival!" Black Elk said. "We have lost the advantage of surprise. And now we must lose more time shaking these gnats."

Already the first carbines were spitting orange licks of flame. Black Elk yanked his pony around.

"Now we must rely on the second plan we discussed. We will split up and lose them out on the plains. Do not waste ammunition firing upon them. Just outride them. Then we will recruit at the white-skin wagon road. Soon it will be light and traffic will be heavy there. Warning or no, we will seize hostages and force the blue blouses to give us their powerful medicine."

\* \* \*

"I'm damned if I know how they got away, sir," Sgt. Nolan Reece apologized. "But they're gone for a fact. We've turned over every rock in that scree. Hanchon and the rest of them red Arabs slipped off slicker'n grease through a goose."

"You still so all fire sure it's a bird's nest on the ground?" Carlson demanded. "Damn it all, soldier, we've been here hours with our thumbs up our sitters, and who knows how long they've been riding."

"Well, you said he was a slippery bastard," Reece said lamely. " 'Pears to me you was right. Him and every buck with him."

"Sir!" a corporal called out, snapping off a salute as he rushed up to Carlson. "The men are standing by their mounts as you ordered. But McQuady's horse is gone. Them Cheyennes must've boosted it!"

Carlson cursed again. He turned back to Reece.

"We can't let Hanchon get to the fort. Col. Neusbaum is no Indian lover. But he's a rule-book commander. And the rule-book says a request for humanitarian aid should be honored if possible, even when it's from savages. Once Neusbaum knows about the epidemic, we can't touch Hanchon or his bunch."

"So what's the plan, sir?"

"Sweat and guts, man! Their horses are tired. Ours are fresh and strong from grain and good graze. We'll push our mounts hard and try to catch them. If we can, I swear they won't shake us again."

Despite the unexpected friendly reception at the bluecoat work camp, Touch the Sky knew they still had a long, dangerous ride to Fort Bates. Desperation had settled deep into his features. Already nearly two sleeps had passed. Delays had cut the already dangerous margin even shorter. Honey Eater might already be dead and the rest past all help. Lt. Westphal's telegram would indeed help. At least the fort knew why the braves were coming. With incredible luck, with unquestioning cooperation from the soldiers, there might still be time.

But one more serious delay, and the Powder River camp could be beyond all help. With Honey Eater's death, he would lose his main reason for all this suffering and fighting to survive.

That meant he could make no careless assumptions—especially the assumption that the warning telegram guaranteed Black Elk's band would be removed as a threat. And Carlson was out there somewhere too, meaner than the white man's Satan with a sunburn.

So as they followed the old Sioux Trace south toward the fort, he relied on a scouting trick once the morning sun was up. Despite the additional loss of time, he halted his band several times to hastily climb a tall tree. From there, he kept a wary eye on both their backtrail and the road ahead. Thus it was that he spotted double danger approaching them like the tongs of a deadly pincers closing.

"Brothers," he called down, "trouble on the hoof, and enough for all!"

Ahead, toward the fort, he could see a clear stretch of the freight road. A stagecoach rocked and bounced, making its way south toward Bighorn Falls. The passengers' carpetbags and portmanteaus bulged out from under the leather boot. The four-horse team strained against their tug chains, fighting a long slope. And hidden in a cutbank at the top of the slope was Black Elk's band!

As if that weren't enough trouble, more bad news approached from behind them. Seth Carlson's platoon raced along a second trail in sets of four, their swallow-tail unit guidon snapping in the breeze.

Touch the Sky needed no shamanic eye to see that Black Elk intended to seize the passengers as hostages. He glanced again at his Cheyenne enemies. Then he shifted on the tree limb to once more study his white enemy.

They couldn't have spotted each other yet. Touch the Sky estimated how fast the soldiers were approaching. Then he guessed how much time remained before the stagecoach reached that cutbank. And all at once, despite seeming hopelessness, a grin split his face.

"Little Horse," he called down, "are you as crazy as you boast?"

"None crazier. Test my fettle, buck!"

"Then I shall. We are about to offer ourselves as free targets to the bluecoats!"

Rapidly, Touch the Sky climbed down. He explained the situation to his comrades. "Brothers," he concluded, "there is no time to keep fighting these running battles. "Let us see if we can lure one enemy onto another."

The trail Carlson's unit currently rode would take them wide of Black Elk and the stagecoach. Touch the Sky's band quickly mounted and rode straight into the teeth of Carlson's advance.

When he was sure they'd been spotted, Touch the Sky doubled back toward the freight road, which wound to the southwest of Carlson's current position. He looked back over his shoulder and watched both columns veer in his direction.

"They have taken the bait!" Little Horse gloated. "Now we will give them a merry chase, brothers!"

Despite these bold words, however, Touch the Sky knew the chase would be anything but merry. Their Indian ponies were the pluckiest on the plains. But they had been ridden hard lately and had rested little, they were nearly exhausted from covering too much ground in too little time. The big cavalry horses, in contrast, were strong and sleek, well grazed and rested.

Several more razorback ridges had to be crossed before the soldiers would be able to spot the stagecoach and the drama unfolding on the freight road. In the meantime, Carlson's veteran

Indian Killers were closing the gap. At first the pursuers' rifle shots had sounded like the insignificant popping of chokecherries. The rifle cracks grew louder, and the fleeing Cheyennes heard bullets fly past their ears with angry-hornet sounds.

"Hi-ya!" Little Horse shouted, thoroughly enjoying this sport. "All they can do is kill us, brothers! Fall on enemy bones!" He raised his streamered lance and shook it at the hair-face soldiers. "Hiii-ya!"

Touch the Sky felt the game little calico's muscles straining beneath him. Now and then wet foam blew back onto him as she started to lather from the pace.

The next time he glanced back, he spotted Seth Carlson's determined face under the turned-up brim of his officer's hat. The soldier's eyes stabbed back, sheening with livid hatred. He was focused on the Cheyenne buck like a bobcat on its prey.

A bullet whanged past Touch the Sky's ear, chipping bark off a nearby cottonwood. The calico was blowing harder, starting to slow noticeably. Once she nearly stumbled.

The cavalry thundered so close that Touch the Sky could see divots of ground being ripped loose by their horses' iron-shod hoofs. Now, Touch the Sky knew, came the most delicate part of this maneuver. It would be a tricky combination of feinting and timing.

When the braves topped the last ridge, Touch the Sky spotted the stagecoach again. It was perhaps a double stone's throw from the cutbank where Black Elk's band were hidden, waiting to pounce. Touch the Sky hoped to expose the attack after it was under way, but before the driver or shotgun were killed.

He watched the stage roll closer and heard the thunder gathering behind his band as the troopers pressed on. The air was deadly with bullets, and the Cheyennes were riding in their low-and-forward defensive postures.

However, Touch the Sky's timing was perfect. Black Elk's band shot forth from the cutbank, yipping, even as Carlson crested the ridge and spotted this new trouble.

For a moment Touch the Sky again met his white enemy's eyes. He read the agony of indecision there. Clearly Carlson longed, with all his heart, to continue dogging his enemy until he had finally killed him. But just as clearly, even an officer as corrupt as he could not forsake such an obvious duty. How would he explain, if anyone on the stagecoach survived, why he had let renegades attack innocent civilians?

Even from there, Touch the Sky could read the curse on Seth Carlson's lips. Mocking him with his eyes, Touch the Sky led his band off toward the southwest.

Carlson and his troops continued on toward the freight road. The bugler blasted out *Boots and Saddles* to hearten the victims and frighten the attackers. While one enemy thus routed the other,

Touch the Sky and his loyal comrades raced toward Fort Bates.

But despite this elating victory over two enemies, Touch the Sky did not feel like reciting coups. After all, telegram or no, they were still approaching the soldier house of enemies. Nor could he stop seeing the image of Honey Eater's fever-drawn face and wondering over and over if he would ever see her alive again.

# Chapter Nine

No one at Fort Bates had yet learned about the aborted Indian attack on the stagecoach bound for Laramie. Seth Carlson's platoon was officially listed in the company roster as on extended maneuvers. He was not expected back at Fort Bates until rations ran low. Unwilling to forego one more chance at killing Hanchon, Carlson did not want to report his action and risk being detained in garrison. He ordered his men into a bivouac near Beaver Creek.

Meantime, Fort Bates remained in a state of high alert. A telegram from Lt. Westphal had warned of an attack on the settlement of Bighorn Falls by desperate Cheyenne renegades. Two rifle companies had been dispatched to patrol the valley. So far, neither had returned.

The morning was still young when Pvt. Colin Padgett and Pvt. Hoby Cunninghan reported for four hours of guard duty at the main gate of Fort Bates. This was one of the last walled forts on the frontier, an enclosure of spiked cottonwood logs with gun towers at each corner.

The huge, iron-reinforced front gate was always kept open since serious threats from Indians had been eliminated in this sector. Padgett and Cunningham stood just outside the open gate, their carbines at sling arms.

"Lord, this dust does get thick on a man's tongue," Padgett said, winking at his comrade. He uncapped his bull's-eye canteen and took a hasty swig from it.

Even from six feet away, Cunningham could smell the strong odor of cheap 40-rod.

"Ahh, rock me to sleep, mother," Padgett said, smacking his lips in appreciation. He glanced back over his shoulder toward the company office, then passed the canteen to Cunningham.

Duty on the frontier was deadly boring—long hours and days and weeks of monotony punctuated by sudden violence. Things were so bad that one-third of all new recruits took French leave, as deserting was called. Those who stuck it out often fell victim to Old Knockumstiff, which the wily Fort Sutler always had ready to hand.

The corporal of the guard had informed both sentries of the special orders concerning a renegade band of Cheyenne loose in the territory.

Somehow, though, the news about a second Cheyenne band approaching the fort for assistance had never reached the guards. So Padgett's voice tightened an octave with nervousness when he suddenly said, "Damn my eyes! Look out there!"

He pushed himself away from the wall he'd been resting against and unslung his carbine. He pointed out across the vast and rolling scrubland.

Cunningham squinted. "I can't tell a Cheyenne from the Queen of England. But them's Injuns, and four of 'em, just like we was warned."

"They're Cheyennes," Padgett said when the band had moved even closer, dust puffs rising behind their horses. "Those are black feathers in their bonnets. Crow feathers. Sioux wear white feathers."

A moment later, squinting against the distance, Padgett added a long whistle. "Damn, boys! One of 'em's riding a cavalry hoss! They've killed at least one trooper!"

Padgett had gone on some scouting details, but neither private had yet faced combat. The army of that day figured it was cheaper to replace a man than to train him. Consequently, neither trooper had ever actually fired the new seven-shot Spencer carbines they'd been issued.

"The crazy red bastards just keep a'comin!" Cunningham explained. "They can't be soft brained enough to attack a fort, can they?"

"The hell they can't! It's a suicide mission!"

Padgett said. "That white rag don't mean jack. Shut the gate!"

The tower guards had spotted the riders racing toward the post too. Cunningham and Padgett quickly unlooped the ropes holding the gate open and swung it closed, dropping the huge wooden bar. The gate was loopholed to allow for defensive fire.

"We're being attacked!" Padgett shouted toward a knot of soldiers just then emerging from the messhall. "On the line, we're being attacked!"

The soldiers scrambled, racing toward the armory, where the enlisted men kept their weapons when not in the field or on guard duty. A moment later, the first shots rang out from the gun towers.

As his band approached Fort Bates, Touch the Sky had not been unduly alarmed. Even from far back, he could see that the gate stood open as usual, and no soldiers were patrolling outside.

Indeed, it was difficult to focus his attention on the fort. Returning to the river valley where he had been raised had planted a sharp spike of nostalgia inside his breast. If only things were different, he could have visited his white parents on their mustang spread. And though Kristen Steele was long gone, this was where he had met and fallen in love with her. Lost is such reflections, and mired in worry for Honey Eater, he didn't realize the new danger until Tangle Hair's shout roused him.

# Death Camp

"Brothers! They are closing the soldier town against us!"

Only then did the tall brave see the gate swinging shut. He should have halted his band, he thought. But halt them to do what? Waste more time they couldn't afford to waste? A white flag flew from his lance, clear for all to see. Lt. Westphal had telegraphed ahead. There was nothing else for it. They must gain the fort and get help or die trying.

Touch the Sky didn't see the first muzzle puffs as the tower guards commenced firing. But he was fully aware when a bullet ripped through the truce flag, leaving a hole dead center. Plumes of dirt shot up all around them as the tower sentries opened up in earnest.

The Cheyenne ponies began their defensive zigzagging, making it difficult for the enemy to lead their targets when aiming. But Touch the Sky realized it was already too late to turn back. Yet each step hurled them closer to death and the end of all hope for Honey Eater and the tribe.

Capt. Tom Riley was one of the first soldiers to hear the shouts and shooting from the south wall. He had just finished the morning formation of his company. Now he was seated in the officers' mess over a plate of sourdough biscuits and side meat when the racket broke out.

Riley had only recently been posted back to Fort Bates after a long stint of duty down south on the

Llano Estacado, or Staked Plain, Comanche country. He had served here early in his career as a mustang lieutenant promoted by brevet from the enlisted ranks. In recognition of superior service and courage in battle, his brevet rank had become permanent.

As he raced toward the gate, unsnapping the holster of his cavalry .44, suspicion bothered him. Riley knew what Lt. Westphal's telegram had said about the renegade Cheyenne Indians. But never did he suspect which Cheyenne was among those approaching the fort until he peeked out the Judas hole in the gate.

"You idiots!" he snapped at Padgett and Cunningham. "I know you two are fresh fish when it comes to combat. But don't you know the rules of engagement? Never fire on a truce flag!"

"Sir, we got orders."

"Trooper, you're out of line! You have new orders now. Open that damn gate or I'll have you doing barrel drill all night!"

His face red with anger, Riley turned toward the two south-facing towers. "Cease fire! Cease fire, you hayseed halfwits! Those are friendlies!"

Padgett didn't look too happy, but he threw the gate open again and then backed off with his weapon raised.

"Lower that piece, trooper!" Riley snapped. "Don't point a weapon at a man unless you mean for sure to kill him. Besides, I can see from here you haven't got a round in the chamber. Did you trade your ammo for rotgut whiskey again from that thieving sutler?"

Padgett noticed his empty chamber and blushed pink clear to his earlobes. "Hell, I had me a bullet in there, sir," he muttered sheepishly.

But Riley waved him off with a disgusted shake of his head. He turned around and ordered the men now assuming battle positions to stand down and secure their weapons.

The Indians pressed onward, if anything deliberately increasing their speed in defiance as they neared the fort. Dust boiled up behind their ponies, and the nearly exhausted animals blew foam. Then they flew through the wide gate at a dead run, scattering slow and surprised soldiers like driftwood in a flood. Then the ponies stopped as if on cue, in half the distance a cavalry horse would have needed.

Touch the Sky's face showed nothing as he surveyed the ring of gawping soldiers. Then his eyes met Riley's, and in spite of his warrior training, a glad smile divided his face.

"Tom Riley!"

"Mrs. Riley's best-looking boy at your service."

Riley deliberately avoided saying Touch the Sky's Cheyenne name, knowing Indians believed their names lost their medicine when heard by white ears. "I heard about Westphal's telegram. So your tribe's up against it?"

Touch the Sky nodded grimly. "You've heard enough, I see. Good, because there's no more time for talk. It may already be too late."

Riley nodded. "C'mon. I'll take you to Col. Neusbaum right now. I'll warn you. He's a better man than some the Army is sending out here to command forts. But he sure's hell ain't no friend of the red man."

When Tom Riley finished hastily explaining the situation, Col. William Neusbaum nodded with a distracted air. He looked across his wide, immaculate desk at the dirty and wild-looking Indian standing in front of him. Old blood stained the fringes of Touch the Sky's leggings, and a violent history was told in the many knife and burn scars covering his chest and back. So far the Cheyenne had said nothing, respectfully holding back despite a desperate urgency clear in his eyes.

"You say he speaks some English?" Neusbaum said doubtfully to Riley.

"Yes, sir." Riley added tactfully, "I'm sure you could talk right to him, sir, instead of through me. It would save time."

Neusbaum grunted at this response. He was in his early fifties, a heavy-jowled man with thick silver hair plastered back by pomade. He spoke with exaggerated enunciation, slowly and raising his voice as if to an imbecile. "Pleased to meet you." After a moment's hesitation, he offered his hand across the desk.

"Uhh, sir," Riley said, "Indians don't shake—"

"Oh, hell," Touch the Sky said, taking the colonel's hand in a powerful grip, "there's no time for all that, Tom! Colonel, it's a very sincere pleasure to make your acquaintance. My chief, Gray Thunder, sends his respect. He thanks you straight from his heart for doing a far better job than the other eagle chiefs sent here before you. He told me you are the first to enforce the treaty that keeps white miners off our land without our permission."

At this clearly spoken English, Col. Neusbaum stared as if a dog had just sung "The Homespun Dress." The surprise turned to a brief smile at the compliment. "Well, you tell Gray Thunder we've had no trouble from his band. I appreciate that. This business with your people, it's very unfortunate. But there's a problem. The U.S. Army does not have its own medical corps or doctors out here. We contract with civilian surgeons. I can't order a contract surgeon to do anything that's not in his contract. And the contracts say nothing about helping savage—uh—I mean, Indians."

"Sir," Riley said, his tone more urgent, "are you sure we couldn't put a little more priority on this. Maybe we could arrange something with Dr. Ladislaw?"

Neusbaum's eyebrows shot up in annoyed surprise at Riley's peremptory tone. Riley was not one to gainsay his superiors. But Neusbaum decided to let his irritation pass. Riley was the best officer on his staff, and good officers should be humored now and then. And this Cheyenne smelled bad, but he was likable enough.

"At ease, Captain. I've sent for Ladislaw. We'll see what he says."

Even as he finished speaking, several quick knocks made all three heads turn toward the open office door. A civilian wearing a faded leather weskit stepped into the room. Dr. Hinton Ladislaw was about ten years younger than Neusbaum, a balding man with timid eyes and a string-bean build. He shrank back, startled, at sight of the tall Cheyenne. Clearly he was a greenhorn around Indians and wished to remain that way.

Quickly, Col. Neusbaum explained the situation. "How 'bout it, Hinton?" Neusbaum said when he'd finished. "You willing to take some medicine and go back to their camp with it?"

Ladislaw's jaw suddenly dropped. "Go to an Indian camp?"

When the Colonel nodded, Ladislaw shook his head like a man who didn't like the look of a horse's teeth. " 'Fraid not, Bill. I didn't take this job so I could get separated from my topknot or what's left of it, anyhow. I don't know much about Indians, but I've heard they kill a medicine man if he fails. You say it's been several days now since the fever hit. There's a damn good chance it's already too late. I'm not too eager to put my bacon in the fire for a lost cause."

Riley was about to object. But Touch the Sky,

his face and voice fighting back the frustration, beat him to it.

"Dr. Ladislaw, listen to me. I promise on my life that no one will hurt you, no matter what happens. I and my friends waiting outside will see to that. Sir, you're a doctor. You took an oath, and nothing in that oath said that Indians don't count. I know that my people and your people have often raised our battle-axes against each other. But we Cheyennes never take the fight to your women and children or let any whites die of disease if we can help.

"This last winter was hard. My tribe was short of meat and firewood. But when a white-skin wagon train foolishly set out from the settlements too late, getting caught in the mountains all winter, we kept the people alive until the spring melt. We were not happy about it; many of us grumbled. But we did it."

Ladislaw had heard about this from the survivors. The heartfelt appeal clearly touched him.

"Aw, won'tcha, Hinton?" Riley said. "I'll give you that little sorrel mare you're so sweet over."

Hinton looked at Neusbaum. The colonel was getting caught up in the appeal too as he listened to this young Indian who mingled manly respect with a sense of his own authority.

"Hell," he said, "if you go, Hinton, I'll put through a generous per diem for you and hazardous duty pay on top of that."

Still Ladislaw debated, trying to overcome years

of sedentary and safe routine. Finally he sighed a long, fluming sigh and nodded his head.

"I still fear it's too late," he told them. "Lord, I hope not, but mountain fever does its work quick. Quicker'n scat. If you get the medicine too late, you're gone beaver. But this young buck is right, I took an oath. If I say no, like I sure's hell want to, I guess I won't rightly get any sleep tonight nor deserve it. Saddle that mare, young Thomas. I'll go get my bag"

# Chapter Ten

At first Honey Eater felt a terrible, unrelenting heat and a thirst so powerful it ached through her entire body. But then, gradually, like pain easing away under a soothing poultice, Honey Eater lost herself in the dream.

She was waiting alone in a secret, fragrant bower of willows well hidden from camp. The wind was a gentle kiss on her face; it blew tendrils of her long black hair back across her temples like soft wing tips. She wore her new blue calico dress. She had just bathed in the nearby river, and the soft dress clung to her like a second skin. It traced the dimpled swells of her nipples, the long, sweeping dip of her hips.

At first she was all alone and softly crying. But then, with the sudden and unexplained reality of dreams, Touch the Sky was beside her. His muscles felt hard, but his hold on her was gentle. She felt his lips tracing a hot, needful line from her lips, down her neck, into the front of her open dress. Then she felt an incredible, warm, wet pleasure ease over her nipples as he slid first one, then the other, into his eager mouth.

But then something was wrong. Just as something was always wrong for her and Touch the Sky. Before the horrible fever squeezed her in its death grip yet again, she realized this was no dream, but a real memory. They had met that way once before and held each other after she boldly declared to him that she considered herself his wife and would lie with him if he sent for her.

But as always when they stole time together, danger had reared its familiar head before their bodies could find the blissful release each sought in the other. Black Elk was coming along the bank, looking for her!

There was no bliss—only this burning hurt, even worse than the tortures of the blazing Staked Plain, where she had been the prisoner of Comanches and Kiowas. And the voice, gentle and sad, at the back of her awareness. The voice of her mother, Singing Woman, who was cut down by Pawnees before Honey Eater's eyes.

"You must remember to sing your death song soon, little daughter, or you will never cross over in peace."

# Death Camp

*    *    *

Sharp Nosed Woman had not felt so sad inside her chest since the terrible attack that killed her brave Smiles Plenty. Looking at Honey Eater, seeing that momentary smile suddenly twisted in a paroxysm of fever pain, made her realize it was too late. The beautiful daughter of the proud Chief Yellow Bear was about to join her father and mother in the Land of Ghosts.

It was too late, too, too late. Neither Touch the Sky nor Black Elk had been able to defeat this grim champion of death, this warrior called mountain fever who needs no bullets to kill. Both Honey Eater and her little niece Laughing Brook had broken out in the faint rash, both had begun the final, desperate panting. It was this terrible dehydration that would kill them. If given water, they would lose twice as much from violent vomiting. All Sharp Nosed Woman could do was bathe them with cool cloths.

"Two pretty little flowers," she whispered, looking at the withered columbine petals in their hair.

Behind her, a baby cried piteously, a steady, hopeless puling. It was so terribly sad that even some brave warriors had tears in their eyes as they stopped and joined the chant groups outside the pest lodge. Night and day, without pause, these groups sang the ancient cure songs given to the people by Maiyun and the high holy ones.

For a moment Sharp Nosed Woman crossed to the entrance and glanced across the camp clearing. Her tired brow wrinkled with weary, disgusted anger as she glanced at Medicine Flute's tipi. The sly young brave, and his champion Wolf Who Hunts Smiling, made much of his shamanic powers and his supposed loyalty to his tribe. Yet the skinny, lazy, cowardly little weasel sat well away from the danger, blowing on that stupid bone flute. He claimed he was curing the sick ones, and he had made it clear that, if the cure failed, it was only because of the white man's stink clinging to Touch the Sky.

Medicine Flute was clever, she thought. His pronouncements were always such that he could claim credit when magic worked and blame Touch the Sky when it failed. But her anger was short-lived. It cost too much effort. And all this death and dying had made her far too weary for any needless effort.

She glanced back at Honey Eater, at the girl lying next to her. Best to sew their new moccasins, she told herself, so they'll be ready for their final journey.

"Are you surprised, cousin?" Wolf Who Hunts Smiling said bitterly. "These white skins are his old childhood friends. He drinks strong water with them, hides messages in trees for them, and in many other ways plays their dog. Can we truly be surprised that they would help the one called White Man Runs Him?"

The two braves and Swift Canoe sat their ponies

in the lee of a sandstone butte overlooking Fort Bates. Stone Mountain had been killed in the skirmish with the soldiers. Below, they watched Touch the Sky and his companions ride out on fresh, strong cavalry mounts. The paleface with them, who looked as if he had already been scalped once, must be the white-skin medicine man.

"There is nothing else for it now," Black Elk said grimly. His black eyes burned with murderous rage. "I do not care that there are only three of us now. With ammunition, I would attack them alone. But we are out of bullets, down to only a few arrows thanks to those bluecoats Woman Face led to us. We cannot mount another strike now."

"No," Wolf Who Hunts Smiling said, "not a full strike. But we can still make their life a hurting place."

Black Elk nodded. Exhaustion and determination combined to make him look as fierce as Wolf Who Hunts Smiling had ever seen him. He scowled so often that deep frown lines were etched into the cured leather of his face. Thick alkali dust coated his braid, his detached ear hung like a door falling off a white-skin lodge.

"Nothing of can," he told his cousin. "We will make their life a hurting place. I have been humiliated enough by Woman Face. I will not let him return with that white skin and his medicine."

This threat secretly thrilled Wolf Who Hunts Smiling. Black Elk's hatred for Touch the Sky, like his own, had finally grown so all consuming that he would even let fellow Cheyennes die rather than allow that tall, pretend Cheyenne to best him!

"I have ears for this, Black Elk! What about me? Do you know what it has been like for me, stripped of my coup feathers by an act of the headmen? White Man Runs Him cost me the right to show others my battle record! Our Sioux cousins visit and sneer at me when they see I have not once counted coup. I, whose coup feathers nearly reached the ground like yours."

"As you say, cousin. We will not let him humiliate us again!"

Swift Canoe had been listening to this with a puzzled frown. "Brothers," he said slowly, "I hate him as do both of you. He killed my only brother with his cowardly treachery! But is this thing right, this letting our people die so that—"

"I have no ears for this womanly softness," Wolf Who Hunts Smiling snapped. "He who would be a leader of men cannot shirk back from hard duty."

He looked at his older cousin and held his eye, steadying Black Elk's resolve. "As you say, war leader, we cannot stop Woman Face and his companions. But we can kill that skinny, hairless white man. Without him, his medicine is useless."

"You say Ladislaw is with them?" Seth Carlson demanded.

"Yes, sir," the scout named MacGruder said. "Old Quinine himself. I saw his bony ass bumping up and down on that little mare Capt. Riley refused to sell you."

"Riley!" Carlson spat the word out with disgust, as if it tasted bitter on his tongue. "I should've know that Indian-loving bastard would mix in this. Prob'ly used his influence with the old man. That hick rail splitter hasn't even been to West Point, and Col. Neusbaum thinks he's a top hand."

MacGruder wisely held his counsel. Like most of the enlisted men, he knew that no officer at the fort would ever call Tom Riley a bastard to his face. Nor would any enlisted man call him that behind his back. Riley had been appointed from the ranks; he was not an elitist and a petty martinet like Carlson. Also unlike Carlson, Riley never touched a bite of food until he knew all of his men were eating. In the same spirit of warrior camaraderie, he never issued any order he wouldn't be willing to follow himself. As a result, his men would follow him into hell carrying empty carbines.

Hanchon's brazen move in forcing Carlson to halt the attack on the stagecoach had left the officer dangerously quiet. When he swore at his men and roweled his horse and threw his hat to the ground, he was mad. But when he clammed up as he was doing now, the men stood by for one hell of a blast. In one of these tempers, he had suddenly gone insane and beaten a stubborn pack mule to death with a trace chain.

For a long time Carlson squatted beside Beaver Creek, brooding. His company was bivouacked along the grassy bank. Shelter halves and dog tents were grouped by squads, carbines stood upright in groups of five at stack arms. The men were enjoying this duty. They had a tacit understanding with their commander. They kept their mouths shut while he broke every regulation in the operations manual; they, in turn, were permitted to slack off whenever possible. While Carlson steamed and fretted, they had thrown trotlines across the creek. Now the smell of fresh trout and bass frying filled the camp.

"All right," he finally said, making up his mind, "they've got to pass Lookout Bluff again on their way back to the Powder country, right?"

MacGruder nodded. "If they're in a hurry like you say, sir. They could cross farther upriver on the Shoshone, but that adds a half day's travel."

"No danger there. They'll ford at Crying Horse Bend."

Carlson paused, remembering a Blackfoot hunting party he had once obliterated in the Bear Paw Mountains with special weapons. It was true that Gatlings and such were virtually useless if Indians knew you had them. The Indians weren't fool enough to obligingly ride in front of the guns for you. But if they were caught by surprise, the dying would be over faster than a hungry man could gobble a biscuit.

"The new spur line from the fort is finished," he told the scout. "We're authorized for special munitions for these field maneuvers. The recruits haven't had their familiarization fire yet. I'm going to give you a requisition for the armory. Then I want you to oversee the loading."

"Of what, sir?"

Carlson smiled and stood up, swiping at some dust on his blue kersey trousers. He stretched his stiff back until it popped.

"Gatlings and Parrot artillery rifles," he finally replied. "This time we're going to blow those flea-bitten blanket asses off the face of the earth."

Tom Riley had a scout out too. But the man wasn't keeping track of the Indians. He was watching Seth Carlson's movements. Touch the Sky had warned Riley of the attack at Lookout Bluff. And since Carlson hadn't returned from maneuvers yet, it was a cinch bet he had more grief in store for Touch the Sky.

Despite his decision to help, Col. Neusbaum had drawn the line when Riley asked if a detachment could be sent with Ladislaw and the Indians. The most recent treaty signed at Fort Laramie strictly forbade him from risking his men in a potentially hostile movement without higher authorization. There was no time for that anyway, Riley knew.

As he turned the haggard-looking Indian ponies over to the private in charge of the graze guard, he made up his mind. "Thompson, graze these ponies with the rest and make sure they get a double ration of grain tonight. But before you do that, ride up to the stables and search out Cpl. Moats. Tell him to pick ten of his best sharpshooters and draw a few days' field rations. Then he's to stand by at the stables until I get there."

"Yes, sir!" The private saluted and turned, running toward his mount picketed nearby.

"Trooper!"

Thompson stopped and turned back around. "Sir!"

"Tell Cpl. Moats each man is to clean his weapon well and have thirty cartridges crimped and ready."

# Chapter Eleven

By now Touch the Sky and his Cheyenne companions had been pushing themselves on sheer will alone. They had not slept since they'd left their Powder River camp, nor had they eaten anything more substantial than the pemmican in their legging sashes. They had not wasted even enough time to shoot and cook a few rabbits.

Their exhaustion showed in a certain dull glaze over their eyes. Like their enemy Wolf Who Hunts Smiling, their eyes shifted constantly on the alert for the ever expected attack. They rode in a four-point diamond formation—Touch the Sky at the fore, Little Horse to the rear, Tangle Hair and Two Twists riding the flanks. Ladislaw rode in the middle, as protected as a man could be when death lurked everywhere like a dry-gulcher.

It had not taken Ladislaw long to realize exactly how dangerous this mission really was. He knew those braves weren't protecting him out of courtesy. He had learned enough to know that he was caught up in some barbaric tribal power struggle. Time and again, despite the warm sun, he shivered inwardly as he pictured the two Indian factions dividing him in half like King Solomon axing that child in two.

Ladislaw had already made himself useful by disinfecting and bandaging Two Twists' wound. Now the contract surgeon chucked up his horse and moved up beside the tall Cheyenne leader.

"No need to give me the evil eye," Ladislaw groused, partly as a cover for his jitters. "I'll go back to my spot. Just want to suggest something."

"You're the doctor," Touch the Sky said with no trace of humor in his face.

"That's right, I am. And a good one, too, though these shit-for-brains malingerers at Fort Bates are too stupid to know it. They call me Sugar Pills and Old Quinine. But it doesn't need a doctor to see that you and your friends are getting sleep simple. You keep this up, one of you is going to make a serious mistake. Each of you swallow two of these."

Touch the Sky's glazed eyes dropped to the dark gleaming pills in Ladislaw's outstretched palm.

"What are they?"

"The soldiers call 'em Night Owls. Basically, each pill is the equivalent of drinking two cups of strong cowboy coffee, the kind that can float a nail and raise a blood blister on saddle leather. Soldiers on night picket take them, and settlers in wagon trains give 'em to the little children out on the plains. The littlest ones get so bored in that emptiness they pass out, fall off the bone shakers, and get crushed under the wheels."

When Touch the Sky hesitated, Ladislaw said, "Fine. You're the one said you're in a hurry, said you got loved ones to save. I'm just trying to help."

"Thanks."

Touch the Sky took the pills and signaled to the rest. All four braves swallowed the pills, grimacing.

"If this is how white soldiers eat, "Two Twists said, "I would rather eat horse droppings."

But soon Touch the Sky did feel more alert, and he could see that his friends did too. And just in time, for now they had ridden into perfect ambush country: a series of rolling hills covered with clumps of pine trees and hawthorn bushes.

At every moment Touch the Sky expected to take his last breath as a bullet found his lights. Sweat beaded along his scalp and rolled down his nape with a tickling sensation like lice digging at him. If was not merely the thought of death that gnawed at him. He wore that familiar fear like a pair of old moccasins. But he was intensely afraid of failure—the failure to get Ladislaw and the medicine back to camp in time.

Again he glanced all around, squinting against

the advancing sun. His eyes traversed the hills, scoured the trees, and delved deep into defiles and coulees. Now and then, after searching a sector normally, he would turn his head and study the same area from the corners of his eyes. Arrow Keeper had once showed him how peripheral vision could pick up some movements that straight-on vision often missed.

But at least they made fair, if not rapid, time on the cavalry mounts. The Cheyennes were not accustomed to such heavy and elaborate saddles, yet they could not dispense with them for fear of making the horses rebel. It was bad enough that these horses were not used to the smell of Indians. They obeyed well enough, being hard broken by the cruel methods of the whites but they were nervous and skittish. As for the Indians, they cringed inwardly as they thought about the iron bits white men shoved in a horse's mouth to control the animal. But urgency called for strong, well-trained mounts, and they had them. Unfortunately, the horses were trained for endurance, not speed. It was doubtful they could outrun Black Elk's band in a dead race, even though the Cheyenne ponies had seen brutal riding.

Touch the Sky was leading the little party up a long rise when, all in a moment, someone leapt at him from behind a boulder. He swung hard in the saddle, his feet caught clumsily in the stirrups, and brought his Sharps .45-120 up to the ready. His finger curled inside the trigger guard.

# Death Camp

Then the heat of shame came into his face when he realized the figure had only been his own shadow suddenly catching his eye on the gray face of the sunlit rock. Perhaps he had trained his side vision a bit too well if it was going to turn him into a nervous girl who started at every owl hoot.

Luckily, no one had seen him nearly shoot his own shadow point-blank. Despite the Night Owl pills, he saw that he was clearly still nerve frazzled from exhaustion and worry. He must get control of himself and settle down. He was a leader. In a sense his entire tribe was behind him right now, pushing him on even as they needed him to pull them to safety. He could not give in now. If he was hurting, what was it like for Honey Eater and the rest?

That last thought focused him like a hard slap to the face. No more of this jumping at shadows. He turned in the saddle to check the progress of the others, and he was just in time to see an arrow zwip past Ladislaw's nose, missing his head by a hairbreadth.

"Brothers!" Touch the Sky bellowed. "Look hard to your flanks and shoot for vitals! Our enemies are upon us!"

The arrow had thwacked into a tree so hard that the shaft still vibrated when Touch the Sky reached the ashen-faced doctor.

"I know you're a healer and not a fighter. But even the gentle beaver reacts to danger! Don't sit your horse, catching flies with your mouth, when you're being shot at!" Touch the Sky told him. "Either spur your mount or dismount and take cover. If you sit still, you're just helping your killer adjust his aim after the first miss."

"Spur my mount?" Ladislaw said in a voice made tight with fear. "Lad, you and I live in two different worlds. While you're dodging bullets and arrows, I'm usually soaking my feet in Epsom salts and reading poetry. Spur my mount? Cheyenne, that damn arrow nicked my nose! It's all I can do right now to keep from pissing myself!"

Little Horse had moved in close with his shotgun ready, all four revolving barrels loaded with buckshot for close-in killing. Two Twists and Tangle Hair, meantime, had boldly rushed a nearby ridge. Touch the Sky could hear the sound of unshod hoofs retreating behind the ridge. There would be no more attempts for now—not from Black Elk's band anyway. This arrow meant one good piece of news: His enemies must be out of bullets.

But where, he thought nervously as he craned his neck to glance all around them, was Seth Carlson?

"That's the last gun emplacement, sir," Sgt. Nolan Reece reported proudly. "Supervised 'em myself. We got the entire draw below covered for saturation fire. A titmouse couldn't slip through there."

Seth Carlson dropped into a squat behind the

Gatling. It had been unhooked from its clumsy wooden carriage and mounted in a sturdy base of rocks and dirt. Its notched sight overlooked the Old Sioux Trace as it wound past the steep headland of Lookout Bluff.

"The other Gatling is set up over yonder at the southern approach," Reece said, pointing.

"Who's firing it?"

Cpl. James, sir. I got Pvt. Lanier feeding rounds into the hopper."

"Good." Carlson approved this strategy with a nod. "They did a good job on the Blackfoot camp."

"That James is a Kentucky boy, sir. Them ol' boys don't bother with this fancy-ass scientific shooting. They lick their thumbs to get their windage, and then they just peddle it to 'em."

Carlson was in a touchy mood and simply dismissed Reece's needless talk with an impatient wave of one hand. "What about the Parrots? You space 'em out even like I said?"

"For a fact, sir. Paced it off myself. Six artillery pieces about fifty feet apart." Reece rubbed a knuckle across his teamster's mustache.

"Whoever rides through below has got to get past two Gatlings firing three hundred fifty rounds a minute, six artillery rifles throwing twenty-pound exploding shells, and a few dozen sharpshooters with full bandoliers. It's gunna be hotter'n the hinges of hell down there. Couldn't a pissant slip through that draw."

Carlson did not look so convinced. "I'd agree,"

he said, "if it was anyone but Hanchon. I'm start-ing to wonder if his life is charmed."

"Ah, all due respect to your rank, sir. But that's what they say about that blanket-assed Apache Geronimo too. But if his red ass is so charmed, how come he always hauls it deep into Mexico so's he can cover it good? Hanchon ain't charmed; he's just been uncommon lucky."

"That he has," Carlson said. Reece was often ir-ritating, but he had hit on a home truth here, and Carlson found his opinion encouraging.

A trooper on lookout near the southern ap-proach trotted closer and saluted Carlson. "Sir! We got us a herd of elk heading this way hell-bent for election. They'll be pushin' through the draw in a few minutes."

"Could have a couple of the men shoot us some fresh meat," Reece said. "The troopers're tired of desecrated beef."

Knowing Reece meant the new desiccated meat rations issued to soldiers in the field, Carlson nod-ded. Then his big, bluff, sunburned face split in a slight grin as he thought of something else.

"Sergeant, have the men fired the new guns for battle sights?"

"Battle sights?" Reece grinned as he caught his superior's drift. "No, sir, they have not, for a fact."

"All right. Have them load and then stand by to fire."

"Right, sir!"

Reece relayed the order to the gun crews while

Carlson walked the length of the bluff, returning to the Gatling gun that marked the first emplacement in this deadly gauntlet. He tilted the black brim of his hat to cut the glare of the westering sun. Then, below, he spotted the small herd. Perhaps a hundred head, racing at full speed and raising dust puffs as they approached.

"Listen up!" Carlson shouted. "I want every swinging peeder in this man's outfit showing me how to shoot! Let's see who's got the biggest pair on him. We're going to turn those elks into stew meat. Think of them as that much less for the savages to eat so they can go on killing soldiers.

"But wait for my command before you open fire. I want them killed after they enter the draw. That way the Indians won't see the dead animals until it's too late."

The men whooped and grinned. They welcomed this bit of sport to break up the monotony up here on the bluff. The fishing had been first-rate at Beaver Creek, the shade cool and inviting. Up here a man could only sweat and slap at gnats.

Rounds were stuffed into the magazine hoppers of the Gatlings. Elongated, fin-tailed rockets were dropped into the rifled bores of the big Parrot guns. The riflemen crammed rounds through the butt plates of their carbines. The herd thundered closer.

Carlson moved down the line and shouted, "Ready on the right?"

"All ready on the right!" Reece said.

"Ready on the left?"

"All ready on the left!"

"All ready on the right, all ready on the left. All ready on the firing line. Watch your targets. Targets!"

The Parrots kicked back hard and belched smoke and flames. The Gatlings chattered and bucked. The precision carbines cracked with the solid report of good tooling. Below, great chunks of earth and rock and bloody elk intermingled as they flew high into the air. The herd never had a chance. Those not killed by the artillery shells fell under a wall of bullets.

"Cease fire!" Carlson bellowed when the last animal lay twitching in its own gore, dead but still nerved for motion.

A cheer flew up from the men. Reece flashed an ear-to-ear smile. "Holy Hannah, Cap'n! If them woulda been Injuns, it'd be raining feathers in Laramie right now!"

It wasn't Indians. But Carlson couldn't help sharing a grin with his platoon sergeant. It had indeed been an impressive slaughter.

"No, sir," Reece said. "A pissant couldn't slip through that trap."

The ride was hard and dangerous, and no amount of pills could defeat the exhaustion threatening to overwhelm Touch the Sky and his Cheyenne companions.

Soon enough they would reach Lookout Bluff.

Since he had no idea where Carlson was, Touch the Sky knew he should expect trouble there. But for now Black Elk's band was again worrying him. Enough time had elapsed since their last attempt on Ladislaw. By now they must have a new scheme in hand.

Once again Ladislaw was riding in the center of a four-point diamond formation. They stopped briefly at a runoff rill so the horses could drink. Touch the Sky could not remember being this tired since his vision quest to Medicine Lake when enemies closed in from every quarter and sleep was impossible. The situation was similar now. Only this time it wasn't just his life that hung in the balance.

He dismounted, threw the horse's bridle, and watched the animal stretch its long neck out to drink from the little streamlet. Everything was a blur, as if his tired eyes saw things underwater. For a moment, just a blessed moment as the horse drank, the tired Cheyenne let his head fall forward and closed his eyes.

When he opened his eyes again, a shock wave of fear slammed into him. Dr. Ladislaw had wandered well away from cover to relieve himself, and none of the others had yet noticed him.

Touch the Sky shouted a warning even as Little Horse looked up and also spotted the danger. Both of them started forward with the swiftness of charging cats, closing the distance between them and Ladislaw. Touch the Sky steeled his muscles for the jump, then saw Wolf Who Hunts Smiling stepping from behind a deadfall, an arrow notched in his bow.

Touch the Sky leapt at the same moment Little Horse did. They crashed down onto Ladislaw and toppled him. But they were an eyeblink too late to completely avoid the deadly arrow—as Touch the Sky landed on the doctor, he felt a pain like white-hot fire rip into his back.

# Chapter Twelve

"I know it hurts like hell," Ladislaw said. "But it missed all the important places. You're just gonna feel stiff for a while."

Touch the Sky nodded, grimacing against the pain. He was sprawled out facedown on the ground. "I've had arrows in me before," he said. "Just push the tip through quick. We're losing more time."

He gritted his teeth against the anticipated pain. But Ladislaw shook his head. "Can't poke it through."

"Why not?"

"The tip is made out of tin."

At these words, Touch the Sky's expression alerted his companions. He translated this news for them. Nothing was more deadly than an arrow tip made from white man's tin. Once in the body, it bent easily and clinched to bone. Instead of sliding out easily, like chipped flints and stone points, the tin became a deadly blade inside, tearing and gouging and severing vital arteries.

"You said it wasn't bad!"

"It's not, right now. It's in a great spot. But it'll play hell on you if I just poke her through. Might even make you bleed to death."

"Then go," Touch the Sky said desperately. "Get back to camp now. There's no time for fancy surgery on me."

"Never mind fancy surgery," Ladislaw muttered, snapping open his kit. "I told you I'm a damn good doctor. I invented a little something for these injuries. We'll be in the saddle in ten minutes."

He pulled a length of oddly looped wire out of the leather kit. "The problem with these tin points is how they're deliberately tied loose to the shaft. That way it breaks off inside. You have to loop the whole thing and just lift it out following the entrance wound. You do that"—he paused, squinting as he lowered his homemade instrument into the jagged tear—"and you're in business." As he pulled the point out and proudly displayed it to the others, Little Horse grinned in amazement, as did his two companions.

"Whoa!" Ladislaw protested when Touch the Sky started to rise. "Stay there just a minute while

I rinse the wound with disinfectant. Then we can ride."

Touch the Sky winced when the alcohol was splashed onto his injury. But it was a small ordeal, indeed, and blessedly brief. Ladislaw was right—he was stiff. Still, very soon they were riding north again, approaching the huge headland of Lookout Bluff.

"Brother," Little Horse said, "do your thoughts fly with mine?"

They were riding side by side, staring up at the prominent land mass. Sister Sun was slowly dropping toward her resting place in the west. But enough light remained to make them good targets.

"If your thoughts are bloody and colored Soldier Blue," Touch the Sky said, "then, yes, buck, mine fly with yours."

"What is there for it? As you say, we have no time for scouting. Some kind of trap is waiting for us. Do we risk it and take our losses?"

Touch the Sky glanced back toward Ladislaw. "Our losses could be accepted. But there is one loss we cannot risk."

"Straight words, buck. What, then?"

"They are up there," Touch the Sky said. "They must be. We cannot afford to wait until darkness falls and attempt to elude them again. What did we do when we needed to sneak past Pawnee sentries and save our village?"

Little Horse grinned. "We created a diversion."

"We did, buck, and we shall again. You know

that horses cannot ride past on the west side of the bluff?"

Little Horse nodded. "Even more scree has fallen back there than lies in the pass around front. A mule could not easily manage it."

"No, so of course they will not be looking for us to use that route. But what if one of us went back there—one of us with shotgun shells full of black powder? What if there was a loud explosion, war whoops, and arrows flying up over the brim onto the soldiers from the back?"

"They would think," Little Horse said slowly, "that an attack was being mounted from that side, that a war party was ascending. Then they would rush in that direction to defend themselves."

Touch the Sky nodded. "They would. Then the remaining braves would have to make a rush for it to get past. The lone brave would be on his own. He would have to fend for himself and get back to camp on his own."

Like Touch the Sky, Little Horse knew the plan was an extreme long shot. But also like Touch the Sky, he realized there was no other option. Little Horse had sniffed the wind again, and he smelled the strong presence of many cavalry mounts—far more than the few they presently rode. Carlson and his Indian Killers were waiting for the braves.

"We both know that I will be the lone brave," Little Horse said. "Be ready to make your move when you hear the attack begin."

"Take Tangle Hair too, so there will be more

racket and shooting. Be careful getting into position," Touch the Sky warned him. "If they spot you and we lose the element of surprise, we will all be feeding the worms."

Even as more time passed, making Touch the Sky chafe at the delay, he had no regrets about this decision. Despite any concrete evidence, he was utterly convinced a powerful attack force lay in wait for them.

He had carefully explained the plan to Two Twists and Ladislaw. Two Twists had not even blinked an eye; Ladislaw, in contrast, lost all the color in his face and fell silent. But Touch the Sky watched the sedentary, timid man nerve himself for this dangerous move. And the Cheyenne realized that he and his comrades were used to danger; indeed, it was the ridge they lived on. For Ladislaw, this was a real effort of bravery. He was even more admirable for remaining so stoic and determined in the face of his fear. The three of them had taken cover in a cutbank well back from the shadow of the bluff.

"Be ready," Touch the Sky said in a voice just above a whisper. "Little Horse should be making his move soon. We must take advantage of the very first moments after he detonates his powder, when the white skins are likely to panic and leave their positions to check behind them."

But as things turned out, it was Touch the Sky's horse, not his friend, who triggered the desperate break. And not when it was supposed to happen. Busy listening for the explosion from behind the bluff, Touch the Sky failed, at first, to notice the angry, buzzing rattle when his horse moved forward a little. He noticed it just in time to yank his own mount around and out of danger. But Ladislaw's mare, with all the medicine on her back, suddenly spooked and jerked away from the contract surgeon before he could secure his grip on her reins. In numb horror, Touch the Sky watched the mare break toward the narrowing draw below the bluff.

In seconds the animal would break into a withering field of fire. The death of a horse could mean the end of this mission. How would they get that medicine once the horse went down in sight of the soldiers' weapons?

All these thoughts flew through Touch the Sky's head in the space of an eyeblink. So did another: the thought of the magic bloodstone in his parfleche. Arrow Keeper had left the stone when he parted from the tribe to build his death wickiup. The old shaman swore the stone, when empowered by sacred words and faith in the supernatural, could make the holder invisible to his enemies. Desperately, Touch the Sky lunged at the horse as it flew past and managed to grip the saddle horn and cantle. His muscles straining like taut cables, he threw himself onto the panicked mount.

They were only seconds away from a clear field of fire. He dug the stone out of his parfleche, gripped it hard, then quickly and fervently sought

Maiyun's help, not for himself, but for the people.

He heard the sudden shout from above, a hateful voice he recognized all too well: "Here they come! Put at 'em!" Then the panicked mount broke into the open, and Touch the Sky braced himself for death.

"Here they come!" Seth Carlson shouted. "Put at 'em!"

Eagerly, he rushed to the brim and stared down, ready to direct the artillery and Gatling fire. He could hear the charging horse, its hoofclops as clear as hail on a tin roof. Hoping for the first shot at Hanchon, Carlson had eased his finger inside the trigger guard and taken up the slack. But staring below with his face frozen in eager expectation, he slowly took his carbine out of his shoulder socket and stared harder below.

What the hell? There was plenty of light yet—at least an hour's worth. And he could hear a horse down there as plain as anything. So where in the hell was it?

"Reece?"

"Sir!"

"You see anything?"

"My hand to God, sir, there ain't a damn thing down there."

Suddenly, an explosion behind them made Carlson flinch and almost drop his carbine. The explosion was followed by hideous Cheyenne war whoops, then a few arrows flew straight up and clattered down onto them.

"We're being attacked from the rear!" Sgt. Reece bellowed. "Reverse positions or they'll cut us down!"

"Wait!" Carlson screamed. "Delay that command! It's some kind of damn trick. It's a feint!"

But it was too late. His men, convinced they were about to be overrun by scalp-crazy savages, hurried to the opposite side of the bluff to counter this new threat.

The first part was over before Touch the Sky could even believe he was still alive. The cavalry horse had bolted straight through the draw. Once Touch the Sky had glanced overhead and spotted Carlson. The befuddled officer was staring right at him, yet failed to shoot. And miraculously, he was safe on the other side of the drainage gully, out of the line of fire.

As the din began from the back of the bluff, Touch the Sky frantically signaled to Two Twists and Ladislaw. While the soldiers were distracted, the other two made their break. Ladislaw rode Touch the Sky's pony. His face was as white as new snow by the time he joined the tall Cheyenne on the other side.

"Now fly like the wind!" Touch the Sky told them. "We must make the river before they can catch us!"

But it was already too late. Carlson, never having bought the ruse anyway, had corralled a few gunners and returned to the east brim of the bluff. Now he spotted his enemies, and though they were out of effective rifle range, the Parrots could still play hell with them. The first rockets lobbed in, and suddenly the earth was exploding all around Touch the Sky and his companions.

The horses panicked as dirt and debris rained all over them. Fighting for control cost the little party even more time. Now the soldiers were racing down to form an attack force below the bluff.

The plan had come close to working. But as Touch the Sky savagely fought to control the recalcitrant cavalry mount, he realized with a sinking feeling that they were losing their slim margin of safety. How could they outrun their enemy without enough lead? But, faintly at first, then louder, came the rousing bugle notes of *Boots and Saddles*.

He glanced behind them and saw a squad of soldiers racing toward the bluff at a gallop, and they weren't shooting at the Cheyennes. They were directing their fire onto the bluff!

A grin tugged at Touch the Sky's lips as he realized Tom Riley was once again riding to the aid of his Cheyenne friend. He knew Riley would detain Carlson so the Cheyennes could escape. But even as he got his horse under control and led his friends toward the river, he couldn't help wondering if their efforts were all for nothing. Had too much time passed? Were Honey Eater and the rest already dead?

# Chapter Thirteen

"Gather near me, little ones," cried the old grandfather, "and hear the story about Mouse Road, the great warrior. When the battle was finally almost over, all of Mouse Road's Cheyenne brothers lay dead. But Mouse Road had fought with such skill and courage that his Crow enemies sent a word bringer to his rifle pit.

" 'We will not kill you,' they said, "for you are a brave and honorable man, a worthy enemy. In you we see the same traits we admire in our men. We will draw off now while you ride away in peace. Go, brave one.'

" ' I will not thank you for your praise, 'Mouse Road replied, 'for your words are only truth and I have earned them. I also trust your word. But there around me lie my comrades, dead as stones.

146

I trained for war with them, learned the secrets of the hunt with them and bounced their children on my knee. How will I return to my village without them? Why would I want to? Come and finish this sport. I am for you!'

"And three more enemies were sent under that day before the last Cheyenne brave was slain. . . . "

With a guilty start, Sharp Nosed Woman woke from her dream. The exhausted woman had nodded out for a moment. Now she crossed to Honey Eater and lay her hand on the girl's forehead.

"Maiyun help us!" Sharp Nosed Woman pulled her hand back as if the touch had burned her, and in fact it had burned her. For an instant it felt as if she had plunged her hand into glowing embers.

More deaths, more dying, more suffering, more grief—when would it end? Only when the last of them had died? Fortunately, the tribe's quick work in tracing the source of the infection had allowed them to quickly isolate the sick and infected. But even so, more than 30 lay dying, with six others already crossed over.

The latest one to go into the final phase was little Laughing Brook. Her heartbeat was fainter than the pulse of a baby bird, and her normally flawless skin was splotchy from the fever raging inside her and thinning her blood dangerously.

"Maiyun help us," Sharped Nosed Woman said again.

But she knew that Maiyun, for His own inscru-

147

table reasons, would not save them. Nor would that stupid, toneless music coming from Medicine Flute's bone instrument. More and more of the people had gathered around his tipi, hoping his medicine could help.

Sharp Nosed Woman believed it was too late for white man or red man's medicine. She no longer held out any hope for assistance from Touch the Sky or Black Elk. Indeed, perhaps the two jealous stags had locked horns in mortal combat even while their tribe lay dying. Men were that way, she thought, everything with them was always war, fighting, pride, and their sacred honor. Was life not hard enough? Why did they have to make it harder with their incessant fighting?

"No, little Honey Eater," she said, "this time your tall, strong brave cannot save you. But if any man might have, he is the man. Black Elk will not shed a tear for your loss. But this Touch the Sky? His is a love beyond all words to measure it. I fear the very grief from your passing may kill him or drive him to fall on his knife. I would gladly burn my beaded wedding shawl if it would mean he could touch your living hand only once more before you cross over."

Sharp Nosed Woman had spent the time, when she wasn't trying to uselessly comfort one of the sick, sewing new moccasins for Honey Eater and Laughing Brook. Both were in her clan, so it was proper to perform this final service. It would be she too who would wash and dress their bodies for the final journey to the Land of Ghosts.

Outside, the sad, monotonous chanting of the cure songs went on. The rhythmic sound comforted her, made her feel her link to the rest of the people during this terrible tragedy.

And clearly there was more suffering ahead. Since she had given up all hope, she just wanted the suffering to be over as quickly as possible. Indeed, it was customary among the Southern Cheyenne to smother young children who caught mountain fever.

Looking at the twisted masks of pain that had replaced Honey Eater and Laughing Brook's pretty faces, she was tempted to do the same. A few moments of weak struggling over each one of these poor sufferers would bring peace.

Just then, from the back of the crowded pest lodge, she heard a gurgling, gasping noise like a sucking chest wound: the death rattle of another infant choking in its own mucus and giving up the ghost. At least the child's pain was almost over.

Quickly, Sharp Nosed Woman rushed to the child's wicker cradle. The importance of this moment was holy, and even her exhaustion could not dull the love in her as she lay her hand on the babe's scalding head.

As the child measured out the final breath of its brief existence on earth, Sharp Nosed Woman sang the sad words of the Cheyenne death song:

*Nothing lives long,*
*Only the earth and the mountains.*

Judd Cole

Tom Riley's squad of sharpshooters had arrived in the nick of time to ensure that Touch the Sky, Two Twists, and Dr. Ladislaw would face no more harassment from Seth Carlson. But Touch the Sky knew that, once again, he and the others would have to ford the dangerous Shoshone River at Crying Horse Bend. This would be especially difficult for the inexperienced Ladislaw. And what better time for Black Elk and Wolf Who Hunts Smiling to make their next deadly move?

At least the tall young warrior's mind was set easy on one point: the fate of Little Horse and Tangle Hair. Thanks to Riley's intervention, they were able to slip away and join their band again.

"Brothers," he told his three weary companions while their ponies drank from the last water hole before the Shoshone, "this should be the final leg of our journey—also the most treacherous. Black Elk will be desperate to save face before the tribe. He cannot let me best him again, as he sees it."

"Save face," Little Horse said bitterly. The constant pace of this mission had finally told on the sturdy little warrior. He no longer made jokes about death being merely one more pony to ride. "Save face, he calls it. As if a warrior's pride is more important than the life of his own good wife."

Exhaustion had made him careless. The moment Little Horse finished speaking these words, he regretted them—not for Black Elk's sake, but for Touch the Sky's. The last thing that worried and battered warrior needed was to be reminded of Honey Eater's danger—a danger that might well have become a death.

"Brother," Little Horse said, "I regret those careless words."

But Touch the Sky was not one to show whatever deep feelings they may have stirred up. Nor was he one to leave any friend feeling awkward in front of others.

"I regret them too, buck. Not because you spoke them, for no offense was intended or caused. But only because they are true. However, are we white men who discuss the various causes of the winds even while our people need us? Let us ride and swap our regrets over the firepit during the cold moons."

Since Ladislaw had learned his lesson, he stayed close to his Cheyenne protectors. They bore straight north toward the Shoshone, feeling a little safer as the ground cover thinned to a few dark clumps of juniper and a scrawny jackpine or two. But once again the cottonwood and willow thickets began to proliferate as they entered the broad tableland close to the river.

Touch the Sky's exhaustion had settled deep into his bone marrow. Huge, dark pockets filled the hollows under his eyes. But despite the bone-numbing weariness, he forced his mind to remain clear and sharp. They were approaching the river. He must come up with some kind of plan to help ensure their safe fording of the flood-swollen river. He would rely on his braves to help him.

When they crested the last ridge overlooking the river, Touch the Sky halted them. For a long moment, he studied the terrain on the opposite bank carefully: every bush, every tree, every cluster of boulders or up-thrusting ledge.

"Brothers," he said slowly, "let us assume that our tribal enemies are lurking at the river."

"A wise assumption," Tangle Hair said grimly.

"As you say, brother. Now, where would they strike?"

"Clearly, at Crying Horse Bend," Little Horse said. "Where else?"

"Yes," Touch the Sky said, eyes still scouring the river below. "But on which side?"

His words left his companions silent as they tried to catch his drift. Ladislaw watched their faces intently, not understanding a word but knowing this was important to the longevity of his white hide. Little Horse started to catch on. "We have, each of us, assumed that they shall have forded by now and will attack from the opposite bank. But the cover is much thicker on this side."

"Much," Tangle Hair said, grasping his meaning. "So they could leave their ponies much closer. Which they must do, for they plan to kill us and take the medicine and whiteskin shaman back with them."

Touch the Sky nodded encouragement. Thus the warriors thought aloud as one. "Now, if you were on this bank, where is the spot you would choose to leave your pony?"

"The nearest place," Two Twists said, "where they would be hidden, yet close to hand."

"Straight words, buck. A place such as that big deadfall just before the bend."

Slowly, the rest nodded, seeing how sensible all this was, and Touch the Sky said, "Either they are there or they are not. We will assume they are. If we are wrong, little will be lost because we are cautious. Tangle Hair!"

"I have ears, buck, and no thread in them like Black Elk."

"You have a stout heart too, warrior. The rest of us will swing to the east and approach the ford from an angle, diverting Black Elk's band from watching to the west where their ponies are probably hidden. You swing wide to the west and come up on that deadfall from the other side of the bend.

"They will make their move when we are in the water. At the first sign of trouble, leap into the open with their ponies' tethers in your hand. Fire your weapon to gain their attention; then wait long enough to let them start after you before you leave with their mounts. Ride hard and scatter them to the four directions, or bring them back to camp if you can."

It was a desperate plan, one based on scanty information and half-formed hunches. But all agreed it was at least a plan and the best they could hope for under the current time constraints.

Touch the Sky explained the strategy to Ladislaw in English.

"We got to cross that river?" he said, staring at the boiling, churning foam.

Touch the Sky nodded. "Unless you have pills that will grow wings on us."

As agreed, Tangle Hair dropped back behind the ridge. Staying below the crest, he angled off toward the deadfall. Meantime, staying conspicuously in the open, Touch the Sky led his small band down to the ford.

The cavalry horses showed more nervousness than the Indian ponies had. But the mounts were well trained for obedience. Rolling their eyes until they were all whites, they nonetheless bravely plunged into the raging water.

Ladislaw looked like a man about to walk the plank. Touch the Sky and Little Horse, constantly watching for attackers, kept him close between them as they splashed into the swirling waters. Two Twists waited behind them, his British trade rifle at the ready as he scoured the bank.

"Holy Hannah!" Ladislaw said as a geyser of foam soaked the front of his shirt.

"Hold on!" Touch the Sky shouted. "Hold on! If that current gets you, you're worm fodder!"

Despite their fear, the cavalry mounts were strong from regular graining. They held up well enough against the vicious pull of the current. But in their nervousness, the Cheyennes had failed to check the cinches on Ladislaw's saddlebag.

"Brother!" Little Horse shouted above the din of the raging river and the wild nickering of the horses.

Touch the Sky looked where Little Horse, wild-eyed with panic, was pointing. And then he spotted the saddlebag containing the medicine. The bag had just been ripped loose, and it was about to tumble out past them into the middle of the swift current!

Every muscle tense with instant desperation, Touch the Sky leapt off his struggling mount. He hit the ice-cold water, felt himself being sucked under, and struggled to the surface again. He swam hard, legs scissoring madly, trying to reach the floundering bag before it was swept under and away forever. Meantime, Little Horse had all he could do to keep Ladislaw in the saddle.

Touch the Sky groped, but missed. He tried again and just missed again. Then two figures stepped out from the thickets behind them. Suddenly, deadly arrows were flying into the river all around his head. Two Twists, frustrated, could see the arrows, but could spot no target from his position on the bank.

But Tangle Hair made his move, exactly as planned. He jumped into the open and fired his weapon to get the attention of Black Elk's band. Knowing they were ruined without mounts, Swift Canoe instantly gave chase. Tangle Hair tore off, heading the ponies by a single leadline.

This startling turn of events did indeed distract

their tribal enemies. And Two Twists had spotted Black Elk and Wolf Who Hunts Smiling. His trade rifle cracked over and over, forcing them to cover down while his companions finished the ford.

The saddlebag was inches from Touch the Sky's grasping fingers. It was on the verge of hitting the main current and floating away forever. He kicked, felt water rush into his lungs, and gasped for breath. Blindly, he struggled while his head was pulled inexorably under. He made one final grab and his fingers locked onto leather.

He was well downriver from the ford by the time he finally dragged himself ashore. But the dripping bag, medicine safe in its waterproofed vials, was in his hands. And his friends were safe—dripping like drowned rats, but safe.

"Brother," Little Horse said when he could speak again, "Tangle Hair has saved us! He stole their ponies, and there is no livestock anywhere in this area. We have finally turned Black Elk and his roosters into impotent capons!"

Touch the Sky nodded. Black Elk and Wolf Who Hunts Smiling were finally out of the picture. But now began the final desperate battle against the most terrible enemy of all: time.

# Chapter Fourteen

Sharp Nosed Woman hardly cared when she heard the camp crier racing up and down the village streets, announcing the arrival of Touch the Sky and his band. What did it matter? This white-skin medicine man they had in tow was too late, far too late. Sharp Nosed Woman knew the progress of mountain fever. Once the victims went into deep unconsciousness and the rapid, choking breathing started, death soon came on swift wings to claim them. And every last one of them had reached that stage. It was dawn of the third sleep since they were stricken—far too late.

Weary, glad the suffering was nearly over, she crossed to the entrance and lifted the hide flap. There, about to raise the flap, stood Touch the Sky. His face was an agony of uncertainty. A nervous-looking white man accompanied him.

"You are too late," she said to Touch the Sky, and Ladislaw got an instant translation by watching the young buck's tortured face.

It was as if he had been struck a fatal blow, which, nonetheless, left him standing, waiting to topple. "She is gone?" he whispered, unable to find voice for the words.

After Ladislaw hurried inside, Sharp Nosed Woman said, "Not yet, but any moment now. They are all past help."

The warrior started to step inside, but Ladislaw's sharp command cut through the fog of his grief and worry. "Don't come in here! They aren't contagious in the initial stages, but all of these poor souls surely are contagious now. I've had the vaccine; you haven't. It's not just your own safety. You'll give it to the rest in your tribe."

Ladislaw stopped briefly beside each patient, then sighed, shook his head, and stood up. He looked at Touch the Sky and shrugged helplessly. "They're too far gone. Way too far, all of them. Their souls belong to the Creator now."

His words pierced Touch the Sky with the force of bullets. From where he stood, gripping the hide entrance flap, he could see the inconspicuous mound where Honey Eater lay in her robes. Ladislaw closed his bag and mopped at his sweaty pate with a handkerchief.

"I'm awfully sorry, young fella," he said sincerely. "Lord knows you done your best. You got us here as quick as you could under the circumstances."

"There's nothing you can do?"

Ladislaw shook his head. "We're about eight hours too late for the best among them—maybe a whole day late for the sickest. It's hopeless."

Touch the Sky looked at Sharp Nosed Woman's weary, grief-ravaged face. She too had gone through a terrible ordeal, just as he had. Then he looked at Ladislaw, for he had just made up his mind.

"I want you to treat them anyway," he said. "Hopeless or not, treat them."

"You don't understand, son. They're—"

"I understand, Doctor. Treat them anyway."

"But—"

"Treat them anyway," Touch the Sky said. "Treat all of them, any with a breath still left in their nostrils."

"Son, what's the point, they—"

"Treat them!"

Touch the Sky's tone would brook no debate. Ladislaw shrugged, a shadow of worry passing over his face. Touch the Sky saw that worried look and understood. "Forget the stories you've heard about other tribes. You will not be killed if your medicine fails. I will not let you be touched, but treat them."

"It's blamed foolishness, but I'll do it. You might just as well go about your business instead of standing there gawking at me. Even if they had a chance, it would take the better part of a day for the medicine to work."

Touch the Sky dropped the flap and turned. Then he slowly and carefully wove his way through the mourners and chanters. From the corner of his eye, he saw Tangle Hair return to camp leading the ponies he'd stolen from Black Elk's band. But Touch the Sky failed to greet him because all of his attention was focused elsewhere. Little Horse, not liking the grim set of his friend's lips, fell into step behind him. At least, Little Horse consoled himself, neither Black Elk or Wolf Who Hunts Smiling was here, or blood would surely flow.

The knot of people who had gathered around Medicine Flute parted when Touch the Sky strode through them. Medicine Flute was about to sound yet another toneless note when Touch the Sky seized the leg-bone flute from his lips. A sharp crack sounded when Touch the Sky snapped it in half against his thigh. He pitched both broken halves off into the trees.

"You skinny, lazy coward," Touch the Sky said. "It is bad enough that you hide in your tipi while your brothers are on the warpath, that you eat a generous share of meat you never kill. It is bad enough that you play the conniving dog for Wolf Who Hunts Smiling and Black Elk and the rest of the Bull Whips. It is bad enough that you pretend to visions and shaman powers and thus not only mock the high holy ones but prey on the faith of the people.

"All this is serious enough. But while our people lie dying, you will not mock true shamanism and waste the prayer energy of all these believers. If I hear you blowing on another flute, I am going to string a new bow with your guts. Do you take the meaning of my words?"

Medicine Flute could put up an arrogant front when surrounded by his supporters. But he truly was a coward, especially when his chief allies were not at hand to lend him false courage. He merely dropped his lidded gaze from that of this stern warrior and said, "As you will. My medicine is strong enough to survive a broken flute."

"Your medicine, white liver, is even more faint than your manhood."

With that Touch the Sky walked off. He saw Ladislaw emerge from the pest lodge. Touch the Sky searched the doctor's face until Ladislaw nodded, assuring him he'd completed the treatment, hopeless though it seemed.

"Brother," Touch the Sky said to Little Horse, "feed the white skin and find a place for him to rest. Then go to your tipi, eat something, and rest yourself. Soon I will come to wake you up. I need your assistance."

Little Horse looked at him asquint. He did not like the look or feel of this. "Assistance in what, brother?"

"You will find out all in good time, buck. Now eat and rest."

Touch the Sky followed his own advice. He returned to his tipi, ate a handful of venison, then told the crier to wake him when the morning sun had traveled the width of four lodge poles. He fell into his robes and slept like a dead man until the crier shook him out.

Like a she-bear eating for her cubs, Touch the Sky forced himself to eat more venison when he awoke. For he knew he would need much strength to face the ordeal looming before him.

One last task remained before he roused Little Horse. Touch the Sky walked down the long, grassy slope to the river. A huge sweat lodge had been made by stretching hides over a frame of bent saplings. Touch the Sky stepped inside and built a fire to heat a circle of rocks. When they glowed red-hot, he filled a rawhide pail with river water, stripped naked, and stepped back inside to pour the cool water over the glowing rocks.

Instantly the lodge filled with billowing steam. For a long time Touch the Sky sat silent and still, letting the vapors rise all around him and permeate his pores. He cleared his mind of all thought, preparing himself for the ordeal ahead. Once again, as so many times before, the time was coming—the time when he would have to visualize his pain as a bright red ball and then place it outside of himself, as Arrow Keeper had taught him. Only thus could a man endure as he had endured.

Touch the Sky had made up his mind and there was no going back. Ladislaw had already told him it took the better part of a day for the medicine to work—if it was going to. But Touch the Sky knew it was far too late to simply sit back and pray for a miracle from the white man's God.

No. He was his tribe's shaman. Arrow Keeper was no longer here to tell him what to do. It was up to him to act, to do something that might add strength to the white-skin medicine. And only one thing could help this late in the tragedy: an agonizing vigil of suffering as an offering to the high holy ones.

He stopped at Little Horse's tipi and roused his tired companion without waking Ladislaw, who slept on the other side of the center pole. "Come, buck," Touch the Sky said. "Shake out the cobwebs and wake to the living day. I need your assistance. I am going to set up a pole."

Little Horse knew his friend well and had been dreading something like this. Once before, up north in the Bear Paw Mountains, Touch the Sky had undergone self-inflicted torture to strengthen a prayer. That time, he had persuaded Little Horse to heap rocks onto his back until he was nearly crushed to death. But his suffering had induced the rare and powerful Indian magic known as the Iron Shirt—bluecoat bullets turned into sand and failed to kill even one member of Shoots Left Handed's beleagured Cheyenne band. But this disease seemed even more hopeless.

"Brother," Little Horse said, "you have done more than ten braves could have to save our people. But we were too late. You have suffered too much on this hard mission. Setting up a pole now could kill you."

"It could, buck. But so could the alternative."

Little Horse understood his meaning. His friend was telling him that, if Honey Eater crossed over, life would mean nothing to Touch the Sky. Reluctant, but knowing protest was useless, Little Horse followed his companion to a copse near the river. Touch the Sky selected a strong cottonwood limb and cut it free with his ax. He filed one end to a point while Little Horse reported to the lodge of the Bow String Troopers.

He returned with a crude leather harness, which was designed to be cinched over one end of the pole. Detachable metal hooks dangled from the harness. They fixed the harness to the pole, and Touch the Sky carried it to a small rise overlooking the entire camp. There, in the blazing midday sun, he dug a hole and lowered his penance pole into it.

"Drive the hooks in, brother," he said, "and don't be squeamish."

Wincing, trying to be quick and careful, Little Horse gouged two hooks into the muscles of Touch the Sky's chest. He had been sure to push the point between the cords of muscle, not through them, so there was not much blood. But the pain made Touch the Sky suck his breath in through his teeth.

"Now hook me up." He said with a gasp.

A few moments later, he dangled a few hand breadths above the ground—all his weight suspended from the hooks in his chest. For the rest of that day, while Sister Sun beat down on him mercilessly, Touch the Sky dangled in a welter of sweat, blood, and pain. Like a man riding through patchy fog, he drifted in and out of consciousness. Each time he surfaced to awareness, he saw Little Horse, Two Twists, and Tangle Hair gathered faithfully at the base of his pole. Despite their deep sympathy for his pain, however, not one of them lifted his hand to comfort Touch the Sky. Such a gesture could ruin the voluntary penance.

At first, only his loyal band had gathered. But soon Chief Gray Thunder heard of this sacrifice and came out to join them in silent camaraderie. As the day progressed, more and more of the people joined the group around his pole. Despite her deep pessimism, Sharp Nosed Woman had been struck by the tall brave's noble gesture. After all, where was Black Elk while his wife lay dying? Thus reasoning, she overcame her exhaustion and led the people in a spirited prayer to Maiyun.

Little Horse had taken Ladislaw to briefly meet Chief Gray Thunder before leading him to his own tipi for sleep. Now the wide-eyed white man stood at the bottom of the rise. He stared at Touch the Sky and at the growing ring of people. These Indians knew he was trying to help. But most either ignored him or treated him with cool civility, some were openly hostile.

Little Horse rose and gazed west toward the Wolf Mountains. Touch the Sky had said to bring him down when the sun's belly touched the peaks. The tall brave was conscious, but only barely.

Little Horse nodded at Tangle Hair and Two Twists. Then he gazed toward the pest lodge, dreading what was about to happen. Already, Ladislaw was slowly heading that way to check on the victims, who were probably cold corpses by now.

Little Horse knew that Touch the Sky had faced down every danger known to a warrior. But as was true with all brave, strong men, the wells of feeling in him, though silent, ran deep. What bullets and arrows and torture could not accomplish, the death of Honey Eater might achieve: the end of Touch the Sky too.

"Lift him," Little Horse told his friends, "but gently. I fear he must now face what the Wendigo himself would flee from."

# Chapter Fifteen

For some time Touch the Sky lay in the cool grass where his friends had placed him. The pain in his chest muscles had long since sent roots and branches throughout the rest of his body.

He opened his eyes. Wincing at the sharp lance points of pain, he sat up; then, wobbling, he stood. Through all this, his sympathetic friends nonetheless refused to help him. There was no shame in requiring help, but it would have insulted him to offer it before he requested it. It was important for Touch the Sky to show the tribe that he did not need it now.

He looked at Little Horse, Two Twists, and Tangle Hair. Beyond them stood Chief Gray Thunder and Spotted Tail, leader of the Bow String Soldiers. Beyond them were the members of the tribe, except for his worst enemies, and any of the Bull Whip Soldiers. These last, following the instructions of their leader, Lone Bear, remained near Medicine Flute's tipi.

No more avoiding it, Touch the Sky knew. So much easier to face the awesome trick rider Comanche Big Tree, who could launch ten arrows before the first one struck its target; the mad renegade Blackfoot Sis-ki-dee, who killed a whiteskin infant by braining it against a tree in front of its mother; or even the Cherokee policeman Mankiller, whose huge and powerful hands could snap a man's neck like a dry sotol stalk.

How much harder to face the fact of seeing Honey Eater with no life in her. There were no muscles to tense for this blow, the one soft place in him that could become a hurting place for life.

"Where is the white-skin shaman?" Touch the Sky finally asked Little Horse.

"Brother, he went into the pest lodge some time ago. He has yet to emerge."

Touch the Sky fought back waves of dizziness and darker waves of pain from the badly abused muscles of his chest. He stared across the clearing at the hide-draped lodge. Then he nodded. His face wincing again at the incredible, fiery pain, he set off across the clearing.

Each step shot a jolting agony of pain through him. His friends followed close behind; then came Gray Thunder, Spotted Tail, and the rest of the people. There was an eerie, ceremonial importance to all of it that humbled everyone, even Touch the Sky's harshest critics.

Little Horse was given to making morbid jokes to help his comrades ease their battle fear. But he understood that such comments would be as wrong as small talk during the Renewal Prayer. He felt he was seeing something more important than the daily suffering—the elemental, powerful holiness of a right and pure and strong love.

Two Twists openly let a tear course down his cheek, and the defiant scowl that accompanied it dared any man to call him a woman for it. Not only was his favorite uncle inside that lodge, probably dead, but he was Honey Eater's closest friend besides Touch the Sky. Often had he risked his life from Black Elk's wrath to slip her a comforting word about Touch the Sky.

Touch the Sky was perhaps a stone's throw away from the lodge when the entrance flap was thrown back and Dr. Ladislaw emerged. The white man's eyes met the red man's. His face looked like that of a man suddenly waking up in a strange room in a strange town. Touch the Sky couldn't quite read that expression. But he felt a cold rock replace his stomach when he saw Ladislaw shake his head in what could only signify a gesture of final defeat.

Touch the Sky spoke in English. "Is it over?"

The contract surgeon stepped aside. He stared out over the serrated peaks of the mountains, as if he had a feeble brain awed by his first view of the West. "Can't be," he muttered.

"Did you hear me?" Touch the Sky demanded.

Ladislaw clearly heard nothing at that moment, except some secret and private music in the spheres. He stared at Touch the Sky. "You know, I promised myself that if God ever showed Himself to me once, even just once, I'd quit my sinning. Well, He called my hand today!"

The contract surgeon's distraught face and odd mutterings had sent some of the people nervously backing away. Clearly, the sight of all the death had unnerved him, many thought.

"Ladislaw!" Touch the Sky snapped. "To hell with your chatter. How are they?"

"Go see for yourself," Ladislaw replied, stepping farther aside.

It was only a few steps, but the longest walk of Touch the Sky's life. His legs hung back like stone weights, so reluctant was he to look inside that lodge and face perhaps the cruelest fact of his fate. Blood still oozed from the punctures in his chest as he finished crossing to the pest lodge.

Again Ladislaw shook his head. "There's only one word for it," he said quietly, even as Touch the Sky steeled himself to look inside. "Miracle."

Touch the Sky heard the word just as his eyes found Honey Eater's. Hers were open. And even from there, he could see the weak but clear glint of vitality in those eyes!

"Tall warrior," she said, her voice faint but recognizable, "Sharp Nosed Woman says we all owe you our lives—once again. As always, I see from looking at you that you have paid dearly for sending death away."

Not just Honey Eater—all were recovering. Trains the Hawk, Two Twists' uncle, mustered a weak smile. Even little Laughing Brook, though not yet living up to her name, smiled weakly at the handsome young warrior.

"A miracle," Ladislaw said again. "They were gone. I only administered that medicine to humor you."

The people outside the lodge were abuzz with exclamations and praise as the words flew through camp: The sick ones were healed! White man's medicine had combined with red man's medicine, and the sick ones were recovering!

An exultant cry of praise was lifted to Maiyun. The camp crier leapt on his pony and tore through the village streets, announcing this miracle to the rest. Excited word bringers were sent to bring the good news to the far-flung Cheyenne bands.

"Touch the Sky," Gray Thunder said, "your acts during council, when you seized the voting stones, amounted to treason. But as I told you then, the act would be vindicated by success. Soon, thanks to you, our distant clans will join us for the feasting and celebrations. We will never forget those we have lost to this terrible disease. But better to dwell on the number who were saved."

His eyes flicked from Touch the Sky to each of the braves who had ridden with him—and to the white-skin doctor who, in spite of his obvious fear, used his skill to save suffering Indians.

"Arrow Keeper spoke the straight word," Gray Thunder told Touch the Sky, "When he said your path would be a violent and bloody one. Trouble comes looking for you like a bear grubbing for beetles. But I will never forget what that wise old shaman also said. You are a taller man by far than the tallest, and you have the true and rare gift of the vision seeker. More trouble is coming, surely. But in you, buck, trouble has met a worthy foe!"

Despite Gray Thunder's public vote of confidence, Touch the Sky and many others did not miss his reference to more trouble coming. Indeed, the main source of all future trouble returned to camp the very next day—or rather limped into camp.

Touch the Sky was still resting in his tipi when he heard a ripple of scornful laughter flying through the camp. He also heard taunting jeers. He rose, stiff with pain, and lifted the elkskin flap of his tipi. At first he saw nothing unusual. Then he spotted Black Elk, Wolf Who Hunts Smiling, and Swift Canoe. Surely it was the most humiliating moment of their lives. For all three rode old, swayback mules obviously stolen from some white-skin corral or mining camp.

"Returned are the mighty heroes!" someone shouted. "They have swapped their ponies for fine mules with mange!"

# Death Camp

"Look! Here is Black Elk, one day after his squaw is saved! Too bad he was not here to see it!"

Touch the Sky could not help a wide smile at the ridiculous sight these three braggarts presented. Wolf Who Hunts Smiling looked especially ludicrous. His mule's back swayed so deep it left the Cheyenne's moccasins dragging on the ground. This, plus the brave's deep scowl, sent some warriors to the ground in laughing fits.

The entire camp had crowded into the clearing, laughing, staring, pointing. His face furious with rage, Wolf Who Hunts Smiling stopped in the middle of camp. As if defiantly, he refused to get off the mule.

"Cheyenne people! Have ears for my words!" His eyes found Touch the Sky's as he spoke. "Enjoy your mirth! Well do I and certain others note the faces of those traitors to the Cheyenne way who mock us now. The simple brains among you have not yet seen the truth. A war is coming and soon! Not a war with bluecoats or Pawnee or Crow—a war within the Cheyenne tribe!"

His words were sobering. Now no one laughed. "Those who mock my cousin and me, look closer. Look over by Medicine Flute's tent. Count the Bull Whips gathered over there. Count their scalps. You who mock are many in number. But many of you are elders or women. Those gathered over by that tipi are warriors in their prime. They do not laugh at pretend Indians who secretly play the dog for white-skins!"

Wolf Who Hunts Smiling had always been a commanding speaker, and he was in his prime now. He continued to stare at Touch the Sky, murder clear in his eyes.

"You call this one your shaman and let him keep our sacred arrows. He who defied his chief openly in council, who went over the entire Council of Forty. I tell you this: From where I stand now to the sun's resting place there is no spot for this one to hide from my wrath! I will kill this false shaman! And many more will die with him if they are foolish enough to follow him."

In a flash, Wolf Who Hunts Smiling had drawn back his arm and let his lance fly. Only at the last moment did Touch the Sky move his head in time. The lance missed his throat by mere inches and struck the cottonwood beside his tipi.

Wolf Who Hunts Smiling threw back his head and laughed. The tribe was silent as they watched the three new arrivals cross to join their Bull Whip brothers. For a moment, before he went back inside his tipi, Touch the Sky's eyes lifted across toward the tipi where Honey Eater was resting, getting her strength back.

Wolf Who Hunts Smiling was right, he thought. A war was coming, and many would die. Just as Arrow Keeper had told Touch the Sky, just as his vision at Medicine Lake had confirmed. The battle lines were clearly drawn; the sides marked out.

# Death Camp

Once the war cry sounded, the holy ones must have mercy on his enemies, for Touch the Sky would not.

"Wolf Who Hunts Smiling!"

The voice startled everyone. Wolf Who Hunts Smiling turned, as did everyone else, to stare at young Two Twists. He stood next to Little Horse and Tangle Hair.

Contempt starched into every feature, Two Twists lifted his clout—a gesture of mocking derision clearly reserved for outright enemies of the tribe.

Wolf Who Hunts Smiling's rage was instant. But Little Horse's raised shotgun persuaded him to leave his Colt in its sheath. So angered was Wolf Who Hunts Smiling that he could not immediately speak. Medicine Flute, ever loyal to his master, hurried forward.

"Many call themselves shamen," he shouted in the voice that had never quite lost its adolescent tendency to break on the high notes. "But any man can put the trance glaze over his eyes and pretend to visions. I say only this. Wolf Who Hunts Smiling has spoken straight arrow. The importance of his words will soon be confirmed in a sign."

Before Touch the Sky could worry what new treachery this prediction meant, Wolf Who Hunts Smiling's mule made it come true. It suddenly lifted its tail and left a huge pile of droppings in the middle of the camp. The roar of laughter throughout camp was instantaneous.

But as he dropped the flap of his tipi again, a smile still dividing his face, Touch the Sky could not help again hearing the words of old Arrow Keeper: *Laughter, while necessary, always gives way to tears.*